Chaos
In The
Capital

Chaos
In The
Capital

Rob Shumaker

With thanks to Special Agent Dave for all his great advice, willingness to answer all of my law-enforcement questions, and offering his own tactical insights.

"Four score and seven years ago our fathers brought forth on this continent, a new nation, conceived in liberty, and dedicated to the proposition that all men are created equal. . ."

– Abraham Lincoln, Gettysburg Address, November 19, 1863

CHAPTER 1

The White House – Washington, D.C.

"'Four score and seven years ago.'"

William Cogdon let his eyes drift to the ceiling as he pondered the writings of the sixteenth President of the United States. The West Sitting Hall on the second floor of the White House enjoyed the rare sound of peaceful quietness on this Monday morning as the President of the United States and his one-time chief of staff and now full-time campaign manager enjoyed a light breakfast and perused their selected reading materials. They met there most mornings – with Cogdon routinely arriving before the President would exit the First Couple's bedroom across the hall. President Anthony Schumacher had settled in for a morning review of yesterday's box scores – the great Pujols and his three home runs in leading the Cardinals to victory sure to brighten the President's day. He loved the box scores and the late summer tally of league leaders and started every morning with a quick trip around the American and National Leagues.

William Cogdon, known as Wiley to those who knew him best, had taken less of an interest in baseball since he was placed in charge of running the President's election campaign. Instead of box scores and division standings, Cogdon spent every waking hour on the phone with consultants, reading the latest poll numbers, and poring over historical mementos that might be of use to the President when he was out speaking on the stump. Friends for over thirty years, the President had grown accustomed to Cogdon reading and thinking out loud.

"'Four score and seven years ago,'" Cogdon said again before pausing. "That's eighty-seven years, isn't it?"

"Uh huh," the President said without taking his eyes off the realization that the Cubs had been no-hit the day before by the Padres. He must have missed that little nugget of joy as he traveled back to the White House from his weekend away at Camp David.

"So eighty-seven years before 1863 was . . ." Cogdon said, subtracting the numbers in his mind. "That would be 1776."

"Uh huh."

"'Four score and seven years ago our fathers brought forth on this continent, a new nation, conceived in liberty,'" Cogdon continued in his deliberate contemplation.

"Born in freedom," the President interjected to show he was in fact listening and offering a different take on the wording.

"'Conceived in liberty and dedicated to the proposition that all men are created equal.'"

"'*All* men are created equal,'" the President emphasized.

Cogdon put down his copy of the Gettysburg Address. Down the hall, the Lincoln Bedroom actually contained a copy signed and dated by Abraham Lincoln himself. The giant of American history who wrote the 267 word speech might have contemplated, or maybe even penned a few of those very lines while living and breathing within those very walls prior to his journey to the dedication ceremony in Pennsylvania over 150 years ago. Cogdon had a healthy admiration for President Lincoln. Himself a lawyer, Cogdon grew up near Gentryville, Indiana, in the same Spencer County where Lincoln spent a good portion of his boyhood years. Now his friend and boss was President of the United States and both could roam the halls wondering what the Great Emancipator must have been thinking while he agonized and navigated over the worst crisis in American history.

"You know, the anniversary of the Gettysburg Address is this November," Cogdon said. "We should come up with a speech to commemorate the occasion."

The President neatly folded his sports page and finished off his glass of orange juice. He then folded his hands in front of his face. "Don't we have something a little more pressing beforehand to worry about?" He smiled slightly, as if to tell Cogdon that his mind should be focused on a more pressing matter. "I think that something happens to fall on the first Tuesday in November."

"I'm on top of that," Cogdon replied. "The campaign is in full swing, the polls are looking good, and I'm confident we will defeat whatever the Democrats throw at us." He did his best to make it sound like a campaign victory was in the bag. But to the President's biggest worrywart, nothing was ever in the bag.

"As long as there are no October surprises," the President said as he rose from his seat at the table and put on his suit coat.

Cogdon squirmed in his seat. His eyes were now closed and the dread would soon send shivers down his spine.

"Don't say that," he pleaded in a whisper.

He put a closed fist up to his chest, most likely another bout of early morning indigestion. It only increased his worry. His blue tie hung loosely around his neck. He just gave up tying it tight anymore. That, along with his growing girth and rumpled appearance, made him look like a man in disarray.

He would never be seen on the cover of any magazines, unless it was the *National Enquirer* or some other gossipy rag seeking to bring ridicule on him or, to a liberal editor's amusement, some embarrassment to the Schumacher Administration. Cogdon had been no stranger to tabloid fodder, most often a result of his longstanding drinking problem and his proclivity for female, and at times multiple, prostitutes. He, however, had reformed his questionable behavior and dedicated his energies to defeating the Democrats who had taken so much joy in witnessing his public floggings. It was no secret the liberals hated Cogdon with a passion, like he was some evil conservative cross between Karl Rove and Dick Cheney, and the Left considered him a great threat to their agenda. In turn, Cogdon took the weight of the President's world on his shoulders and made it his own.

Although he had been a political strategist for over thirty years, he had no idea what was coming. The election was less than two months away. And with the way things had been going, something was bound to come up that would surprise, if not shock, the entire country.

The President seemed to be a magnet for all sorts of surprises.

President Schumacher had been in office for a little over seven months. The former Vice President rose to his current position after former President Ronald Fisher tried to have him killed by going along with a plan to have his Marine Two helicopter shot out of the sky. When the plan failed and the plot became known within the Fisher Administration, the President and his co-conspirator/lover, CIA Director Jillian Franklin, took their own lives before the public and a jury of their peers could condemn them for their heinous crimes.

Once in control in the Oval Office, President Schumacher settled in and took the war on terrorism up a notch. He reopened the detention facility at Guantanamo Bay and hauled the terrorist detainees out of civilian courts in the United States and paraded them back before the military tribunals at Gitmo. Enraged, the terrorists responded with a daring attack on the National Archives where they sought not to harm the Charters of Freedom but the President's youngest daughter who worked as a volunteer docent. The attack killed twenty-five Americans but Anna Schumacher was unharmed.

When the President responded with decisive military action in the Afghan and Pakistani training camps where the terrorists had plotted and practiced their dastardly deed, the American people hoped for peace, quiet, and a return to normalcy. Instead, a broken arrow of a Supreme Court Justice decided his allegiance was with Allah and not the Constitution and tried to blow himself up with a suicide vest during the President's speech to a Joint Session of Congress. Only the quick action by the Director of the FBI saved the life of the President of the United States as well as the lives of countless members of Congress, Justices of the Supreme Court, and Cabinet secretaries.

The President was indeed a magnet. The terrorists would no doubt pick up the pace lest they be obliterated by President Schumacher's military. He had promised to go to the ends of the earth to hunt those who sought to harm America. The constant threat of terrorist attacks kept Cogdon up at nights. He worried the American people would come to the conclusion that President Schumacher was too much of a lightning rod, too much of a risk to have in the White House, and then decide to settle for someone who could give a good speech and promise peace and tranquility for all mankind.

And then, of course, there were the Democrats still to worry about. Who knew what type of tricks they had up their sleeves. Hell, the former Democrat Speaker of the House knew of a plot to kill then Congressman Schumacher and didn't do anything about it. She was eventually kicked out of Congress, tried and convicted in federal court, and sentenced to spend the rest of her life in prison.

Cogdon prayed President Schumacher had weathered his last storm and gotten the bad luck out of the way so he could then focus on governing the country. Something, however, told Cogdon not to bet on it. He reached into his shirt pocket for a cherry antacid, a generous supply that would be gone by mid-afternoon.

"Come on," the President said as he started for the hall. "Let's just worry about our agenda and keep focused on the finish line. It'll all work out in the end."

The usually effusive Cogdon said nothing as he packed up his materials. Another fist to his tightening chest didn't soothe his mind any.

He had a bad feeling about something.

CHAPTER 2

Chicago, Illinois

"Were you followed?"

The first question was the same every time they met. It had become as routine as "How are you doing?" or "Nice to see you again." But the two men seated in the lobby of the Palmer House Hilton were not old friends looking to get together for idle chit-chat or to talk about the Windy City weather or yet another worthless season from the feckless Cubs. They met in a different place every time and watched their backs at every opportunity. Cell phones were purchased, used once, and then discarded. Little was written down, and all messages, whether on the phone or on the web, were in code.

People act that way when they are plotting to kill the President of the United States.

Moamar Abbed took a look around the opulent lobby and even up to the ornate ceiling. Nothing seemed to say "You're being followed." He had taken two different El trains from his one-bedroom apartment on the north side of Chicago. He disembarked near Union Station and proceeded to Grant Park where he walked around Buckingham Fountain twice, all the while studying those sitting on the benches, jogging along the gravel paths, and taking pictures of the surrounding landmarks and skyline. He never once looked over his shoulder. Instead, he turned in every direction, hiding behind his sunglasses and pretending to be on the phone yapping away just like a hundred other people. The phone, however, was off. It was simply a prop on that late summer day.

Even in the middle of September, tourists and school groups had flocked to Chicago to visit the Shedd Aquarium, the Museum of Science and Industry, and Navy Pier. Between stops, they headed to Grant Park to parade around Buckingham Fountain, pose for pictures, point at the boats on Lake Michigan, and look at their maps again. Then they spread out in search of food. And Abbed was right behind the longest line of tourists crossing Michigan Avenue hoping to blend in.

He had walked two blocks north and took a left on Monroe. The sidewalks were filled with pedestrians during the lunch hour, many were in business suits and in a definite hurry to get back to the office before the boss found out they were late. Abbed was sure he had not raised any suspicions. He entered the revolving doors of the Hilton at Monroe and State Streets and found still more people, most of them waited patiently in line at the Starbucks inside on the ground floor. He bypassed the line and turned around. He saw no one he had seen before. He entered the gift shop and purchased a Coke and a copy of the *Tribune*. After one more look around, he took his Coke and paper up the escalator to the lobby level and found Mohammed Akbar sitting with his back to the wall across the way. The site had been chosen because of its heavy foot traffic and boisterous surroundings. The louder things were, the less likely an eavesdropper would gain the advantage.

Mohammed Akbar had been waiting for twenty minutes, and the frequent glances at his watch indicated he was either worried about his guest's absence or desperate for one of his Dutch Masters grape cigarillos. Given that he couldn't smoke inside, he tapped his foot under the table. After he spotted Abbed, he had given him the nod that it was safe to approach the table.

"I don't think I was followed," Abbed said, pulling out a chair and sitting down. "I was very careful. That is why I am a little late. There are a lot of people out there."

Akbar nodded. "I am glad you took precautions. We must not rush lest we ruin our business plan."

Akbar had placed on the table before him a bevy of bar graphs and pie charts that described the operating appropriations for the Illinois state budget. There was $9 billion for elementary and secondary education, another $8 billion for health and human services, and $12 billion for the Department of Public Aid. The graphs showed ominous rows of downward facing red lines as the State of Illinois had no money to pay for all the fruit baked into the pie and had been borrowing the filling for some time. It might make any observer, especially an Illinois taxpayer, hot under the collar, even more so considering the genius Democrats in the General Assembly sought to pay for their incompetence in fiscal governance by raising taxes on all hardworking citizens in the Land of Lincoln.

But Abbed and Akbar couldn't care less about the figures or the state's dire financial straits. They had no connection with Illinois Government. They had no love for Blago or the Daley political machine. They had never even voted. They didn't pay any taxes either. Their way was fully paid for them by their families in Saudi Arabia. Abbed brought the documents simply as props to distract any nosy passerby intent on hearing what the two nicely dressed men were discussing. The setting was simply a business meeting between two professionals.

Mohammed Akbar had been in the United States for twenty years. He came on a student visa, obtained a degree in Muslim theology, and became one of Chicago's premier Muslim clerics. With a nicely trimmed beard framing his thin face, he was a quiet man by nature, not one of those rabble-rousing clerics who rant and rave about Allah demanding the death and destruction of the Great Satan and its citizens. Sure he believed it. But he was smart enough to realize that such vitriolic and outspoken anger only caused American law enforcement to take notice. And notice was a bad thing when waging war against America. The last thing he needed was *60 Minutes* setting up a satellite truck outside his mosque and an inquisitive reporter asking questions. Instead, martyrdom in the name of Allah required a bit of quiet patience. So Akbar decided early on that he would fly under the radar in his attempt to spread the type of jihad never seen before. In public, he spoke calmly about the peaceful Muslim religion and the need for tolerance of all religions. Even the Jews must be respected, he would state with sincere believability. Although this brought condemnation from some of his radical comrades, he would always remind them the prowling tiger is silent just prior to attacking its prey.

Akbar had spent the last ten years coordinating a campaign in Chicago, Detroit, Los Angeles, and New York to set up an underground network of Muslim men who would start the path toward his grand jihad and the destructive downfall of the United States. Instead of just focusing recruitment at big city mosques, Akbar trolled college campuses where he could find young men, some of whom had been radicalized since birth, but others whose minds just needed a little more convincing that America and her deviant ways must be defeated in the name of Allah. Akbar sought out male students, American or foreign born, studying engineering, biological sciences, and medicine.

The thought was the students' expertise in these areas would only enhance their value to the cause. Engineers could offer insight on taking down buildings, bridges, and the like. Biologists and chemists would not only have knowledge of toxic substances but also the knowhow to spread them over large populations. Medical professionals could also be utilized to increase the carnage once the war began and the casualties started rolling in. The ideal students would be those who blended in with their surroundings – a cell phone in one hand, the ubiquitous white ear buds stretching to their iPods, and a wardrobe of Tommy Hilfiger apparel and a pair of Nike shoes. Along with a hatred for America, of course. It would be a new breed of terrorist – one where its warriors wore a suit and tie or a white lab coat over the bombs strapped to their chests.

In search of engineering students, Akbar had traveled an hour and a half southeast out of Chicago to Purdue University in West Lafayette, Indiana. Its renowned engineering school, the ninth best in the country according to *U.S. News & World Report*, enjoyed connections with such out-of-this-world luminaries like Neil Armstrong, the first man on the moon, and Eugene Cernan, the last man on the moon, as well as lesser-known engineers like Charles Ellis, the designer of the Golden Gate Bridge, and Elwood Mead, the chief construction engineer on the Grand Coulee and Hoover Dams.

The university was Big Ten, but the campus had a small town feel to it. Of course, much of Indiana is that way. With not much effort at all, Akbar found two recruits in the five member Society of College Muslims and watched with great anticipation as they progressed through school.

At the same time, Akbar's current mosque was undergoing a major construction project on the southside of Chicago and he was in charge of seeing to it that it was completed on time. Although, that wasn't the only thing he had on his plate.

"I got a call from the office yesterday," Akbar said. The code had been practiced for some time now. It was best to speak the business lingo whenever they met. "The boss wants the project completed by the fifth of October."

Abbed looked across the table with wide eyes. "The fifth of October! That only gives us a little more than two weeks," he whispered in shock. "Construction will take longer than two weeks to complete. You know that."

"That is why we must pick up the pace."

Abbed shook his head back and forth. "You have to ask for more time."

"Impossible," Akbar responded. "The first stage of construction will end on the fifth. We must move forward quickly."

Abbed nodded. Both of them knew the importance of the fifth of October.

That was the day when the boss's son would be put to death.

The Boss, also known as Sheik Abdullah Abulla in Saudi Arabia, was the Crown Prince's half-brother's nephew. He ruled his own little part of the kingdom with his own ocean full of oil under the sand. He was a billionaire many times over but his only male offspring had confined his father's travels to the Middle East for over a decade now. He was no longer welcome in the West, in part because of his violent hatred for the Jews and like-minded Americans. The other part had a little something to do with his son taking part in the plot on 9/11.

The Sheik's son, Muqtada Abdulla, had grown up in the mosques of Saudi Arabia learning to hate America and its sinful ways of drunkenness, debauchery, and homosexuality. Allah demanded that all the infidels be killed, and Muqtada set his course to violently follow that order. He had conspired with bin Laden in the mountains of Afghanistan and personally trained seven of the terrorist hijackers. He watched the attacks live with the al-Qaeda leadership and was hoisted on the shoulders of joyous thugs when the Twin Towers came down. He was promised, and received, a large portion of the vast wealth of the terrorist network and built his own fortified compound in Pakistan to live out his days and offer his services to up-and-coming terrorist organizations that wanted to strike the Great Satan – kind of like a terrorism consultant for the 21st century. His dream of living as a hero was derailed, however, when U.S. Army Special Forces knocked on his front door. They then broke down the door, killed his bodyguards, and captured the scum of the earth and hauled his sorry ass back to the U.S. detention facility at Guantanamo Bay, Cuba.

Three years later, Muqtada was found guilty in a military tribunal and sentenced to death. His appeals had dragged on for ten years until the Supreme Court upheld his conviction and sentence. Two days before Akbar and Abbed's meeting at the Hilton, the Federal Bureau of Prisons issued its final directive:

Office of Public Affairs
Washington, D.C.

For immediate release – Federal execution date set for Muqtada Adbulla

Today, the Federal Bureau of Prisons set October 5th as the date on which to carry out the death sentence of inmate Muqtada Abdulla at the United States Penitentiary, Terre Haute, Indiana. Abdulla was found guilty of conspiracy to commit a terrorist act in connection with the attacks on September 11, 2001, in New York City.

The Federal Bureau of Prisons formally notified Abdulla, in writing, of his scheduled execution date. The execution will occur at 8 p.m., Eastern Standard Time. In accordance with federal regulations, the method of execution will be by lethal injection.

Further notice regarding the procedures for viewing the execution by victims, victims' family members, and members of the media pool will be sent in the upcoming weeks.

Now Sheik Abulla wanted to exact revenge on the United States. How dare America do this to his son. He wanted America brought to her knees. The thought of attacking the prison had been debated and rejected. Instead, the plan was to kill the President and demand the release of Muqtada. The Sheik wanted a big score, a lasting legacy that would make him a hero in the Middle East and his son a likely martyr in the eyes of the Muslim world. He knew the chances of success were slim but he was willing to take the risk at cutting the head off the American snake. Killing the President would remind the American people that the destruction was their own fault brought about because of their immoral and godless ways and their unlawful occupation of foreign lands. And if a dead President did not lead America to changing its course of evil, the Sheik would unleash his terrorist network on the United States in the post-assassination chaos.

"Do you have the work schedule?"

Akbar pulled a sheet of paper out of his folder. "It looks like the job site will be ready for the second stage by the middle of next week. We need to start our preliminary operations and get our people in place."

"I will get Malik and Ahmed ready to head to the job site," Abbed said. "They are some of my best young workers. Malik will be ready within two days."

"Good. Let's get to work."

CHAPTER 3

Capitol Hill – Washington, D.C.

Congresswoman Rosita Sanchez sat in her Capitol Hill office basking in the sunlight that filtered through the windows offering stunning views of the Washington Monument and the Lincoln Memorial. Most of the members of Congress were at home pressing their constituents' flesh or holding town-hall meetings, but Sanchez found her plush office the best place to conduct business. After rising out of the depths of poverty to her current position as House Minority Leader, the newspapers across the country were heralding this new star of the Democratic Party.

Because today she was one step closer to becoming the next President of the United States.

Rosita Sanchez was born in Los Angeles to parents who had illegally crossed the U.S./Mexico border some ten years before her birth. Her mother worked as a maid for two hotel chains, while her father made a living in the back-breaking work found in the Southern California farm fields. Often left alone while her parents worked, Sanchez grew up in a dirt poor section of L.A. – dodging bullets from drive-by gang bangers and sharing the streets with drug pushers and dope dealers. She had friends in the gangs, some more in prison, and even tried the dope on a few occasions. But she decided early on she wanted a better life for herself.

And she wanted to take her countrymen right along with her.

Sanchez worked her way through law school and returned to her hometown to start representing those in her community – those who, in her mind, were wrongly targeted by the police because of the color of their skin and routinely forgotten by the politicians because of the lack of money in their wallets. She began organizing community protests and navigated the bureaucratic maze to obtain welfare checks for the poor, food stamps for the hungry, and decent legal representation for the indigent. Feeling she had done more for the citizens' well-being than the local representative who spent most of his time in Washington, she ran for a spot in Congress and won the seat on the backs of the large Hispanic population in the district. With her flowing dark hair and good looks, the 45-year-old Sanchez was never at a loss for attention. Plus, she was articulate and fiercely determined to wage war with those she felt were holding her people down. Some in the media called her the Hispanic Obama, and many more believed she would be the first woman to occupy the Oval Office.

"Did you see the President is going to El Paso tomorrow?" Sanchez asked, her face hiding behind a copy of that morning's *Post*.

Also hiding behind his own copy was Niles Julius Bongiorno III, Sanchez's campaign director and highly respected political guru. A graduate of Yale, with degrees in political science and law, Bongiorno had become a master political strategist, one who commanded big bucks to retain his services. Sharply dressed in a blue pinstriped suit with white pocket square and matching tie, he had made the Capital's best-dressed list the past three years and he was always a hot topic of discussion when he paraded into the ubiquitous cocktail parties throughout the Beltway. With his Ivy League milieu, he was the exact opposite of his political competitor William Cogdon – rich, debonair, and telegenic. He was a star in his own right and had the credentials to back up his elite smugness.

Over the last two decades, he used his family's vast banking wealth and his own political skills in running congressional campaigns across the country before moving on to statewide contests for the U.S. Senate. Now it was the big show – where the stakes involved the entire world not just some trivial congressional district. He had signed on with Sanchez even before she had thought about running for President. He could tell she was going to be the future of the Democratic Party and scooped her up before any of the other political vultures had a chance to latch on to her.

Bongiorno's candidate had outlasted six other Democrats seeking to take down President Schumacher in the upcoming election. It had been a bruising battle – six rich, white males from the country clubs against the Hispanic female Sanchez from the barrio. She was the least experienced of the bunch – three had been governors, two had been senators, and one was a retired three-star general. The two senators had over twenty years under their belts, their start coming when a twenty-something Sanchez was still a sophomore undergrad at Southern Cal. But Bongiorno had helped Sanchez weather the political storm and pushed her to the precipice of power – with only one more election to go.

"We are going to have to hammer the President on his stance on Hispanics," Bongiorno said, folding up his paper and placing it neatly on the table in front of him. He crossed one leg over the other and flicked a speck of paper off the knee of his creased trousers. He could practically see his reflection in the top of his shoe. He had both of them shined everyday on Capitol Hill – in part to show his fastidious nature but mostly to flaunt his wealth and power. He especially loved watching newbie Dem congressmen, some of whom slept on their office hide-a-bed, parade by the shoe-shine stand in their wrinkled suits and genuflect in his direction while he looked down from his royal perch and the commoners buffed, brushed, and otherwise fawned over his fine Italian footwear. He repeated his brilliant idea. "Hammer him like there's no tomorrow."

"Does he even have a stance on Hispanics?" Her tone insinuated the President probably never gave Hispanics a second thought. African-Americans either. Any person of color for that matter.

"Doesn't matter," Bongiorno shrugged. "We make it sound like he wants to ship every Spanish speaking person back to Mexico, whether they are illegals or born and raised American citizens."

"Do you really think that would work?" Sanchez asked, finally putting down her paper and turning her eyes to Bongiorno.

"It's worked so far, hasn't it?"

The Sanchez campaign had been hard-core liberal – focusing most of its attention on minorities, the poor, the downtrodden – all those people who had been voting for Democrats for the last thirty years but, to the surprise of no one on the Right, had nothing to show for it but an addiction to government handouts. Thus, the primary campaign was one full of grand promises. Sanchez promised to be their savior, the one who would finally unshackle them from their bonds of destitution and provide for their every need by redistributing wealth and sticking it to those rich fat cats who had kept them down for so long. Sanchez was well-known for playing the race card, the female card, or any other applicable card she had in her deck that would instantly shut her opponents up. Just the idle threat of being called a racist or a bigot or a xenophobe by Sanchez was enough to buckle the knees of even the most liberal of Democrats.

"Hell, we got Senator Cravens to drop out of the race just because he had a Hispanic housekeeper," Bongiorno said, reminiscing about one of the highlights of the primary campaign. "She was legal and they paid her above minimum wage. But when you asked him at that second debate about his Mexican slaves, he almost shit his pants."

Sanchez smiled with delight. "Yes, he did." The zinger by Sanchez and Senator Craven's deer-in-the-headlights look of political fright had been replayed countless times on TV and the Internet. It was a classic low blow, and Cravens, who was thereafter inundated with angry calls from Hispanic groups to drop out, could not recover from the hit.

"He withdrew from the race three days later."

"Health reasons," Sanchez said with feeling.

"Health reasons, my ass. He was just afraid you would call him on something else that we didn't know about yet. He probably had an illegal gardener or something. Maybe a Mexican mistress that he had on the side."

While it was fun to relive the good times of the campaign, Sanchez knew the battle for the White House was just starting to heat up. They had already discussed shifting to the political center to grab the moderates and independents. And she had to make a final decision about running mates. The right Vice-Presidential candidate could mean the difference in a close election between winning and losing. And given that a large portion of Americans still wondered whether Congresswoman Rosita Sanchez had what it took to be President, the right running mate would have to be someone Sanchez and the American people could trust and rely on when a crisis arose in the White House.

"What have your polls said about the VP slot?"

Bongiorno opened up his black briefing folder and pulled out a sheet of paper showing the latest numbers. "Thirty-three percent say Governor Thackston, thirty percent say General Graham, twenty-three percent say Senator Mason, and a couple of idiots want Senator Cravens on the ballot."

Governor William Thackston had led the State of Minnesota for the last eight years. He had pushed through state-run health care and raised taxes – two items the Republicans would pounce on if he became the VP candidate. Still, he had weathered the "Great Flood" that hit St. Cloud two years ago with courage and confidence. In that liberal-leaning state, he had good executive skills and a great campaign organization. Sanchez could rely on him to bring home the white Midwesterners and the middle-of-the-road, big-city undecideds. He had made the short list of most TV prognosticators.

But while Governor Thackston had his positive attributes, Sanchez had already made up her mind. She had thought about it long and hard, considering both the political realities and the real-world problems she would face as President. She needed someone with a military background. She needed General Thaddeus Graham.

Originally from New York, General Thaddeus Drake Graham, ret., known as T.D. to his friends and colleagues, had three stars on his shoulders from his days in the U.S. Army. After graduating from West Point, where he ranked in the lower third of his class, he received the Purple Heart in Vietnam. He then worked his way up the chain of command stateside when the war was over. After an early retirement, he marched back into the field commanding a blue helmeted United Nations force in central Africa. There, he distinguished himself as a left-wing pacifist, bowing down to the wishes of the third-world communists and tyrannical despots in the U.N. and never doing much of anything without their approval. A French newspaper cartoon once showed him on all fours and tethered to the leash of the U.N. Secretary General, and the conservatives never let him hear the end of it given the weak-kneed French were poking fun of his military skills. O mon dieu!

After making little progress in the fight to stop the multiple African genocides, General Graham returned to America to lecture those who would listen on the evils of superpower politics. MSNBC even gave him a late-night talk show that only a handful of die-hard liberals managed to watch. And half of them were simply flipping through the channels after Letterman signed off for the evening. Buoyed by his television appearances and his résumé, Graham sought the Democratic Presidential nomination, figuring his medals and ribbons would entice moderates to his side. All he had to do was sound tough on terrorism and the job would be his, he thought.

Running consistently near the bottom of the polls, he made it through the Iowa and New Hampshire primaries, Super Tuesday, and two debates before bowing out in late May. He was smart enough to see that he didn't have the campaign operation to win. Not a great feather in the cap for a former commanding officer but maybe next time, he thought. Slightly prone to verbal gaffes, he often brought moments of levity to the campaign trail and cartoonists never failed to exaggerate his big head, his 1980s comb over, his bright white teeth, and his supersized ego. But most importantly to his political career, he had sidestepped the wrath of Congresswoman Sanchez, came out of the primary campaign relatively unscathed, and set himself up for a spot on the ticket. Or at the very least a Cabinet post.

"This campaign is going to be all about national security," Bongiorno said. "We need someone with some military experience to reassure the American people that they will be safe under a Sanchez Administration. I really think General Graham would give us that lift that we need. He'll put us over the top."

Sanchez was already on board. "And we need to make the campaign about how dangerous the Schumacher Administration is and will be in the coming years. How many more attacks will America have to endure under this President? He is the greatest recruiting tool al-Qaeda has. Even more than the second Bush and his Gitmo prison."

"General Graham has already pounded away at President Schumacher and his cowboy brand of diplomacy."

"And I can let him keep on pounding," Sanchez said. "It will carry a lot more weight from a military man."

Bongiorno nodded his head in total agreement. "We need someone who can bring peace to the world," he said with feeling. The liberal mantra was always peace – whether it be one-sided negotiation or all-out capitulation. And it would be the mantra of a President Sanchez. "We need someone who will finally bring the radical Muslims to the table and listen to their needs. Maybe it's time for America to realize it cannot keep dropping bombs all over the world in hopes of making peace."

"I agree. Why don't you put a call into General Graham," Sanchez said. "Tell him we need to talk about the future of America."

Chicago, Illinois

Mohammed Hamda's head was looking in every direction but the one where the danger was coming right at him at a quick pace. To the left, the right, and the rear, he saw nothing but people – laughing, talking, focused on everything but him. At least that was a good thing. But he was not focused on what was happening in front of him.

"Heads up!"

"Watch out!"

"Incoming!"

Hamda flinched on all three warnings, his head snapping to the northwest, his wide eyes looking for the problem that was on its way. He could feel his heart pounding away inside his chest. He was a split second away from diving for cover to save his own life. Luckily, his eyes caught the missile just off to his right.

It landed on the concourse, and after one bounce a horde of middle-aged men piled onto each other in their quest for a $12 Major League baseball.

In the relative silence that followed. Hamda regained his breath, the rhythmic crack of the bat echoing throughout the stadium helping to calm his nerves. His heart rate began to return back to normal. He had picked U.S. Cellular Field as a meeting place because of open space and the large number of people. The White Sox were hosting the Yankees that evening, and it was sure to be a sell-out since the Bronx Bombers were a huge draw wherever they went. The chances of undercover cops listening in on his conversations in that pack of humanity made it an ideal place to have a discussion with the man he had recently met on Facebook.

The man was supposed to meet Hamda on the main concourse behind the center-field bleachers. Looking for the man for the past twenty minutes, Hamda never once looked at the batting practice taking place on the field or the balls that were flying into the stands and into the hands of the ball hawks. In hopes of getting out of the glare of the soon-to-be setting sun, he settled in the dark shadow of the statue of Hall of Fame catcher Carlton Fisk.

Hamda had never been to a baseball game before, never even watched a full game on TV, and he had never witnessed the great Fisk strap on the chest protector and shin guards and squat behind home plate at the Old and New Comiskey Parks. Hamda had no idea who Fisk was, or that he was once the all-time home run leader for major league catchers – the most famous dinger, of course, being his dramatic shot off the Fenway Park foul pole, after some gentle coaxing, in the twelfth inning of the '75 World Series. Notwithstanding his lack of baseball knowledge, Hamda gleaned the man affectionately known as Pudge must have been popular given his current bronzed state and the large collection of #72 jerseys in the crowd.

But baseball history was not on his mind today. Hamda's eyes looked toward the left-field line and then to the right-field side. He had told the man to wear a White Sox hat so he would know who he was. Unfortunately, every other person in the place was wearing a Sox hat. A smattering of others showed their support for the Yankees. Hamda only had a poor quality picture of the man from his Facebook page. He glanced at it every so often hoping to put a face with the photo.

Mohammed Hamda had just turned twenty four years of age. He worked at a dry cleaner during the day but earning a paycheck had been the last thing on his mind in the last two and a half months. He had grown up in Yemen, came to the United States when he was eighteen, and enrolled in a community college hoping to become restauranteur. But then the attack on the National Archives occurred, and he quickly decided the restaurant business would offer none of the glory that international terrorism had to offer its martyrs.

With his healthy ego, he envisioned himself on par with bin Laden, maybe a younger version but with similar dreams, and he was determined to make a name for himself in the United States. And that could only be done by killing a large number of Americans on their home soil. Being self-radicalized, he had yet to immerse himself in the network of like-minded jihadists who could carry out destruction on a scale to his liking. He hoped that would change today. The man he was to be meeting shared his views, and this was the first face-to-face meeting to discuss their planned holy war against the United States.

Hamda turned to look at the field, the players hurrying off after the end of batting practice. The game would start in less than an hour, and rows of fans began making their way to the concession stands and restrooms before the first pitch.

"Is now a good time for prayer?" the man said quietly into Hamda's ear.

Hamda flinched, his head turning to his left. He had not seen him coming. The man next to him was wearing a Sox hat just like he said he would. Hamda recognized the beard. The picture he was holding showed the man with a nicely trimmed beard.

"Fayez?" Hamda asked, looking the man over. The man was wearing khaki pants and a black Sox T-shirt. He blended in nicely with his surroundings.

"Mohammed," Fayez Harraj said. "It is nice to finally meet you."

Hamda gripped the man's right hand with his own. He was noticeably nervous. He had begun to sweat, and his palm was moist. Today was the first day he had ever entered into a conspiracy to wage war against the United States of America. His heart was beating like a drum it was so exhilarating.

"Fayez, my friend, shall we take a seat?" Hamda asked, nodding his head to his left.

Hamda and Harraj sat in the last row of the bleachers and exchanged pleasantries. Harraj had been born in the United States but became increasingly disillusioned with the American way of government and its prosecution of the war on terror. He hated the U.S. occupation of Iraq and Afghanistan and feared the imposition of Western-style democracy would hold down the true Islamic believer. He took to the Internet to find like-minded Muslims in the United States, and his search led him to Hamda, who fancied himself as an up-and-coming voice for angry Muslim men.

After an hour of getting to know each other, which helped allay Hamda's fears that Harraj might be an undercover cop, neither of the men realized the game had started. Hoping not to draw attention to themselves, they had stood for the Star-Spangled Banner. But Hamda took notice when Harraj did not remove his cap. He took it as a good sign, one of disrespect for the Great Satan and its blood-drenched flag. Now, after the Yankees went in order in the top of the first, Hamda motioned for Harraj to the aisle.

"Why don't we take a walk."

Hamda and Harraj walked to the concourse and headed for the left-field line, the smell of fresh-baked pretzels and cinnamon churros filling the air. Hamda, however, was in no mood for food. He was constantly looking over his shoulder and into the eyes of those passing by with their eight-dollar cups of beer and four-dollar hot dogs. He was suspicious of everything and everyone. Oblivious to the sudden roar of the crowd, he almost jumped out of his shoes when the fireworks started booming overhead, the aerial bombs and the famed exploding scoreboard with its flashing pinwheels denoting the Sox had led off the bottom half with a home run. For a second, he thought the stadium was under attack.

Over the Sox organist's traditional rendition of *Na Na Hey Hey (Kiss Him Goodbye)* belting out from the loudspeakers, Hamda leaned over to Harraj and yelled into his ear. "Let's get out of here so we can talk some more!" he said, pointing to the exit.

"We're leaving the stadium?" Harraj asked.

"Yes, let's go." There were security people in yellow jackets all over the place and Hamda did not want to risk cops listening in on their conversation. He just knew the authorities were looking at him and waiting to haul him off to some windowless room where they could throw him in with the drunks and the ticket scalpers and then interrogate him like some common criminal. Hamda and Harraj would be the only people walking out of the ballpark, and that would help Hamda keep an eye on things.

They crossed 35th Street and walked around the lot to the north of the stadium where Old Comiskey once stood from 1910 to 1990. There was a parking lot of cars around, a few trash cans, but nothing that caught Hamda's attention. The absence of security put his mind at ease. Finally, they had some peace and quiet.

"Your brother in Yemen has called for jihad against President Schumacher," Hamda said to Harraj, who was not related to the man but a devout follower of his ramblings.

"Yes, he is stirring up a lot of anger back home."

"I want to do the same here," Hamda said, looking north to the Chicago skyline. He envisioned a world of possibilities that the city offered, but he was growing impatient. He read stories about his Muslim brothers, some of whom were leading the fight, others who had become martyrs for the cause, and he could not stand waiting any longer to make a name for himself. "But I want real action, not words."

"What do you have in mind?"

"I want something big," Hamda said, his mind full of dreams. "I want big numbers that will make the history books."

Harraj could see the madness in the man's eyes. He then threw his thumb over his right shoulder. "We just left thirty thousand plus inside the stadium."

"It will not work," Hamda said, shaking his head. "You cannot get a bomb close enough to kill many people here. They were even checking bags at the gate when I walked in." He acted like he knew what he was talking about, like he had thought it all through and decided against it. "A truck bomb would be lucky to kill a couple hundred with all the cement and steel of the stadium. I don't want to kill a hundred." He then looked directly at Harraj. "I want thousands to die."

Harraj nodded. He had made it clear to Hamda in their e-mail discussions that he wanted the same. He knew people in and around Chicago who could put a plan together if the right opportunity presented itself – some who were just waiting for the right time to strike.

"You need a big crowd," Harraj said.

"Yes, a mass of people."

"Like all those people in Times Square in New York City on New Year's Eve."

"Yes, but without the security."

Harraj looked at his watch and checked the date. The World Series wasn't too far around the corner. The eyes of the world would be on the games, and the spectacle would attract large crowds. But the chances of it happening on the South Side were slim, given the White Sox were eight games back of the rival Twins. Only a late September rally could push them into the postseason. And it went without saying that there would be no chance of a Fall Classic on the North Side of the Windy City. The Bears had started their season, but Soldier Field would not be a viable target. Again, too much steel and concrete to unleash the carnage Hamda was looking for.

"What about the marathon?" Harraj asked.

Hamda stopped in mid stride. "Marathon?"

Hamda hadn't even thought about the Chicago Marathon. Although well-known in the running community as well as with the die-hard locals who lined the streets in their respective neighborhoods on race day, the marathon did not get a lot of press around the sports world. It could be easily overlooked. But it did provide Hamda with a tempting target. There would be no stadium facade in his way, not even the worldwide hoopla of the World Series or the NFL that would attract armed personnel from multiple law-enforcement agencies. Just a sea of people for as far as the eye could see.

"How many people would be in the marathon?"

"You could be talking thirty to forty thousand," Harraj said. "That's not even counting the spectators."

"And it covers a large area?"

Harraj pointed at the ground and then to the north. "From here to Wrigley Field on the North Side and just about everywhere in between. It goes all over the city."

"Would security be tight?"

"Doubtful," Harraj said. "Since the marathon doesn't make headline news and because they can't secure the entire course, security would probably consist of a couple of cops on the corners directing traffic."

Hamda nodded his head and smiled. He looked north at the 110 stories of the Willis Tower and the rest of the skyscrapers standing tall in the Chicago skyline. He now had the target he wanted. The 9/11 terrorists targeted a large number of people concentrated in single buildings – the World Trade Center and the Pentagon. But he would do the same but without the buildings. His targets would be congregated together in a few city blocks. He didn't see the need to go looking for anywhere else to unleash his dream of destruction. He wanted to get started immediately so he could become a star in the Muslim world.

"You say you know people who can help put something together?"

Harraj nodded. "I have a couple of guys that feel the same as we do. They have been trained to kill but will only act when they know an attack is of a significant size that it will make a difference. They are not interested in putting a bomb-laden backpack on a park bench to kill a couple of people. You however will offer them the opportunity to get into the game so they can use their skills."

"I can get them money."

"I will make some calls," Harraj said. "I take it you want a bomb?"

"Yes, a truck bomb would do nicely," Hamda said. Thinking better of it, he added, "maybe two."

"You are aiming big."

"Yes," Hamda said. "I want it to be spectacular."

CHAPTER 4

The White House – Washington, D.C.

President Schumacher stepped off the elevator on the ground floor of the White House and made the stroll along the Colonnade on his way to the Oval Office. The Indian summer air could be felt even at that early hour of 7 a.m. Alongside him was the head of his Secret Service protective detail, Special Agent Michael Craig, who had been by his side ever since Schumacher had become Vice President. The tall and lean forty-year-old Craig had a head of graying hair that caused many observers to mistake him for the President, even though the latter was fifteen years his senior. They both got along well, talked about each other's families often, and respected each other's job.

"Are your guys all ready to head to El Paso tomorrow?" President Schumacher asked. His sly smile indicated the question was not about family vacation plans or a nice tranquil conference with lots of coffee, orange juice, and cream-cheese pastries. It was work. Stressful work.

Agent Craig's "guys" consisted of over 125 Secret Service agents, men and women, who had worked for two weeks on the President's scheduled trip to El Paso, Texas. The trip was meant to give the President an appropriate backdrop for his speech on border security, a major platform in his campaign. An advance team had gone over El Paso with a fine-toothed comb – mapping out the route from the airport to the convention center, as well as any escape route in case there was trouble, coordinating with local police and hospitals, and also keeping their ears open for rumblings of trouble.

"If it were up to me," Agent Craig said. "I'd keep you inside the White House bunker twenty-four-seven."

Agent Craig knew what he was talking about. He had a front row seat to President Schumacher's brushes with danger. He was on the Marine Two helicopter carrying the Vice President when it was shot out of the sky after departing from Camp David. They were the only two survivors of the eight on board. He was standing next to Vice President Schumacher when President Fisher drank a bottle of cyanide-laced tea to take his own life. Agent Craig had also been the one who forcefully carried the President out of the House Chamber when Supreme Court Justice Ali Hussein tried to detonate his suicide vest.

Agent Craig was beginning to wonder if the President's luck was going to run out sometime in the near future. Maybe it would run out for both of them.

"You're not burning out on me, are you?"

Agent Craig responded with a smile and added, "I'm just being paranoid."

"Good, that's what I need," the President responded. "Always on your toes."

Agent Craig opened the door to the Oval Office for the President. Once inside, they saw the Director of the Federal Bureau of Investigation, Tyrone Stubblefield, talking with the Director of Homeland Security, Bradley Michaelson, and the Director of the Secret Service, Allan Defoe. National Security Adviser Carl Harnacke was talking on his cell phone as he stood near the fireplace.

"Good morning, gentlemen," the President said.

"Morning, Mr. President," the four men responded.

While most Presidents would utilize the two couches in the Oval Office with a crowd of this size, President Schumacher liked to sit behind his desk and write notes so he asked the four men to pull up chairs. Agent Craig stood guard by the door to the Colonnade.

The President rocked gently in his leather chair as he thumbed through the Presidential Daily Brief that he had brought with him from the residence. A CIA officer had dropped off the PDB earlier that morning, and the President had looked over the highly classified material right along with his box scores.

A knock on the door leading to the President's secretary was followed by the bald head of CIA Director William Parker popping in.

"Director Parker, come in," the President said, waving him to the assembled group.

"Sorry, I'm late, sir."

"No problem. I was just glancing over the PDB one more time."

Director Parker pulled up the last remaining empty chair. "Am I taking Mr. Cogdon's chair?"

"No, he won't be joining us this morning," the President said. "We've decided Mr. Cogdon will take a leave of absence from his duties as chief of staff to run the campaign full time. But, given his control issues, he probably hasn't delegated the duties to his deputy yet." The President closed his PDB. "Now, why do you look so glum, Director Parker? You look plum tuckered out, like there might be problems out there in the world."

Director Parker nodded. "Yes, sir. There is always something."

The President shook his head. Every day was the same. "Just once I'd like to come into the Oval Office and have you tell me the world is quiet today. Nothing to worry about, Mr. President."

"That probably won't happen until your last day in office," Parker said. "And even then I wouldn't put it past those who seek to do you harm."

The President sighed. "Well, what's the matter with the world today?"

Director Parker leaned forward in his chair and opened up his leather folder. "Mr. President, as you know the CIA, with the help of the NSA, captures a tremendous amount of conversational traffic from all over the world. The chatter we normally hear fell off dramatically after the attempted assassination in the Capitol. It was almost like the terror cells were trying to judge the reaction to the attempt. Did Justice Hussein have the backing of a state sponsor of terror? Or was he a lone wolf? I think they were also attempting to see how the attack played out. How did you react? How did the Secret Service react? What precautions have been implemented? What changes have been made in your security?"

"And now the chatter has . . . ?"

"The chatter has started back up again," Director Parker said ominously.

"Let me guess. I'm still a target."

Director Parker did not smile. "I believe so, sir. You will always be a target."

"But you have new concerns?"

"Mr. President, when I first started working for the CIA twenty years ago ninety percent of our assets on the ground were in Russia, China, Afghanistan, and Europe. We rarely received much intel from South America or Central America. But, of late, we are receiving a surprisingly large amount of intelligence coming from Mexico."

"Mexico?"

"Yes, sir. Over the last few years, Mexico has become a country of utter lawlessness. The drug cartels run most of the northern part of the country and a good deal of the southern part at the Guatemalan border. As you know, the violence has escalated even to a point that it has crossed over the border into the United States."

The President nodded his head, noting he was well aware of it.

"The Border Patrol and Immigration and Customs Enforcement are seeing an increasing amount of drug smuggling being attempted across the southern border. And now, what is even more worrisome, is we are also beginning to see Pakistani nationals arriving in Mexico City, foreigners from Somalia and Yemen have been flagged by Mexican authorities in Acapulco. You'd be surprised by the number of phone calls the NSA has logged from Ciudad Juarez to Pakistan."

NSA Harnacke nodded in agreement. He had received the same intel.

The President wrote something down on his legal pad. "Well," he said, "I guess that's all the more reason for me to hit border security hard in this campaign. I'll start tomorrow in El Paso."

Directors Stubblefield and Defoe sat forward in their seats and glanced at each other. Both of them had the same thing on their minds.

"About that El Paso trip, Mr. President," Director Stubblefield said.

The President held up his hands. He knew exactly what Stubblefield was going to say. "Come on, guys. El Paso is one of the safest cities in America. And I doubt Agent Craig will let me walk unaccompanied across the border to Juarez so there's no reason to worry."

Ciudad Juarez, however, was a reason to worry. Situated less than three miles south from El Paso, the Mexican border town had one of the highest murder rates in the world – higher even than Bogota and Baghdad. Many U.S. officials believed the Mexican Government had lost total control of the area now run by drug-trafficking organizations. Gun battles between cartels and the Mexican military were not uncommon even in broad daylight. Several Americans had been caught in the crossfire. Kidnappings were rampant, and the failure to pay the ransom could lead to a family member's decapitation or his mutilated body dangling from a bridge. The situation had gotten so far out of control the U.S. State Department issued alerts to those looking to travel to Ciudad Juarez and recommended they use extreme caution, travel only during daylight hours, or forgo any unnecessary trips altogether. Travel was at your own risk.

"We're just worried right now might not be the best time for a trip to El Paso," Director Stubblefield said. "Some of my compatriots in the Mexican Government are very skittish right now. I don't get the feeling that they are in much control down there. It worries me greatly." He gave the President an all-too familiar look that he wasn't just being overly cautious.

The Director of the FBI was the President's closest advisor in all of Washington, D.C., and more importantly his best friend. Their thirty-year friendship began when they roomed together as new agent trainees at the FBI. Just out of law school, the young fresh-faced attorney Anthony Schumacher was unpacking his belongings at the FBI training academy in Quantico, Virginia, when the massive six-foot-six former linebacker for the Oakland Raiders walked into the room and said they would be bunkmates. Realizing this was not someone you disagreed with, young Schumacher offered a hearty handshake.

Once they became FBI agents, both Schumacher and Stubblefield were stationed in San Diego, where the old guard dubbed the rookies the "Odd Couple." Schumacher was six-two, as Indiana white as Larry Bird, and thin like a marathon runner. Stubblefield, all black with a sleek bald head, was built like bulldozer. A good deal of their work centered on nabbing high-profile drug dealers shipping their illicit wares across the border from Tijuana. Agent Schumacher's career was cut short after he was struck down by a bullet in a foiled bank robbery. The only thing that saved him from certain death was his partner running into the bank and shooting the remaining gunman.

Following his retirement from the FBI, Schumacher practiced law before entering the political arena which eventually resulted in his current seat in the Oval Office. And Director Stubblefield had a hand in keeping him there too. Stubblefield and his FBI discovered the plot of Justice Hussein to blow himself up in the House Chamber. After a race to the Capitol, Stubblefield fired off two shots that took down the Justice before he could detonate his suicide vest. The Director seemed to have the uncanny ability to be in the right place at the right time to save the life of Anthony J. Schumacher. The President owed his life to him.

On a more personal side, the First Lady, Danielle Schumacher, and Director Stubblefield's wife, Tina, had become close friends over the years. They dined regularly, and the First Lady confided in Tina greatly. In part, the First Lady hoped her concerns for her husband's safety would make it up the chain of command in the Stubblefield household.

Knowing the President was ultimately going to travel to El Paso whether anyone in the room liked it or not, Director Stubblefield decided to plant the seeds that people were still out to get him and they might try to come through Mexico. Just to make sure the President knew of the dangers and would take precautions.

"Do you remember when we arrested Raul Camacho?" Stubblefield asked.

Only one other person in the room had ever heard of the name Raul Pedro Camacho. The CIA Director, the National Security Adviser, and the Homeland Security Director were racking their brains trying to remember when and where this unknown individual had been arrested by the FBI. Was he some fugitive on the FBI's Ten Most Wanted list? Or a terrorist they had just forgotten about in the myriad of arrests made in the global war on terrorism over the past several years?

The President, however, was well aware of Mr. Camacho. He remembered him like he was a long-lost relative. "Ah yes, our friend El Diablo."

Raul Camacho was one of the leading drug runners in Southern California when both Schumacher and Stubblefield were rookie field agents with the FBI. At the time, Camacho was on the Ten Most Wanted list, not only for his trafficking in cocaine and heroin but also for the murders of several Mexican police chiefs. Agents were warned the man was heavily armed and highly dangerous. Hiding out on the outskirts of San Diego, he blew his cover one dark night when he tried to pick up a hooker. Agents Schumacher and Stubblefield swooped in to nab him, one of their first arrests. It helped take millions of dollars of cocaine and marijuana off the streets of the United States. And it also put a price on the heads of the two arresting agents.

"Mr. President, given our testimony at El Diablo's trial, we have become wanted men by the Sonoran drug cartel."

"You have got to be kidding me. That was thirty years ago!"

Stubblefield managed a knowing smile. "Yes, but El Diablo is still in federal prison. And El Diablo Jr. is running his own subsidiary of the cartel now."

"So, Junior followed in his father's footsteps."

"Yes, sir."

"Isn't that nice. What's the name of Junior's cartel?"

"Los hijos del diablo."

The President smiled. "The sons of the devil."

"You got it. And he has been out for revenge ever since you became headline news."

Director Parker decided to speak up and join the conversation. "It looks like you have pissed off a lot of people in your life, Mr. President."

The President laughed as he rocked in his chair. "I guess I have." He then added. "I guess we both have," he said, pointing an accusatory finger at Director Stubblefield, whose public stature had grown right along with the President's. "People are going to start calling us the Double Trouble Twins."

Director Stubblefield had a rare laugh in agreement but the moment of jocularity didn't last long. "Mr. President, you now have two of the most dedicated and violent organizations on the planet determined to see you dead."

The Oval Office suddenly grew quiet at the statement, its starkness bringing everybody back to reality.

"They will stop at nothing to protect their radical ideology and their illegal businesses." He then tried to put it all together. "With Director Parker's recent spike in intelligence, there might be something brewing between the cartels and foreign nationals with connections to al-Qaeda. We have nothing specific at this point. There is no credible evidence that something is imminent in El Paso, but I just want you to be aware of it."

"I appreciate the info and your concern. I have the utmost faith in the FBI, the CIA, and the Secret Service, and I know you will all stay on top of this. Now let's look forward to El Paso."

CHAPTER 5

Silver Creek, Indiana

Malik al-Mutallab pulled to a quick stop in the rock-filled parking lot, the dry Midwestern dirt flying past the window of his rented Toyota Corolla. It was ninety degrees outside and the scorching September heat wave wasn't helping his nerves any. The sign outside the establishment read "Maple Ridge Farms," a local outpost for the burgeoning farm industry and one of the hundred roadside stands that littered rural Indiana from May to October. The brightly chalked sandwich board outside the front door of the wood frame building beckoned passersby with an assortment of melons, sweet corn, radishes, and tomatoes that were ripe for purchase.

Al-Mutallab looked at his map and then out the front windshield, then turned the map upside down and gave another quizzical look through his squinted eyes. He cursed under his breath as he threw the map into the empty seat next to him. Not only had the rental car's air conditioner failed, so had the worthless GPS device. His cell phone battery died somewhere north of West Lafayette. He was a native of Chicago and was used to seeing city blocks full of steel and glass skyscrapers, a McDonald's or Starbucks on every other corner, parking lots covered in asphalt, and big green signs with white arrows that pointed people to where they wanted to go. Now he was lost in the middle of nowhere Indiana. The gas tank was heading fast toward empty and his patience was wearing thin.

But he had a job to do. And the job site was somewhere nearby. Per Moamar Abbed's orders, al-Mutallab was to be the first wave of scouts to make their way to Silver Creek in search of President Schumacher's family home. Al-Qaeda had not given up on its plan to bring death and destruction to America.

And first and foremost on the hit list was the President of the United States.

President Schumacher's war on terrorism made him enemy number one in al-Qaeda's eyes and the world's most wanted terrorist organization was determined to kill him at all costs. Al-Qaeda's terrorist cell in Chicago was now implementing the first phase of their plan, and nothing was off the table. A terrorist attack could entail automatic weapons, bombs, rocket-propelled grenades, or any other means depending on the situation in and around Silver Creek. Al-Mutallab was sent to check out the bucolic surroundings, survey any accompanying defenses, and set up the plan of attack.

This, however, was al-Mutallab's initial assignment, and his nerves were on edge. He could not help feeling like he was being watched. For years he was taught to be suspicious of everyone. The locals were not to be trusted. All Americans were his enemy, he was constantly told. Now he had to try to portray a sense of calm and complete his assignment.

Needless to say, the thirty-two-year-old al-Mutallab was not a local. His swarthy Middle Eastern look didn't help him blend in, but thousands of tourists of multiple nationalities descended on Silver Creek every year in hopes of catching a glimpse of the President while he was in town. Or at least take a picture of his two-story, white-brick house, which, much to the dismay of the tourists, could not be seen from the only accessible public road near the Schumacher compound. Still, people flocked to Silver Creek to visit the gifts shops, stop by the grade school the President attended, and have their photo taken with a cardboard cutout of him inside the Donut Palace. One aspiring entrepreneur had even started an unofficial Schumacher museum complete with large photos and political knickknacks on display along with its most prized possession – a Little League uniform the President was said to have worn back in the day on the dusty ball diamonds of west-central Indiana. With all the presidential hoopla, Silver Creek had become the second most visited home of living presidents behind the Bushes' Atlantic Ocean estate in Kennebunkport.

Al-Mutallab ran over the checklist in his mind one more time. The script stated he was a medical student from Indianapolis on his way back home from a conference at the University of Illinois at Urbana-Champaign. He was really an engineering student at Purdue, but his handler, Moamar Abbed, wanted to keep the college angle quiet as long as possible. No need to tell people where he was really from if it could be avoided. At any rate, al-Mutallab was ready to claim he was "very much" interested in seeing "the sites" on his way back to Indy and wanted to see the President's house. Perhaps buy a T-shirt showing he had visited Silver Creek. Or maybe a postcard to send to his friends.

But now he was lost and had to ask for directions. In the terrorist handbook, having to stop to ask for help was a big no-no, a giant red flag that brought great risk to any operation. All it did was grab the attention of the concerned citizens, who could relay vital characteristics of the suspicious person to the police.

Al-Mutallab scanned the parking lot. The rusted white Chevy truck sitting on the south side of the building had to be that of the proprietor of the establishment – the "EIEIO 1" license plate a dead giveaway. Outside the front door sat a white Cadillac – most likely the preferred ride of an elderly couple looking for an apple pie or a sack of home-grown tomatoes for that night's dinner. Nothing that looked like it might be used by law enforcement. Of course, in this neck of the woods, al-Mutallab thought the local badged posse probably rode up to the place on horseback. He saw nothing but corn, soybeans, and sycamore trees baking under the sun for as far as his eyes could see. He couldn't imagine anyone wanting to live there. He wiped the sweat off his forehead and stepped out of the car. He walked quickly to the door and turned the handle with his sweaty right hand. The ringing of the bell over the door startled him slightly as he stepped inside.

"Hi," the woman behind the counter said. "Welcome to Maple Ridge Farms."

The polite welcome came from Donna Sullivan, a third generation farmer who now oversaw five-hundred acres of prime Indiana farm ground. She was 75 years old but still had more energy than folks half her age. She was well known in these parts and anyone seeking farm fresh produce made their way to Maple Ridge.

The elderly couple who owned the Cadillac made their way out the door with their bounty and bright smiles. Al-Mutallab let them by and walked cautiously to the counter.

Sullivan knew exactly what the man heading her way wanted. She had seen it a hundred times since Anthony J. Schumacher became Vice President and then President of the United States. She knew the President, had three grown daughters who had gone to high school with him, and found him a down-to-earth guy. She had high hopes that he would win the election and stick around Washington for a full two terms – in part because she wholeheartedly agreed with his conservative politics. But the real reason was he was good for business. His two favorite stops in Silver Creek were Maple Ridge Farms and the Donut Palace, the latter being where he used to work as a teenager. Every time he was in town he stopped by. Two pictures on the wall showed the President enjoying the fresh fare from Maple Ridge. He loved the watermelons and sweet corn in the summer and the homemade apple pies in the fall. The smiley-faced iced cookies at the Donut Palace were good year round. Sullivan had come to the realization that giving directions to lost tourists was just part of the job.

"You look like you could use some fresh apples," she said to the man. She had a magnetic personality and could sell eyeglasses to a blind man. She already had the bag opened. "Or maybe some farm-fresh melons or radishes. Picked 'em fresh this morning."

The man took one last swipe to the sweat on his forehead. "No, I'm just looking for . . . " He stopped in mid sentence, his mind screeching to a sudden stop. He didn't know what to say. He had been instructed to find "that bastard's house" in Silver Creek and report back. Luckily for him, his mind stopped him before "that bastard" left his mouth.

Donna read him like an open book and bailed him out. "You're looking for the Indiana White House, aren't you?" It was so obvious.

He nodded and started rambling on how he was on his way back to Indianapolis from a doctor's conference in Champaign and thought he would visit the President's hometown. He had read about Silver Creek in the paper and saw stories about it on TV. After hours of rehearsing, he sounded believable. He smiled too, just like he had practiced.

"You need to get back on the road you were on and head south," she said pointing out the window. When you stop at the intersection, turn right at the stop sign and head west for three miles. Once you get to the next intersection, turn left, and the President's house will be about a mile to the south on the right-hand side of the road hidden behind the trees. You'll see the guardhouse out front." She added with a smile, "If you drive into the river you'll know you've gone too far." She always liked that line.

The man followed the owner's finger with his own. "South to the stop sign, right to the stop sign, and then left."

"You got it. Now, how about a pint of strawberries for the family back in Indy? You doctors know how important it is to eat healthy. Lots of good vitamin C here."

Wanting to blend in and feeling the need to show his agreement with her assessment of the medical profession, of which he was a part in mind only, he nodded his head and reached for his wallet. She said two-fifty but he threw a five on the counter, grabbed the pint, and told her to keep the change. He was late and needed to get a move on. He was supposed to have uploaded a whole host of Silver Creek pictures to Abbed back in Chicago. He thanked her and hustled out to his car to get back on schedule. With tires spinning in the parking lot gravel, he was finally on his way.

But he was not the only one on the move.

Sullivan's antennae were raised as soon as the man walked in the door. A glance out her window indicated he had come alone – a rarity in her mind. Most of the regular gawkers had a caravan full of kids or a Cadillac full of old ladies looking for covered bridges or, at the appropriate time, the abundantly beautiful fall foliage. Young men all by their lonesome and searching for the President's house were few and far between. The car was clearly a rental – the green "e" logo indicating it was from the Enterprise stable. The Indiana license plate indicated the car came from Lake County, home to Gary, Indiana, just outside of Chicago. The capital city of Indianapolis sits in Marion County. The signs might seem innocuous to most, but not this 75-year-old farmer.

Donna grabbed a paper bag from beneath the counter and unholstered the stainless steel pliers dangling on the right hip of her denim overalls. She squeezed the edge of the five-dollar bill with her pliers and dropped it in the bag. She folded over the top of the bag and put it in the drawer of the desk behind her before reaching for the phone.

Maple Ridge Farms was the closest thing to civilization near the President's house. There was little around other than the forests of trees and corn fields. The bustling metropolis of Silver Creek, population 7,800, was eight miles to the southeast and tourists just off the interstate who didn't want to drive all the way into town to ask for directions stopped at her place. Most left with a better sense of where they were headed. And a bag of produce, too.

"This is Agent Ford," the man on the other end of the line said.

"Hi. This is Donna Sullivan at Maple Ridge Farms," she said, looking out the window and losing sight of the man's car down the road. She could still see his trail of dust rising above the fields. "And I just gave directions to a guy who just didn't seem right to me."

She had only made the call once before. Roughly a year ago, a disheveled man with a mess of blonde hair and smelling like he hadn't bathed in a week barged into the shop and asked for directions to the Schumacher residence. The wide eyes and pressured speech of the man scared Donna so much she called the Silver Creek police department and reported that a crazy man was asking where the Schumachers lived because he had a present for Ashley, the oldest of the Schumacher children. She feared he was on his way to harm her. The police department transferred her to the sheriff's department. After relaying the facts once again, her call was transferred to the Secret Service command post. By that time, the determined madman was running through the cornfield toward the Schumacher house. Once he emerged from the corn, and after a short scramble, the man was apprehended and carted off to the mental-health hospital. The Secret Service thanked Donna for her tip and asked for her assistance. If she saw anything suspicious, they asked her to immediately call the guardhouse on the Schumacher property. The Secret Service agents rewarded her by being frequent customers.

Donna gave the man's license plate number and a description of the car. She also told the agent she kept the five-dollar bill he had given her. Agent Ford thanked her and told her somebody would stop by later.

She now began to wonder if the war on terror was making its way to Silver Creek.

Ciudad Juarez, Mexico

The dusty road in the northern Chihuahuan Desert ended at a cattle gate and a barbed-wire fence. There were no signs, no ominous warnings about trespassing, or anything marking the territory of the land owners. But everyone south of the Rio Grande knew what lay behind the mesquite thickets on the other side of the fence. And no one showed up uninvited.

Los hijos del diablo didn't like unannounced visitors.

Raul Camacho, Jr., sat behind the wooden desk his father once occupied before his arrest by the FBI. Three walls of his office were painted white and decorated with only a large map of the United States and Mexico on one wall and a macabre portrait of skulls and skeletons in celebration of El Dia de los Muertos, the Day of the Dead, on another. A dusty statue of the Virgin Mary sat in the far corner on one of the shelves that displayed a fine and deadly array of weaponry. The outer wall of the building was lined with sandbags – just in case the Mexican federales or a rival cartel breached the compound perimeter and tried to take out Camacho while he sat in his office. From the ceiling hung a heavy bag that Camacho used for exercise when he was wasn't beating rivals to a pulp.

Camacho was born in Chihuahua, Mexico, smuggled across the border when he was three, and grew up on the streets of Los Angeles with his mother while his father made a living shipping drugs across the southwest border. The gangs of Southern California offered Junior a criminal education, but the Vice Lords with their five-pointed stars and the Gangster Disciples with their pitchfork tattoos bored him. He found the "Folks" and the "People" too juvenile, too concerned about marking their territory with their fancy graffiti. He, on the other hand, wanted more action. So at age sixteen, and with his father in federal prison, he moved back to Mexico to start his career as a world-renowned drug smuggler.

Now in charge of the Sons of the Devil drug-trafficking cartel, Camacho had inherited his father's ruthless and brutal nature. Nothing was too violent in his eyes to further the business. He once kidnapped the local police chief and used a chainsaw to decapitate the man. The video of the atrocity was shown whenever the police or the Mexican Government thought of cracking down on the drug cartels. When an upstart cartel infringed on Camacho's territory, he had two of their members kidnapped, doused with gasoline, and lit on fire. The men, then fully aflame, were thrown to their deaths off a 600-foot bridge. After another cartel rival was found stealing from Camacho, he had the man killed. He then cut off the man's right hand, shoved his middle finger up his anus, and sent the mutilated body to the man's bosses to show them what would happen if they stole from him again.

Camacho allied the Sons of the Devil with the La Familia, the Sinaloan cartel, and La Mara Salvatrucha, the MS-13 gang organization. The MS-13 leaders initially balked at any alliance, actually claiming with great animosity that Camacho had used the MS-13's devil horns as his own tattoo brand. An unconcerned Camacho relented without violence and designed a flaming pitchfork with devil's horns on each side. He kept the sign language though, the upward facing index and pinkie fingers mimicking the horns while the MS-13 used the same but upside down for a downward facing "m." While attempting to not step on each other's toes, the cartels and gangs ran roughshod over Mexico from the borders of Guatemala to the United States. Robbery, murder, and extortion were just some of the violent tricks of their trade as they engaged in drug and arms trafficking, human smuggling, and illegal immigration.

And none of them liked what they were seeing north of the border.

"El Zapatero is coming to El Paso tomorrow," Camacho said to his most trusted lieutenant, Joaquin Carajas. Zapatero is Spanish for shoemaker. Close enough to use for President Schumacher, Camacho thought. Although he was known to use "el serpiente," the snake, and "el perro," the dog, interchangeably.

"You know he is going to call for more funding for the Border Patrol," Carajas said. They all read the news stories, the Internet proving to be a valuable resource to help them keep up with the developments in U.S. border security. "More cameras and technology to stop the flow of narcotics."

"The President does not seem to be a guy who will back down without a fight."

Carajas agreed with the assessment. He was forty one with a closely cropped haircut. His combat boots were caked with the dust he walked through after surveying the warehouse full of cocaine being readied for transport into the United States. "President Zapatero will not help our profit margins any."

Camacho leaned back in his brown leather chair and clasped his hands behind his head. He fancied himself a successful business man. One whose products were not cars or computers or widgets, but cocaine, marijuana, and heroin. The lavender logbook on his desk kept track of all his shipments – accounts received, accounts payable, shipments in transit, shipments confiscated. – in neatly handwritten columns. He had an accountant on staff to keep track of all these matters, but he trusted no one. Far too many of his employees and confidantes had thought stealing from the cartel might bring them great riches. It usually resulted in their untimely deaths. Camacho was constantly tinkering with his business model to keep one step ahead of not only his competitors but also those who wanted to shut his business down for good.

"That is why we have invited our next guest."

Camacho reached over to the phone on his desk and pushed the button for his executive assistant. The woman, the twenty-eight-year-old daughter of one of the Devils, had worked for the organization since she was eleven. She rarely asked questions and simply enjoyed the fruits of the Devils' labors.

"Yes, sir."

"Maria, please show our guest into the office."

"Yes, Mr. Camacho. Right away."

The Middle Eastern man had been glaring at Maria for the better part of twenty minutes, tapping his fingers impatiently on his right knee. Maria did her best to avoid eye contact and act like she was busy with cartel paperwork. She escorted the man down the hall and made a right turn. At the first door, she knocked once and turned the handle. Her left arm swept forward and the man walked in. She quickly closed the door behind him and hurried back to her desk thankful to be out of the stranger's presence and his angry gaze.

Carajas rose from his seat and offered a hand. Camacho stayed seated behind his desk, his hands still behind his head and a smug smirk on his face.

"I have been waiting for thirty minutes," the man said, shaking the hand of Carajas but not taking his eyes off Camacho. The frown on his face was apparent.

"And yet you are still here," Camacho replied.

The man nodded slowly. The frown did not disappear however. He was not used to being kept waiting. He was a man of violence. A terrorist. Someone people feared. His list of human kills probably rivaled Camacho's. But today he was not on his home turf, and Camacho's reputation for being a violent hothead was not something one took lightly or dismissed out of hand.

"How are you and my friends from Yemen this fine day?" Camacho asked.

The man nodded again. "I am well as are my countrymen. And I bring you greetings on their behalf."

Camacho leaned forward and placed his elbows on his desk. "Sit down, Mr. Rumullah. We have a lot to discuss."

Abdi Rumallah was al-Qaeda's human-resource officer in Yemen, recruiting new jihadists for the war against America. It was not a difficult job in the Middle Eastern part of the world. New recruits would line up with little hesitation after those that came before were either captured or killed. Something about serving Allah and enjoying some virgins in the afterlife made them almost desperate to serve. But a week ago, he had received a phone call from Saudi Arabia. And the request from the desert was one for the fast track. Rumallah would have little time to call for Middle East martyrs and implement a plan across the ocean. Given the time crunch, he thought he might have to outsource the job, maybe look elsewhere for his martyrs. He decided the Chihuahuan Desert of Mexico was the place to look. While his call to Camacho was unexpected, the substance of the call was something Camacho heard everyday.

It was all about "that dog President Schumacher" and the evil United States of America.

Camacho got out of his chair and looked out the bulletproof window as his hired help loaded bundles of cocaine onto a small Cessna aircraft. With luck and a good bit of timing, the load would make its way on to American streets within two days. Camacho's weathered cheeks showed a scar on each side, one the symbol of a long forgotten gang initiation, the other a fight with a rival cartel member in a bloody battle to the death. He stood five-ten and his jeans and red checkered shirt hung loosely on his frame. He took his eyes off the window and focused on Rumallah.

"I understand we have a similar interest in the leader to our north."

"Yes," Rumallah said. "I guess you could say we are brothers in the same cause."

Camacho chuckled at the statement. "I don't know about brothers," he said. "Maybe distant cousins. We have different reasons for not liking President Schumacher. What is it I can do for you, my friend?"

"I have a client from Saudi Arabia who wants to make President Schumacher's life difficult."

Don't we all? Camacho thought to himself. "How difficult?"

"Very."

Camacho nodded his head and walked around his desk. He stopped and took a seat on the corner. "I can understand. President Schumacher is threatening to shut down the border and make my job much more difficult."

"That is why I thought we might be able to work together."

"What do you have in mind?"

Rumallah leaned back in his chair. "My client is Sheik Abdullah Abdulla, and he is the father of . . ."

Camacho cut him off before he could continue. "Muqtada Abdulla," he said. "The 9/11 conspirator. I have heard plenty of stories about him." Camacho was beginning to wonder if he was going to regret this meeting.

"And he is going to be executed by the United States on October fifth," Rumallah said.

Camacho knew all of this, and he wanted to get to the heart of the matter. He had contraband to deliver. "What do you want from me?"

Rumallah shifted in his seat. "My people are in the process of implementing their plan to neutralize President Schumacher for good. But we don't know whether we can pull it off in time before Abdulla's execution." He made it sound like the only obstacle was the fast approaching execution date, that it was simply a done deal if only they had more time.

"And?" Come on, get on with it.

"Given your stature in Mexico and around the world," Rumallah said, laying it on as thick as his own ego would allow, "we want you to take out the President when he travels to El Paso tomorrow."

Camacho scoffed at the idea. He might control northern Mexico, but north of the border? Rumallah expected him to assassinate the President of the United States on a moment's notice? Like it was as simple as counting to ten?

"Don't you think I would have done that by now if I had the chance?" he said, looking down at Rumallah. "The guy is going to be a pain in my ass for another four years if he gets elected. And you think it would be easy for me to get the job done?"

"Your way of doing business is well-known, Mr. Camacho. You are the one everyone says can get the job done."

Camacho's eyes widened and he could not hide his grin. He was "The One" everyone talked about? His mind envisioned thugs around the world saying he was the one, and only one, who could take down the President. This new morsel of information, true or not, would circulate amongst the various Mexican drug cartels within hours and further bolster his lethal image. He might one day end up being known as the most dangerous man on the planet.

"Killing the President would benefit us both," Rumallah added.

Camacho left his desk and returned to looking out the window. He could not stop thinking about the notoriety it would generate if he pulled it off. "Do you know how difficult it would be to pull off?"

"My network has many weapons that could help you in your quest."

"Bombs?"

Rumallah nodded. "Bombs, rocket-propelled grenades, suicide vests, whatever you need." He could tell Camacho was thinking it through.

"You have numerous ways to get the hardware into the United States without detection from the authorities?"

"Of course."

"I can have everything you need here by tomorrow morning."

Camacho took his eyes off his workers outside. "I'll think about it," he said. "But my price for entering into your war will be steep."

"Rest assured, my friend," Rumallah said as he stood. "The kingdom of Saudi Arabia has resources you can only dream of ."

Camacho walked over to Rumallah and stuck out his hand. "I'll be in touch."

CHAPTER 6

Capitol Hill – Washington, D.C.

The right hand of the Director of the FBI was held at shoulder level, just like those of his compatriots at Homeland Security, National Intelligence, and the CIA. Their sworn testimony would soon follow.

"I do," they all said before sitting down.

The seats in the hearing room gallery were all filled – those in the front by staff members of the various agencies on the hot seat that day and those in the back hoping to get on TV that night. One red-haired woman wearing a pink T-shirt and a large swath of gray duct tape over her mouth was sent to protest who knows what. Capitol police kept a close eye on her.

The sign in front of the Director read "Mr. Stubblefield." He was a big man even sitting down, and he towered over the other agency heads seated next to him at the table. This was his fifth trip up to Capitol Hill to testify before the House Intelligence Committee, something he never enjoyed doing. It wasn't that he disliked being on camera or was afraid to speak in public. It was the self-righteous know-it-alls on the congressional committees who, although they had no experience in his line of work, liked to lecture him on how he should do his job. The committee hearings were simply sideshows – where members of Congress could show up and make it look like they were doing the peoples' business. Some failed to attend, always citing pressing constituent concerns but the real reason being deliberate indifference to the matter. Director Stubblefield felt he could save everyone's time and present the same information in written form, but even then the reports would just be read by committee staffers who would selectively pass on what he or she thought their boss needed to know. He had to constantly tell himself to remain calm as it would all be over in an hour or two.

Known as the Bureau of Investigation in 1909 before it was officially named the Federal Bureau of Investigation in 1935, the FBI has been cloaked with the jurisdiction to investigate more than 200 violations of federal law, including organized crime, public corruption, white-collar crime, violent crime, and civil-rights violations. After 9/11, the focus of the FBI's investigative expertise turned more toward national security and protecting Americans against terrorist attacks. At its head, the Director oversees 56 field offices, 400 resident agencies, and over 15,000 special agents. More than a dozen men have served as FBI Director, the most famous being John E. Hoover, better known as J. Edgar, who served from 1924 until his death in 1972. In the first year of his ten-year term, Director Stubblefield, the first African-American at the FBI's top job, had the responsibility to thwart any terrorist attacks on the country. And it was a never ending battle.

In his opening statement, he reminded those on the committee about the dangers the U.S. faced on a daily basis. The southern border was a matter of great concern – not only because of the drug trafficking but also the smuggling of humans and weapons into the United States. He believed Muslim extremists were planning to unleash a new round of terror, and intelligence reports indicated their goal was to disrupt the upcoming presidential election. He asked the committee and Congress as a whole to provide the FBI with the tools to investigate and keep America safe.

After thirty minutes of questioning from the ranking committee members of both parties, Chairman Patrick Palladino threw the microphone over to Michigan Congresswoman Moeisha Robinson, the second-highest ranked Democrat on the committee. She had represented the inner-city slums of Detroit for over thirty years, and she returned home to brave the mean streets and ghettos every twenty-four months when it was time for reelection. How she managed to secure a seat on the Intelligence Committee was anyone's guess.

She looked down from her perch and over her half-glasses. The countdown clock indicated she had the floor for the next ten minutes. "Thank you, Mr. Chairman. Director Stubblefield, you have known the current occupant of the White House for some time, correct?"

She couldn't bring herself to call him President so she settled on "the occupant." The Congresswoman had a few run-ins with President Schumacher during his days in the House of Representatives and she rarely went a day without trying to drag his name through the mud. Recently, she started whispering the word "impeachment" hoping it would catch on.

"Yes, I have known President Schumacher for over thirty years."

Congresswoman Robinson reached back to one of her staffers who was handing her a note. They did that a lot. With her instructions now in hand, she made her political points for the evening news and the liberal bloggers.

"Are you concerned about his ability to lead this country?" she huffed. "I mean he wasn't elected Vice President," she rattled off counting on her fingers. "He wasn't elected President either. It's almost like our government has had a coup d'état and the American people have been forced to suffer through it."

Several of the Republicans on the committee could be seen shaking their heads, many wondering why they had to sit and listen to this crap.

"Congresswoman," Director Stubblefield said calmly, "I'm not sure what you are talking about. The Twenty-Fifth Amendment to our Constitution provides for the legitimate transfer of power. So you don't have to be concerned about any type of coup d'état."

Robinson took another note from her staffer before glaring down at the Director. "Are you familiar with the Fourth Amendment, Mr. Stubblefield?"

The Director could feel his blood starting to boil. His top row of teeth were now grinding on the bottom row. He had no patience for the Congresswoman's partisan political games. He considered getting up and walking out. "Yes, I am familiar with it."

"Are you going to comply with it?"

It happened every time Robinson decided to show up at an Intelligence Committee hearing. And it was the same thing every time – baseless accusations or frivolous questions. Stubblefield finally had enough.

"Congresswoman, what in the hell kind of question is that? Of course I'm going to comply with the Fourth Amendment. I'm going to comply with the Constitution. I swore to uphold it when I first became an FBI agent. And I resent having to sit here and have you question my integrity by asking if I'm going to comply with the law."

Robinson grabbed another note from over her shoulder before wagging a finger at him. "We have to keep a close eye over you Fibbies, Mr. Stubblefield," she said in her snarky liberal tone. She then threw in a racial component to bolster her claims. "You know, J. Edgar Hoover had his FBI spy on Martin Luther King, Jr." She insinuated that Director Stubblefield and the FBI had better be willing to redress past civil-rights violations – maybe even use some of its budget for reparations or affirmative action.

Stubblefield looked at his watch. He was going to give her three more minutes then he was leaving. "Congresswoman, I am not Director Hoover. I, along with my fellow agents, are deeply committed to the rule of law and doing everything within our lawful power to protect the American people."

Another note. "Mr. Stubblefield, does the FBI intend on promoting an outreach program to understand why terrorists around the world so hate America and especially this President?"

The Democrats had decided the buzzword for the day would be "outreach," and dutiful left-wing reporters from the broadcast and cable news networks as well as journalists in the print and Internet media would repeat the word over and over again for the next twenty-four-hour news cycle. Congresswoman Rosita Sanchez was making "outreach" a major platform in her presidential campaign, and it was up to Congresswoman Robinson to carry the liberal water when the camera was on.

Director Stubblefield had no desire to agree to any "outreach" programs. And he wasn't going to put a nice face on terrorism or the war by referring to the former as "man caused disasters" or the latter as "overseas contingency operations." He decided to give her the facts as he knew them.

"Congresswoman, we know why Muslim extremists hate America. Bin Laden told us after 9/11. They don't like the godless ways of this country, the sexual perversion of Hollywood as they see it, the acceptance of gay marriage, not to mention the out-of-wedlock births that have broken up the American family. Now, we could debate the root cause of those problems – the liberal agenda of government dependency, the absence of God in the classroom, or the loss of morality in society. But I'm not in that business, and I'm not going to waste any more of my time listening to your frivolous and idiotic questions. We are at war, Congresswoman. The terrorists believe every infidel and unbeliever must be converted or killed and that the lives of every American citizen must be ruled by sharia law. Now, if you want to go make nice with the terrorists, be my guest. But until the terrorists decide to stop their holy war against the United States, I intend to fight back."

The Director pushed his chair away from the table and stormed out of the hearing room, a cadre of reporters and cameramen trailing him down the hallway. The liberal media now had a new man to keep an eye on.

Silver Creek, Indiana

Al-Mutallab was just reaching the last intersection Donna Sullivan mentioned before making the left-hand turn and heading south. Sitting at the stop sign, he reached behind the passenger seat and grabbed the camera bag. He unzipped it and took out two cameras. One he turned on, pressed the record button on the video function and placed it in a homemade cradle on the dashboard. A piece of black electrical tape had been placed over the "on" light on the front of the camera that was currently blinking to indicate it was recording. The camera would record everything out the front of his windshield. He turned on the other camera and checked that the function was set to landscape. After a quick glance in his rear-view mirror to see that nobody was waiting behind him on that desolate stretch of road, he took a picture of the road to his south and to the north. Nothing more than a strip of freshly laid asphalt in both directions. He took one more of the vast forest of trees to his west – no doubt running along the east side of the Wabash. The batteries were fully charged and now it was time for some sightseeing.

He turned on his left-turn signal, looked both ways, and pulled the rented Corolla onto county road number seven. Fields of corn stalks stretching well above shoulder high sandwiched the road for what seemed like miles on end. He drove south. With one hand on the wheel, he used the other to snap a picture of the road in front of him. He was doing everything his handlers asked for. After a minute's worth of driving, he noticed a stand of trees running perpendicular from the trees fronting the Wabash. Another click of the camera.

As he proceeded on, the corn fields soon to be harvested stopped on the right side of the road. The signs reading "No Trespassing," "No Admittance," and "Restricted Area" were clearly visible. What al-Mutallab saw next nearly caused him to wet himself as he dropped the camera onto the floorboard in front of him.

"Oh, shit," he mumbled to himself.

Fanning out across the vast expanse of green grass indicating the start of President Schumacher's property was a six-man team of some of the biggest and meanest looking bad asses the United States Secret Service had to offer. Each man, dressed in full black battle dress uniform and carrying a fully loaded SR-16 automatic weapon, stood glaring behind their sunglasses at the man crawling along in the Corolla. Two others had their high-powered binoculars on the driver. Five minutes ago, they sat quietly behind a bank of monitors in the air-conditioned comfort of two converted recreational vehicles sitting in the driveway. From there they could monitor the surveillance cameras, motion detectors, and ground sensors littering the property. Once the call from Donna Sullivan came in, they filed out to strut their stuff.

Al-Mutallab had every right to drive down that road, but the Secret Service was out in full force simply to intimidate. They had no idea who he was, but if he had any nefarious ideas involving the Schumacher property, the agents let it be known that this is what he or anyone else would encounter if they crossed the line. Or at least the amount of force the Secret Service was willing to show off. Only they knew what the next line of defense would have to offer.

Al-Mutallab had a death grip on the steering wheel. Only his eyes dared move to look at the agents staring him down. Out of the corner of his right eye, he saw the whirring rush of blades of the police helicopter sitting on the helipad. The increasing speed indicated it was ready for takeoff.

"Shit."

Al-Mutallab continued on beyond the road to the west with the guardhouse and headed south. He exhaled heavily. Once he thought he had passed the outer boundary of the property he grabbed the camera off the dash, turned it off, and threw it behind the passenger seat. A part of him wanted to delete the tape. He now knew he should have started it sooner, to make it look like he had been sightseeing in central Indiana. The drops of sweat running down his forehead told him he would not be making another pass of the property. He picked up the Corolla's pace and wound his way into Silver Creek. He began to relax.

That wasn't so bad, he thought.

His joy for a job well done was short lived as he noticed the police helicopter was now off to his right and keeping a steady pace. Al-Mutallab checked his speedometer. He was three miles per hour under the limit. A quick glance out the window indicated the helicopter was still there shadowing him.

His rear-view mirror did not show any police vehicles behind him. He found a McDonald's on the outskirts of town and pulled to a stop. The helicopter banked left and hovered at five-hundred feet, the pilot looking directly toward al-Mutallab's front windshield. He kept telling himself he hadn't done anything wrong. He had to pee now more than ever. He opened the door, kept his head down, and did his best to walk calmly inside. Don't run, he told himself. After a quick trip to the restroom to relieve himself and to wipe the sweat off his forehead, he walked to the window of the dining area and saw the helicopter was gone. He exhaled a worried breath. He noticed a handful of cars in the parking lot. He just knew he was being followed. The Secret Service had no doubt photographed the car as he drove by the property. The dining area had a couple of teenagers and a group of elderly men. No one looked like a cop. Al-Mutallab ordered a large Coke and, once he got back in the car, he did his best to get the hell out of Silver Creek without raising any more suspicion.

As he traveled back toward the interstate he didn't even notice the two Secret Service agents now at Maple Ridge Farms lifting finger prints off the knobs of the front door.

CHAPTER 7

Fort Bliss – El Paso, Texas

While the Secret Service had its worries about taking the President outside the protective bubble of the White House, they were somewhat relieved when the President's handlers decided to use Fort Bliss as the backdrop for his speech on national security. What better place to keep the President safe than the home of the U.S. Army's 1st Armored Division. Nicknamed "Old Ironsides," the Division was the first armored division to see combat in World War II, rolling through North Africa in Operation Torch in November 1942. Its storied résumé included destroying the Iraqi Republican Guard in Desert Storm and fighting the war on terrorism in Operation Iraqi Freedom. Needless to say, the Commander in Chief was in friendly territory. Plus, the grounds were encased with fencing and topped with razor wire and the hangar provided a secure covering. And the cameras focusing on the President never showed the helicopter gunships circling the grounds or the fully armed F-18s circling high in the Texas sky above them.

In a crowd full of troops and a stage lined with American flags, the President put forth the major plank of his election campaign.

"The number one priority of any American President is the safety and security of the American people," he said behind the Presidential seal. "For far too long, the federal government has failed to protect our southernmost borders from those seeking to break our laws. In the last year, the United States Border Patrol confiscated more than 4.5 million pounds of cocaine, marijuana, and heroin. In a three-month stretch, agents were seizing on average more than 6,000 pounds of contraband per day.

"In one month alone, Border Patrol agents seized twelve pounds of methamphetamine valued at $300,000 in Yuma, Arizona; 17,000 pounds of marijuana valued at $13 million in Edinburg, Texas; a million dollar's worth of meth and cocaine in Calexico, California; *eleven tons* of marijuana . . .," the President said before stopping to let the crowd absorb the figures, ". . . that's *22,000 pounds* of marijuana, were seized on rail cars by Immigration and Customs Enforcement agents as it reached the city of Chicago. I could go on but rest assured the list is long.

"And those who seek to send their foreign contraband to America are constantly searching for new places to hide their illegal goods. In Nogales, Arizona, Border Patrol agents seized heroin and cocaine worth three quarters of a million dollars that were hidden inside fire extinguishers. In Los Angeles, fourteen pounds of cocaine were discovered inside Easter egg candies. In Brownsville, Texas, a woman affiliated with Mexican drug cartels was found with heroin hidden in her breast implants.

"Given this relentless assault, I will propose to Congress a doubling in the amount of Border Patrol agents and supply them with the tools and weaponry needed to accomplish their mission. No longer will Border Patrol agents be outmanned or outgunned by drug cartels intent on bringing their poison to the streets of the United States. I will also propose one billion dollars for technological advances such as unmanned drones, infrared cameras, and ground sensors to fight the war in the bright of day and the dark of night. And finally, I will demand that Congress appropriate the funds to finish building the border fence to keep America safe."

The pro-military crowd gave a hearty round of applause for the President's efforts. Most lived in the area, and the increasing violence across the border and encroaching into their back yards was constantly on their mind because it made the evening news every night. They often wondered if they were under attack from the drug cartel and human traffickers.

"Until Congress acts, I am today ordering the call up of 10,000 National Guard troops to help secure the border from Brownsville and Metamoros to San Diego and Tijuana. And they will not be relegated to desk duty. They will be armed and ready to respond if attacked. Also, I have spoken with newly elected Mexican President Felipe Garza who has expressed his country's support for a bilateral agreement whereby the United States would help in the fight against drug cartels in Northern Mexico. From this day forward, the United States of America will be on offense in this war against narco-terrorism."

While those in the crowd might have supported the President's mission, the liberal media types in the rear of the hangar were in shock at the President's forceful tone. One tweeted the President was declaring war on Mexico. Another walked out in disgust. Who was this man with his big-gun, big-fence mentality? Several left-leaning political cartoons would later show President Schumacher atop a tank and rolling across the southern border with a large and bold "Yeehaa!" in the bubble above his Dukakis-style helmet head.

"Now let me take a moment to those who may disagree with my proposals. Yes, we are a nation of immigrants. We have a long and proud history of immigration. But it would denigrate the struggle of those who came before us to allow a border with no laws and citizenship with no responsibilities. An America with secure borders offers safety to descendants of those who came on the Mayflower, the huddled masses who saw liberty's lamp at Ellis Island, as well as those who took the oath of citizenship right here in El Paso this past Fourth of July. Lesser amounts of illegal drugs will benefit the neighborhoods of Americans by birth and Americans by choice. The drug cartels will not stop, and the United States will not stop either."

Silver Creek, Indiana

The two canoes with two passengers each hit the water just under a bridge in Covington, Indiana. It was a favorite starting point for boaters looking to enjoy a day paddling down the Wabash River, the nearly 500-mile long state river of Indiana, or maybe some fishing or picnicking on the shores downstream. Malik al-Mutallab had returned to Chicago to brief the terror leaders on what he had discovered in Silver Creek.

And they were not happy.

Al-Mutallab told them the thought of attacking the President's compound by knocking on the front door was out of the question. The armed Secret Service agents, or at least those he could see, would make a ground-based attack an impossibility. Multiple news reports indicated a no-fly zone extended ten miles around the Schumacher property. And it was rumored the Secret Service manned two camouflaged Patriot missile batteries in case someone had the balls to launch an attack by air. Short of tunneling under the house, al-Mutallab said an attack in Silver Creek would be suicidal.

But his handlers were not ready to give up just yet. An attack by land or by air might be impossible, but an attack by sea might still be in the cards. And the Wabash River flowed right by the President's house.

Fearing his cover might have been blown the last time he visited Silver Creek, al-Mutallab implored his bosses to write a different script. Abbed agreed to let al-Mutallab and his cohort, Ahmed Khalidi, to use their student status. They had driven down from West Lafayette earlier in the day with two hot blondes they bribed the night before at a campus party. Jasmine and Jessica, both sophomores majoring in fashion design, had agreed to the trip after al-Mutallab promised them a day of marijuana and booze followed by an evening of dinner and shopping. He had provided a sampling of the goods the night before and even provided them with a $300 advance. Given that it was early in the fall semester and their design classes did not require much work, along with the fact that two of their engineering friends vouched for al-Mutallab, or at least vouched for the potency of his weed, Jasmine and Jessica promised to be ready at nine the next morning.

When al-Mutallab and Khalidi showed up at nine and after they rousted the girls out of bed, the quartet was on the road by ten-thirty. They stopped once at a gas station for more beer, once at KFC for a bucket of picnic chicken, and once at a rest stop so Jessica could urinate for the second time. Both men wore khaki shorts, fresh off the rack, along with polo shirts, one blue and one black – an ensemble more appropriate for yachting on the high seas than canoeing the muddy waters of the Wabash.

Al-Mutallab took the lead canoe with Jessica in the rear. She had started drinking on the way down and was a bit buzzed already. He snapped a few pictures to start filling up his digital camera with photos that would befit such a peaceful day on the river. Two brand new fishing rods sat unused in the bottom of each boat and the small Styrofoam container of bait sat next to the chicken. Captain Khalidi shoved off with Jasmine in the front and another camera ready to go.

"It's hot out here," Jasmine pouted. They had barely been out of the car for ten minutes before she started pouting.

"Have another beer," Khalidi responded.

"Yeah, have another beer, you dork!" Jessica shouted across the water.

Al-Mutallab steered the boat to the right and flipped a Miller Lite to Khalidi who handed it over to Jasmine. She popped the top and was soon in a better mood.

"Take your shirt off if you're still hot," al-Mutallab said.

Both girls instantly took a liking to the idea and whipped off their T-shirts. Both were wearing pink bikini tops and the lack of tan lines indicated they probably spent more time sunning themselves than frequenting the undergrad library. The men, however, took no notice. Their focus was down river. They could feel the quiet stillness, and the tree-lined canyon held the heat and humidity well. Each man was taking mental notes, looking for anything in the trees or on the banks that would announce their presence to the Secret Service. They figured it would be a five or six-mile trip.

"Hello!" Jasmine yelled as the two boats floated between the forest of trees. Apparently she just wanted to hear her own voice and the echo off the sycamores. "Hello!"

"Hello!" Jessica said. The beer in her hand was her third of the day and tenth within the last twenty-four hours. "Woo!" she bellowed as loud as she could.

"We ought to go skinny dipping!" Jasmine blurted out.

Jessica doubled over in a fit of laughter, like it was the funniest thing she had ever heard. "Woo! Skinny dipping! Yeah, baby!"

"Quiet down!" al-Mutallab snapped harshly. He didn't know how much more he could take. He was not a fan of boisterous American girls. He thought women should be covered from head to toe and speak only when spoken to. He wondered if the drunk coeds would be more trouble than they were worth.

"Don't tell her to be quiet!" Jasmine shot back. The increasing buzz was making her feisty. "And don't even think about getting any tonight, asshole. We're just here for the beer and the shopping."

Khalidi stepped in hoping to calm the situation. The women were there to make the two men blend into the surroundings. Khalidi and al-Mutallab just needed them to stay in the boat for another half hour or so and then they could do whatever they wanted. The flotilla had just passed under the interstate overpass and both men knew it couldn't be much longer to the President's house.

"Who wants to take a couple of tokes?" Khalidi asked. He was more skilled in the ways of the college student than his compatriot. Because al-Mutallab always had his mind fixed on the plan and had a quick temper, he was not always the sociable type. Khalidi, however, knew the situation called for an easygoing, devil-may-care attitude. He fished around in the cooler and found his stash of weed hidden in an emptied can of beer.

He passed the marijuana and a lighter to Jasmine, who promptly smoked it to her heart's content before reaching over and giving the rest to Jessica. Both girls inhaled deeply. Ah, the men thought, things are much calmer now. Jasmine put her tanned legs on the bow and leaned back as Khalidi paddled slowly forward.

"Hey, I forgot my sun screen in the car," Jessica reported to no one in particular.

Jasmine made some remark about not worrying about it before she did actually have a rational thought. "Hey, how are we going to get back to the car anyway?"

Khalidi and al-Mutallab looked at each other. They hadn't thought about that.

Al-Mutallab sounded confident when he responded, "I got a friend not too much farther down the river. He'll give us a ride back."

CHAPTER 8

United States Penitentiary – Terre Haute, Indiana

Situated just two miles south of Indiana's eleventh largest city, the United States Penitentiary, Terre Haute, consists of thirty-three acres within its double fences topped with razor wire. Although it is one of the federal government's nine high-security prisons, the USP in Terre Haute differs in one very deadly respect – it is home to the special confinement unit. Housed in the SCU, inmates serving federal death sentences await their turn in the government's only execution chamber now in use.

The methods used to carry out capital punishment have undergone a lethal evolution, and some would argue they have become more humane, over the last 150 years of American history. Those who conspired to assassinate President Lincoln were hung from the gallows at the Old Arsenal Penitentiary in D.C. following a military tribunal in 1865. Convicted of espionage, Ethel and Julius Rosenberg were electrocuted at Sing Sing in New York in 1953. Bonnie Brown Heady, the last women executed by the government, died in a Missouri gas chamber following her murder conviction. Still others were on the receiving end of a firing squad. Today, those sentenced to death in the federal system are subject to the current method of execution – lethal injection.

And in two weeks, one of the SCU's fifty unfortunate members was set to take the long lonely walk to his death. Muqtada Abdulla, the one-time terrorist, had long since shed his playboy good looks. Gone were the days of his jet black hair, Armani suits, and alligator-hide shoes. Now, his head was shaved and a wispy gray beard reached down to his chest covered by a smelly lime-green top and matching trousers. He had to remove his prison-issued khaki top and pants every time he met with his attorney, and he cursed the guards during every change of apparel. His beady black eyes, those eyes that had seen death and destruction on a scale rarely seen by any living human, were still alive and angry as ever.

"Damn you American dogs!" Abdulla fumed as he sat across the table from E. Bennett Hurt, his well-paid lawyer from the Civil Liberties Alliance. Abdulla's father had shelled out big bucks for Muqtada's defense and even more for his countless yet fruitless appeals. The CLA, a left-wing organization that spent most of its time representing guilty terrorists, had been recommended to Sheik Abdulla because of the CLA's not-so-subtle dislike of the United States. Based out of New York, the CLA had unsuccessfully tried to stop President Schumacher from transferring and trying terrorist detainees at Guantanamo Bay. Having lost that fight but not the desire to weaken the conservative Schumacher Administration, the CLA's best and brightest lawyers took up the cause of Muqtada Abdulla and were prepared to bring the legal process to a standstill.

But they were running out of time and options.

"You American dogs will all die soon!" the now afoot Abdulla yelled through the sound proof door of the lawyer-client meeting room. He was yelling to no one in particular. "You dogs will all die and burn in a fiery hell!" He could go on like this for at least thirty minutes or until his voice finally gave out. Once the yelling stopped and the veins popping out of his neck subsided, he clasped his hands behind his back and shuffled back and forth in his prison-issued sandals.

"Muqtada," Hurt said softly. "Please try to calm down. We have much to talk about today."

With flashes of anger filling his eyes, Muqtada lunged for his attorney and stopped an inch from his face. "I am going to be executed by these bastards in fourteen days and you tell me to calm down."

Hurt could smell the prison-issued vegan chili still on Muqtada's breath. He was not afraid though. He had grown accustomed to his client's belligerent rants. Hurt had represented Muqtada for over two years now. A graduate of Columbia Law, Hurt had taken up the leftist cause in his first job out of school in the general counsel's office at the United Nations. Once fully ensconced and indoctrinated in the U.N. way of doing things, he looked the other way at the atrocities of dictators and blamed all the world's ills on the United States. After his U.N. stint, he took his skills to the Civil Liberties Alliance and its cadre of attorneys out to put America, big business, and all Republicans in their place. He dressed well in dark colors, almost always with pinstripes. The dark blue suit he was wearing today was given to him by the head of the Liuzzi crime family of New York. Hurt had won an acquittal in the mob boss's racketeering trial in federal court leading to his high-profile stature in the legal community. He was now the top attorney for one of the world's most hated terrorists.

"Sit down," Hurt said quietly, gesturing to Muqtada and straightening the edges of a stack of papers they would have to go through in the next hour.

"I want to know how you're going to get me out of here," Muqtada demanded.

Hurt sighed softly. Muqtada was never going to get out of prison. At least not via any legal route. His three appeals failed to turn up any reversible errors. The Supreme Court of the United States had upheld his conviction and death sentence by a unanimous vote. His attorneys had filed numerous *habeas* actions and section 1983 claims – anything to draw out the death sentence and hold out hope for a miracle. His last remaining hope now was to save himself from the death chamber.

"First of all," Hurt said, "it is not helping your cause any when you rack up all these disciplinary infractions." He held up a handful of his client's disciplinary tickets.

Muqtada smiled with pride at the man, his yellow teeth emerging from behind the gray beard. He had accumulated thirty-seven violations in the last year, including multiple infractions for spitting on a prison guard, urinating in the recreation area, and flooding his cell by shoving newspapers down his toilet. He was most proud of cutting the closed end off an old tube of toothpaste, filling it with his own feces, and squirting it through his cell door and on to the shirt of a guard bringing his dinner. The guard had to rush to the prison infirmary to shower the stinking mess off of him, get a new shirt, and endure a myriad of blood tests to make sure he hadn't contracted any communicable diseases. For his prison crimes, Muqtada had his telephone and commissary privileges reduced. He was denied his one hour of recreation time. And, no surprise, the prison authorities took away his toothpaste. The long line of punishments did not lead him to change his ways.

"I will kill all these dogs!" he yelled at the table. He then pushed back his chair and with a full head of steam stomped to the door for another round of America bashing. He took off his sandal and beat it repeatedly against the window. "I will kill all you dogs soon! My people will kill you! You got what you deserved on 9/11! And there will be more 9/11s until your country is destroyed!"

Hurt just decided to keep talking once Muqtada paused for a breath. "The only thing your disciplinary infractions can do to help us is if we say you are clinically insane," he said as he checked off another idea off his list. "Courts are reluctant to go forward with a death sentence if the defendant is mentally ill."

Muqtada turned away from the window and fired the sandal at Hurt's head. It missed and landed with a weak thud against the wall. "I am not insane, you son of a . . ." he muttered in a low growl.

"I know, Muqtada, I know," Hurt said, grabbing the sandal and tossing it onto the floor at his client's feet. "But we need to buy you some time. And we are doing everything possible to stall the process."

Feeling the need to give his voice a rest, Muqtada sat down across the table from his lawyer and folded his hands in front of him. After composing himself, he then nodded at Hurt to continue.

"The warden faxed me the method of execution yesterday," Hurt said as he pulled out another sheet from his brown expandable file. Muqtada nodded again. "What they will do is strap you to a gurney in the execution chamber and insert intravenous tubes into your arms. They'll start off with two grams of sodium thiopental, a barbituate sedative that helps render you unconscious. Outward signs of breathing and movement will most likely stop after fifteen seconds. The sodium thiopental is *supposed* to ensure you don't feel any pain with the two drugs that will follow. They'll next give you fifty milligrams of pancuronium bromide, a paralytic agent that will paralyze your diaphragm and stop your respiration. Finally, they'll give you 240 milliequivalents of potassium chloride, which will interfere with your brain's ability to tell your heart to contract and lead to cardiac arrest."

Muqtada showed little emotion. The only movement was his right index finger tapping on the table.

"Now in the next few days we will file last-minute motions to stay your execution. We'll start off in the federal district court in Indianapolis and go up to the Seventh Circuit Court of Appeals in Chicago after that. Our lawyers have prepared motions arguing the dosages are too small and may cause you excruciating pain, the drugs are made by an unknown foreign manufacturer and not approved by the FDA, and then, of course, our usual Eighth Amendment argument that the death penalty is unconstitutional because it constitutes cruel and unusual punishment."

Muqtada grabbed the stack of disciplinary infractions and hurled them against the wall in a blizzard of paper. He was not getting the information he wanted so he leaned in closer across the table.

"I know all this, you idiot. I want to get back to my first question. What is really being done to get me out of here? You damn attorneys can do nothing for me but file these worthless papers," he said as he swiped at the stack of paper still left on the table. "What are my brothers doing to get me out of here?"

Even the leftist Hurt was uncomfortable with the question. He knew his freedom, the very freedom protected by the United States Constitution of which he so often derided, could be in jeopardy if the authorities became aware of the information he knew and was about to divulge. Lawyers had been prosecuted for passing along plans and instructions to terrorists outside the prison walls. And ten years in prison would not be a good fit for Hurt. He looked at the walls, the floor, and even underneath the table. Nothing indicated the presence of any type of listening device. Taping attorney-client conversations was against the law, but, of course, Hurt never trusted government types to comply with the law. Especially when he was on the government's own turf.

Just to be careful, Hurt leaned in across the table and stopped a short distance from Muqtada's ear. "I talked to your father yesterday," he whispered. "He says your men have been working on a project for the past week but it has been slow going."

Abdulla's eyes glanced at the window in the door and then back at Hurt. "Did they consider the prison?" he whispered.

"Impossible," Hurt replied, shaking his head.

One of the first plans to spring Muqtada from prison was a daring helicopter extraction while he was out for his one-hour per day in the recreation yard. Three problems arose, however. One, Muqtada had lost his yard privileges so often it was never a guarantee he would receive his one hour outside. Plus, the guards changed the yard time every day, and oftentimes made inmates exercise in an unused swimming pool with a wire cage on top. Second, the guards in the towers are heavily armed, and any attempt by Muqtada to flee via helicopter would most likely be met with his body riddled with bullets. Third, navigating the wires crisscrossing the yard would be nearly impossible for even the best helicopter pilots. Tunnels had also been discussed but were quickly dismissed because of the ground sensors and steel bars buried in the Indiana dirt. Bulldozers crashing through the fences and walls would again cause a barrage of bullets to fly. The penitentiary was secured like a Midwestern Alcatraz, minus the frigid waters of San Francisco Bay.

"What is plan B then?"

"Your father's family in Saudi Arabia is currently seeking to intervene on your behalf. I know they have talked with people in Mexico about your upcoming execution. Maybe they will be able to buy us some time."

"Who is the target of their intervention?"

Hurt moved in closer toward Muqtada's ear. "The President."

"Schumacher?" Muqtada was a little surprised. He didn't know whether his father would be looking for such a big score.

"Yes."

"And my brothers are nearby?" Muqtada asked. Even within the hardened prison walls, he could almost feel his rescuers getting closer.

"Yes," Hurt whispered. "Just up the river scouting locations."

Muqtada smiled for the first time in days. He could almost see it now. Killing the President would be the first in a long line of violent acts on the American people if Muqtada was not released and sent back to freedom in Saudi Arabia. Finally the Americans would be treated like the "dogs" that they are, he thought to himself.

"When will it happen?"

Hurt shrugged.

"I want to know when it will happen!"

"I don't know, Muqtada. You must realize the plan might fail. It is very dangerous. They are running out of options and you are running out of time."

Muqtada would have none of it. "No, Allah will make it happen."

He was sure of it.

CHAPTER 9

Silver Creek, Indiana

"We've got two canoes passing south under the I-74 overpass," Special Agent Matt Kincade said into his microphone. With its full compliment of high-tech sensors, the Secret Service mobile command post on the Schumacher property contained a bank of television monitors showing surveillance video from around the area – the perimeter of the house, the roads leading to the property, and even one on the underside of the interstate broadcasting pictures of the Wabash River below. Anytime any pleasure craft passed within view of the camera, the alarms started going off.

Agent Kincade zeroed the camera's focus onto the occupants of the boats. "Two males," he reported. He was unsure of their race, maybe they were Hispanic, maybe Middle Eastern. "Two white females."

Special Agent Zach Levrett, the agent in charge at the Schumacher property, looked in over his shoulder. "Tighten up on that guy in the front there," he said pointing at the screen.

Agent Kincade complied, and the picture showed al-Mutallab in a clearer light. In his black polo, he was angrily pointing at Jasmine and saying something that undoubtedly wouldn't go over well with her.

"That guy looks familiar," Levrett said. "Pull up the photo of that guy who drove by the property last week."

Kincade did so with a few mouse clicks and both compared the photos. It was difficult to tell. One was taken from a hundred feet in the air and the other was at eye level taken when al-Mutallab glanced ever so slightly toward the property. Levrett wasn't going to take any chances.

He reached for the phone next to the television screens.

"This is the Cabin," he said, referring to the mobile command's code name. "Get me three teams up river now. Two canoes. Two males, two females. Approach with caution." He then looked at all the screens again, all appeared quiet. But sometimes appearances could be deceiving when dealing with terrorists. "All units look alive. This is not a drill. Repeat, this is not a drill."

Partly distracted by the noisy women, al-Mutallab had just now remembered his camera and took to filming the shores of the Wabash south of the interstate. Every so often he would take another shot of Jasmine or the other two in the boat next to him. Khalidi was too busy fumbling around for more beer to appease the women and keep their minds occupied. Neither of the men saw the buoys and flotation devices starting to pop up near the bank on the eastern side of the river. Needless to say, the two women didn't notice the buoys either or the interconnected steel chains that would wreak havoc on any trespassing outboard motor making its way to shore. Of course, the women had just weathered through their two-minute stupor and were now yelling about how much fun they were having.

"Yeah, baby!" Jasmine yelled, downing another mouthful. "I love beer!"

"Woo!"

With all the noise and rocking boats, nobody even saw the United States Secret Service roaring up the Wabash to meet them head on. On loan from the United States Coast Guard, the Secret Service patrolled the river with two 36-foot, dual-diesel long-range Interceptors and four smaller Zodiac short-range Prosecutors. Each vessel contained a three-man team, with one member in charge of manning the M240 7.62-mm machine gun mounted on each vessel. As the portion of the Wabash nearest the President's house was the deepest and widest part of the river, the Secret Service had plenty of area to move around and patrol.

Both Khalidi and al-Mutallab looked at each other wondering what they were hearing in between the high-pitched screams of joy from the two women. It sounded like a horde of hornets buzzing toward them. It was then that they realized the noise reverberating off the forest of trees was coming from the three water craft speeding toward them at a good clip.

"Oh shit," al-Mutallab whispered to himself. He had had that same feeling the week before. He looked over at a wide-eyed Khalidi.

"Act cool," he told him. He then pointed to his comrade's canoe. "Hurry up and ditch the weed."

As surreptitiously as possible, Khalidi slowly reached down into the cooler and deposited the rest of his marijuana into the muddy depths of the Wabash. The last thing he worried about was a simple possession offense, most likely a misdemeanor that no one would think twice of, but no sense giving the authorities something to pin on them or give the cops reason to start rooting around in their private lives.

Once the women had stopped their yapping long enough for them to realize they were about to have visitors, Jessica thought it might be some boaters looking for a party.

"Woo!" she bellowed. "Yeah, baby! Over here!" She started waving her arms intent on welcoming her fellow partygoers.

"Be quiet!" al-Mutallab admonished.

It was no use. The Secret Service throttled up the diesels and loudly motored to a stop in front of them, and the two women instantly took a liking to the three men in each boat. All nine agents were dressed in black BDUs with orange life preservers. The three who weren't driving or manning the M240 had their MP-5s readied for action. For some reason, perhaps the combination of being on the water and their rising blood-alcohol levels, the two women thought the agents were in the Navy and gave them a hearty salute.

"We love Navy men!" Jessica announced with admiration. "We go to Purdue!" As if such a spirited statement of collegiate pride would be a great thing for any former or current midshipman to hear.

"Woo! Boilermakers!" Jasmine responded with her own earsplitting decibels. She was a good ways gone.

Special Agent Mitch Abernathy took the lead. "How are you folks doing today?"

Khalidi and al-Mutallab responded that everything was good. It was a beautiful day on the Wabash, and the quartet was just on a sightseeing trip down river.

"You guys want some beer!" Jasmine blurted out. She was a hospitable sort.

Agent Abernathy looked at the two women. He wasn't there for them. "I'm sorry, ma'am, but there's no open alcohol allowed on the Wabash."

"Nice going, you dork," Jessica said.

Agent Abernathy switched his focus to al-Mutallab. "I'm Special Agent Abernathy with the United States Secret Service. I'm afraid you have just crossed over into restricted waters."

Both al-Mutallab and Khalidi looked at each other in astonishment. They looked like it was unfathomable that they had done something wrong.

"These are restricted waters?" al-Mutallab protested. From his perch, he looked at both sides of the river. This was a navigable waterway, wasn't it? How in the hell was he supposed to know? There weren't any signs or markers showing him any boundaries he wasn't supposed to cross. At least none that he had seen. He wasn't about to back down.

Wanting to split up the two groups before they started telling their stories, Agent Abernathy answered the question with one of his own after a quick scan of the canoes. "Do you folks have any life preservers?"

Khalidi and al-Mutallab looked at each other again. Al-Mutallab squinted his eyes at his friend, his jaw now clenched tight. His volcanic temper was slowly percolating. They had brought the babes, the booze, the joints, and the freaking fried chicken. But some idiot forgot to bring the life jackets.

The Secret Service blocked the paths of both canoes and roped them to a separate vessel. Agent Abernathy asked the two women to step into the boat with the two other agents. Jasmine took great delight when one of the agents scooped her up into his muscular arms after she became a little tipsy during embarkation. Once aboard, the agents moved to the far shore and anchored up.

Al-Mutallab and Khalidi boarded Agent Abernathy's Interceptor. Both of the Middle Easterners knew this couldn't be good.

"Welcome back to Silver Creek, Malik," Agent Abernathy said.

CHAPTER 10

San Francisco, California

Congresswoman Sanchez and General Graham spent the last hour pressing the flesh and grinning for cameras as hundreds of liberal fat cats ponied up $10,000 each to line up for a meet and greet with the Democratic Party's ticket for President and Vice President of the United States. After twenty minutes to recuperate, they were off to the penthouse suite of the San Francisco Hyatt Regency where they were to meet with the real big wigs of the liberal establishment. These folks scoffed at the ten-grand handshakes, instead forking over fifty Gs to sit down with the candidates for a full hour to bend their ears and lobby them on behalf of their constituency. Sanchez and Graham would pull in $300,000 for sixty minutes of intense listening and false promising.

Seated around the oval conference table in the penthouse were six of the Democrats' best friends – Art Brennan, the fiery head of the Civil Liberties Alliance; Jane Quinn, the president of the Coalition of Gay/Lesbian Democrats; Tony Riotta, the head of the United Federation of American Labor; Rosario Hernandez, the leader of the Hispanic Democrats of America; DeWayne Jackson, the vice president of the National Association of Black Leadership, and Sonny Zell, the outspoken president of MAMAL, the group advocating to Make American Marijuana Available and Legal.

None of them had much love for the Republican Party nor the GOP's hope and desire for smaller government, lower taxes, and individual responsibility. They all had made their way back to the socialist Xanadu of San Francisco three weeks after the Democratic National Convention to get the quality face time they had originally been promised and paid for. The prior meeting had to be cancelled due to the near riotous crowd of homeless pot smokers, aging hippies, and dirty anarchists filling the streets and looking to light up their bongs, smear those warmongering Republicans, and smash the windows of any greedy bank they could find. A live shot from MSNBC showed the Embarcadero full of protesters with their signs plastered with marijuana leaves and peace symbols, a dense cloud of cannabis smoke wafting over the crowd as they angrily marched toward City Hall. The California governor wondered whether he was going to have to call out the National Guard to protect the local citizenry from the liberals. Given the commotion, the private, big donor meeting was rescheduled for a quieter time when the Sanchez campaign was next in town.

Congresswoman Sanchez and General Graham sat next to each other and faced their six guests. Coffee and tea were provided but little was consumed. Time with the candidates was too precious, and too expensive, to waste sipping drinks.

Sanchez opened the meeting with a polite welcome and told the donors she was always willing to listen to their concerns. And she would do so as President. They were all friends, she reminded them. Soldiers in the same cause. And they would all have a seat at the power table in the White House.

Next up was General Graham, who droned on and on about his accomplishments and how much he brought to the ticket. He thought his presence sealed the deal for victory. Despite his military credentials, he had a certain Woodrow-Wilson-like aura to him – haughty, upper class, a know-it-all professorial type that students, or donors, grew tired of quickly. He was not actually a man of the people, the hoi polloi too stupid, in his mind, to understand his brilliance. With his thinning comb-over that looked like a well-worn carpet remnant from the '80s, it was obvious Sanchez's Hollywood makeup artists and hairdressers would have their work cut out for them during the upcoming televised debates.

When the floor was opened up for discussion, Rosario Hernandez beat everyone to the punch. She looked angry, the perpetual scowl on her face indicating she didn't like it when she didn't get what she wanted. She could make a person's life a living hell if they tried to screw her or her people over. Liberal pols had learned to kiss her feet at every opportunity.

"I would like to hear firsthand what a Sanchez Administration would do on the issue of immigration," she said. She insinuated the fluff she was getting from Sanchez's staff failed to carry much weight in her eyes.

"Of course," Sanchez said. Given her Hispanic heritage and liberal leanings, her open-borders philosophy was well known. "I have a comprehensive plan to deal with immigration reform."

"It must include amnesty," Hernandez interjected forcefully. Her constituency would demand it or threaten to stay home on election day.

"Absolutely, it will. Granting citizenship to undocumented immigrants will be a great boon to the Democratic Party."

"I've heard a lot of Democrat politicians promise amnesty but fail to deliver in the end." She was borderline nasty, like a twice scorned wife looking philanderer number three in the face.

"It'll be a top priority with us, Rosario."

General Graham felt the need to pipe up to show off his political skills. "We just won't be able to talk about it as much as you'd like us to, Rosario, since most Americans are against amnesty for illegals. A majority of the people want a secure border to help stop the flow of illegal immigrants . . . ,"

"*Undocumented* immigrants, Mr. Graham," a glaring Hernandez shot back. She hated when people used the term "illegal" to describe immigrants coming to this country. She felt it was unfair to stereotype those crossing the border in search of a better life simply because they did not follow the draconian immigration laws of the United States. At least Sanchez had the good sense not to use the word "illegal." Hernandez was beginning to think General Graham was an idiot. It was obvious to her that he was not "down for the struggle."

"I'm sorry, undocumented immigrants" Graham huffed before putting Hernandez in her place. "And it's General, Rosario."

Her nostrils slightly flaring, Hernandez was not impressed. "Make sure you get it right before your debates with Vice President Jackson . . . General," she bristled derisively. The "General" remark was laden with a heavy dose of contempt.

Congresswoman Sanchez felt the need to step in lest this meeting of friends turn into a contentious free-for-all.

"Rosario, I promise you that your concerns will be a top priority for a Sanchez Administration. But like General Graham said, we cannot run a campaign advocating open borders and amnesty. It might work well in the barrios and bodegas of Los Angeles, Houston, and New York, but not so much in the white picket fence neighborhoods of the American heartland."

General Graham showed a full mouth of teeth and nodded in agreement with his running mate.

Hernandez relented for the time being. She had been promised a seat at the table many times before by Democrat politicians, who were only interested in the expected votes of her constituency, only to be pushed to the back burner once the election was over. The gays and the blacks felt the same way. That is why Hernandez learned to be forceful in her demands. She inwardly vowed to hound Sanchez and Graham to no end if they won the election.

Sonny Zell wasted no time in the ensuing and awkward silence and jumped right into the fray for his own cause. His pony tail and cannabis leaf lapel pin were a dead giveaway that Sonny Redwood Zell was not a Washington insider or typical political power broker. He had never worked in government, nor could he considering he wouldn't be able to pass the mandatory drug test necessary for federal employment. He smoked a joint every morning with his cup of coffee and bowl of oatmeal. And given the amount of cannabis he went through in a day, it was possible those around the table were getting high just by the third-hand smoke that was emanating from him and his organic hemp line of clothing. He was by far the marijuana lobby's best friend and had made it his mission in life to legalize marijuana from sea to shining sea.

The enterprising Zell had started out twenty years ago in a hole-in-the-wall shop in Berkeley where he sold medical marijuana to those in desperate need of alleviating a whole host of ailments – everything from cancer to glaucoma to bee stings to the cough due to cold. Anxiety was also a common malady. Zell sometimes thought California had an epidemic of apprehensive citizens, so worried about the earthquakes, mudslides, and wildfires, not to mention the traffic jams, that they had to light up just to make it through the day.

Over the last ten years, federal agents had raided the shop on four occasions and shut him down completely on another two. But he soldiered on and opened shops in San Francisco, Oakland, and Los Angeles. His business had a certain ebb and flow to it that largely depended on which political party was in charge in Sacramento or Washington, D.C. Lately, the liberal politicians in California, with what could be best described as a 21st century "Eureka!" moment befitting the state motto, had taken a shine to his marijuana dispensary and allowed him to expand his business with the only caveat being the Golden State would impose an eight-percent marijuana tax on his products to help fill the state's barren and indebted coffers.

"Congresswoman, what are your views on medical marijuana?" Zell asked. "I didn't hear any mention of your position at the convention."

"I'm all for it, Sonny, you know that." She had known Zell for over ten years and been the recipient of numerous phone calls and letters during her time as a member of the California delegation in Congress. "Just two years ago, I co-sponsored legislation that would legalize medical marijuana provided you have a doctor's prescription."

"Yeah, but it went nowhere in the House," Zell said. "I'm not even sure it got out of committee. I know the Senate didn't get a chance to consider the measure."

General Graham stepped in once again. "It's not an issue most Americans support, Sonny."

Like Zell didn't already know that. He had lived the counterculture life since his mother gave birth to him in a hippie commune in northern California under the abundant sunshine and giant redwood stands, hence his name. He was home-schooled. Well, educated more on the streets of Berkeley than an actual school within a home, but he had survived the rough-and-tumble days of the "marijuana gestapo," as he called the authorities, by expanding his business with a line of bongs, trinkets, tie-dyed T-shirts, and other cannabis apparel. He made a killing with the college crowd. Still, his country-wide legalization project was never far from his mind.

"Hear me out on this," Zell said, like he was a man with a plan. "If we legalize marijuana, think of the tax revenue it would generate for the United States. It could be in the billions of dollars. Sure, we're trillions of dollars in debt but a billion here and a billion there will start to add up. We would also save millions of dollars in law-enforcement costs. Instead of arresting, prosecuting, and incarcerating people for dope possession, we let cops focus on more serious crimes and court backlogs will decrease." Zell then pointed at DeWayne Jackson. "Just think of the blacks that we would keep out of jail if we legalized marijuana."

Jackson gave a half-hearted shrug without disagreeing. African-American youths were more often involved in the purchase and distribution of heroin and crack cocaine – hard-core drugs that carried long-term prison sentences. And nobody was calling for the legalization of those drugs. Still, Jackson did not deny it was possible legalization could help the black community.

"Marijuana is legal in other parts of the world," Zell added. "A lot of Americans travel to Amsterdam because it's readily available over there."

"So is prostitution," the worldly Graham said. "Should we open up a line of brothels in Southern California and tax them as well?"

Zell didn't respond to the remark. He was mellow enough not to disrespect the General by rolling his eyes at him too. "Congresswoman," he said turning his focus back on her. "What do you think?"

Sanchez was on the fence but looked like she could be persuaded. "You know President Schumacher would be dead set against any platform to legalize marijuana. He would absolutely hammer us."

General Graham agreed. "He made the argument two days ago that we really don't want our kids to grow up hooked on legalized marijuana. He asked the crowd, I think it was in Kansas somewhere, whether we want our kids to go to school stoned, only to drop out, and wind up on the public welfare rolls because they're too high to get a job. He said marijuana usage among teens is up largely due to the gaining acceptance of medical marijuana. That's partly your fault, Sonny," he said, pointing an accusatory finger at him.

Zell nodded, knowing it was an uphill battle even with Democrats. "We're trying to make some headway here in California. We've got a ballot measure to allow a person to grow a small amount of marijuana for their own personal use. Not to resell it to anyone else like kids, of course. I think it's fifty-fifty that it will pass."

"President Schumacher has already said he'll pull all of California's federal highway money if the measure passes," Sanchez reported. "That's hundreds of millions of dollars that California cannot afford to do without. He's even hinted at requiring a drug test for any recipient of federal aid."

"That's why I am deeply committed to helping you become the next President of the United States."

Sanchez and Graham smiled. Both were intrigued by the possibility of a new federal tax that could raise billions of dollars for them to fund yet another government program. Plus, they could regulate the hell out of it and control the lives of the user, who in turn, based on his or her stoned state of mind, would become more dependent on the government for their well-being. Yes, this was a definite possibility in a Sanchez Administration.

"We're going to have to keep this one quiet, too," General Graham said.

As with much of the Democratic platform, the specifics had to be kept hidden from public view. A campaign promising bigger government, higher taxes, amnesty for illegals, and all the marijuana you can smoke was not a winning strategy. They would have to campaign one way and govern the exact opposite.

"But we can start spreading the word," Sanchez said. "Start laying the groundwork and we'll get right on it after the inauguration."

The hallucinogenic turn of events was followed by the lobbyists for the gays and lesbians, the unions, and the African-Americans imploring the candidates to push for the federal recognition of gay marriage, increased public employee pensions, and more affirmative action. Sanchez and Graham were wholeheartedly on board with each of the groups' cause. They made sure to mention President Schumacher's staunch opposition and the need to fire up their constituents to get out the vote.

After thirty minutes of back and forth, the group quieted down, a couple wondering if the silence meant their time with the candidates was over and whether they should pack up and head for home.

General Graham, however, felt the need to talk some more. "Art, you've been pretty quiet over there," he said.

Brennan had not even opened his folder, hadn't even said a word since the opening round of pleasantries. He was there mainly to listen to what everyone else was asking for. His way of doing business did not depend on which party was in the White House or who controlled the House or the Senate. Most of what he did was paid for by far-left donors. As the chairman of the Civil Liberties Alliance, the intensely hostile Brennan had a thorny burr up his saddle when it came to the United States. Its superpower status and the constant butting in on other nations' affairs required a good comeuppance in his mind. And he was always on the lookout to bash the U.S. Luckily for him, he had the Democratic Party on his side.

"General, I have only a small matter to discuss with you and Congresswoman Sanchez," Brennan said softly. "It can wait until the meeting's over."

The five other donors who plopped down fifty thousand for a semi-private meeting with the candidates looked at Brennan with scornful disgust. The nerve of the man! Wanting a private meeting for the same amount of money!

"It'll just take a second of your time while we walk out."

"Okay, then," Sanchez said. She was ready to head to her next campaign stop. The group stood, exchanged handshakes all around, and promised to work tirelessly on Sanchez's behalf. Brennan was the last of the group to head for the door and he intentionally slowed both Sanchez and Graham to discuss his only agenda item.

After making sure the door to the suite had closed, he spoke barely above a whisper. "I didn't want to mention this in front of the others. I think both of you are aware of the CLA's representation of Muqtada Abdulla?"

"Of course," General Graham said. "He's set to be executed in a matter of days."

"Yes," Brennan responded before taking a deep breath. His request would be a tricky subject, even for liberals. "I need one of you to call for the President to push back the execution date."

Sanchez and Graham stared at Brennan with wide eyes. Both wondered if they heard correctly.

"Are you nuts?" Sanchez asked. "That's even more of a political hot potato than Sonny's marijuana measure."

"She's right, Art. It would be suicidal for the Democrats to call off the execution when we're at war with the terrorists," Graham added. Even he was politically savvy enough to see it.

"I'm not asking you to advocate for calling off the execution. Just postpone it for a couple of weeks."

"The man's a terrorist," General Graham shot back. "A guilty terrorist!"

The fiery Brennan was starting to get worked up. "Both of you are against capital punishment!" he fumed. He had perused their position papers a number of times. He had also read their long forgotten speeches when they were simply novices in the political arena. He pointed at Sanchez. "For over ten years, you have called it cruel and unusual punishment and called for its abolition." He then pointed at General Graham. "And you have railed against the use of military tribunals in the war on terrorism."

Graham stepped in front of Sanchez and was ready to go nose to nose with Brennan. "If we ask the President to postpone the execution we'll look like fools, like we're soft on national security! That's not going to help our chances of winning, Art!"

Brennan gave it right back to him. "I don't need a lecture from you, General. I need that execution postponed!"

Sanchez stepped in between them and looked at Brennan. "Why do you need it postponed?" she asked, not sure if she wanted to know the answer.

"My client needs more time."

"Time for what?" Graham huffed. "He's had a hundred appeals already and they have gone nowhere."

"He just needs a little more time." Brennan strained not to give too much information. "We have a last-ditch appeal ready for the federal courts."

"I'm sure it will be about as successful as the others," Graham responded.

"Please, just a few days might help," Brennan said. "You can say you want to ensure the legal process plays out. If Muqtada is put to death before all his appeals are exhausted it could be used as a recruiting tool for terrorists around the world. Something both of you are concerned about, I'm sure."

Sanchez was shaking her head slowly back and forth. She wasn't stupid enough to jump into the middle of the upcoming execution of a terrorist whether she agreed with capital punishment or not. "Let's just see how it all plays out. There's no sense of me sticking my neck out for a terrorist when the appeals process might conclude before the execution takes place. I'll keep your concerns in mind, Art."

Brennan reluctantly nodded and allowed the two candidates to leave the room. He suddenly needed a smoke, maybe one of his trademark stogies. Of course, lighting up within the San Francisco city limits would bring out the cigarette gestapo right quick. He paced back and forth before reaching for his phone. He called his team of lawyers to tell them to hurry up on Abdulla's motion to stay his execution.

They were running out of time.

CHAPTER 11

Silver Creek, Indiana

Agent Abernathy took the two men to a makeshift boat dock one mile north of the Schumacher property and handed them off to three other agents. The two men were then taken to a mobile unit for questioning.

Special Agent Ben Dorsey took the lead as he sat across the table from al-Mutallab, who had an unopened bottle of water in front of him. "Mr. al-Mutallab, can you tell me what you were doing here today?"

"Boating with friends." What the hell else did it look like? Al-Mutallab was direct in his response, but his tone of voice was flat. He knew he hadn't done anything wrong other than maybe having open alcohol on the river or boating without a life preserver. Barely enough to waste time on writing a ticket.

"Where do you live?"

"I live in West Lafayette. I'm a senior engineering student at Purdue." He sounded believable, but of course, this time he was telling the truth.

Dorsey wrote the city and college on his yellow legal pad. "Where did you and your friends start from today?"

"Just up the river in Covington."

"Where were you heading?"

"Just down river a ways," he said with a shrug. He thought about offering that they were going to meet his friends but since he had no friends down river, he kept quiet.

Agent Dorsey flinched slightly as the cell phone on his right hip started buzzing. He reached for it, read the text message, and placed it back into the holster. The two women speaking with the other agents didn't know a whole lot about the two men they were with. They didn't know the last names of Malik and Ahmed, just some guys they met the night before at a party. They appeared to have simply gone with the two men to enjoy a day of boating and beer. Agent Dorsey made a few more notations on his notepad.

"Tell me about the two women you were with."

Al-Mutallab rolled his eyes. "I don't know why you want to ask me all these fuckin' questions," he snapped. Just another example of the pigs sticking it to the minorities, he thought. "I haven't done anything wrong. We were just boating. If you're gonna ticket me for not having a life jacket or for having open alcohol, well, just give me the damn ticket."

"What are the names of those two women, Mr. al-Mutallab?" Agent Dorsey looked directly at him, his pen poised to write down the response. His raised eyebrows silently asked the question again.

Al-Mutallab glanced down at his folded hands, a dead giveaway his mind was trying to come up with something. The script he was to go off of had become thicker by the day, and the problem with living in the land of make believe was you couldn't keep everything straight. Just yesterday he had added these two women to the story. Now their names had slipped his mind in all the activity.

"What are the names of the two women?"

"Jackie and Jasmine," al-Mutallab said, hoping he was right.

Dorsey looked at his notes. "Did you mean Jessica and Jasmine?"

"Yeah, Jessica and Jasmine," al-Mutallab said, now remembering their names. "We all go to Purdue. We met them last night at a party and they agreed to a day of boating."

"Just met them yesterday and they agreed to go boating with you?"

"Yeah." Was that so hard to believe? al-Mutallab thought to himself.

"What are their last names?"

Now Al-Mutallab thought he had the upper hand. "I told you," he said brusquely, "I just met them last night. I don't know their last names."

"Let's cut to the chase, Malik," Agent Dorsey said, dropping his pen on the desk and leaning forward. "What are you doing back in Silver Creek?"

Had Agent Dorsey asked him whether he had ever been to Silver Creek, al-Mutallab could have simply said yes. But now he was trying to come up with a response and the noticeable silence indicated something was amiss.

"I've never been here before," he stammered. His mind instantly gauged the response and hoped Agent Dorsey would take it at that. He thought back to the McDonald's where he bought the Coke. He hadn't done anything that would leave a mark as to his name or where he was coming from. At least, nothing that he could remember in the last thirty seconds.

Agent Dorsey shook his head like he was greatly disappointed. "Malik, when you start lying to me then I get the sneakin' suspicion you weren't really out enjoying a day of boating on the Wabash with your girlfriends."

"I'm not lying," al-Mutallab protested, his voice rising. He acted like he was royally offended.

"Malik, if you keep lying to me it's only going to make things worse for you. Why are you back in Silver Creek?"

"I told you once before," he said, jamming the end of his index finger onto the table top. He was now fully committed to the story. "I've never been to Silver Creek!"

Agent Dorsey rested his elbows on the table and folded his hands in front of him. "Malik, we have your picture from when you drove that rented Corolla past the President's house last week."

"That wasn't me," al-Mutallab said, shaking his head. "Must have been someone else."

Agent Dorsey reached over and grabbed the file on the table. He pulled out a surveillance picture taken through the front windshield from a camera just off the main road. He placed the picture in front of al-Mutallab, who studied it with care. It had been enhanced a great deal with the best technology the Secret Service had in its arsenal. But he noticed the clarity still wasn't all that good and that gave him a chance at a denial.

"That's not me. What? Do you think because that guy has a dark complexion he must be me? Does every Middle Easterner look alike to you? That's racist, you pig! That's nothing but racial profiling! I told you I have never been to Silver Creek!"

Had al-Mutallab simply confessed that he had been to Silver Creek before and was today enjoying some recreation on the Wabash, the Secret Service might have told him to be on his way. Maybe drop the hint that he should find a new place to enjoy the many of Indiana's fine recreational opportunities. But his insistent denials only made the agents more suspicious.

"Have you ever been to Tarnak Farms, Malik?"

The question shot through al-Mutallab like a bolt of lightning. Both agents sitting across the table from him noticed he flinched ever so slightly at the question. The glare radiating from al-Mutallab's dark squinting eyes indicated he knew exactly what Agent Dorsey was talking about and what he was really searching for in his interview. And al-Mutallab was not amused.

Tarnak Farms was an Afghan camp near Kandahar used by bin Laden to train terrorists prior the 9/11 attacks. And al-Mutallab's age made it clear to all involved that he hadn't been in the vicinity of the camp considering it had long been put out of commission courtesy of a carpet-bombing campaign carried out by U.S. B-52s.

"No, I have never been there." He made it sound like he had never even heard of the place let alone stepped foot on the property.

Agent Dorsey made a note on his pad and asked another question he already knew the answer to. "Have you ever been to *Maple Ridge* Farms?" Maybe *this* farm would ring a bell in al-Mutallab's mind.

"No." Al-Mutallab was prepared to respond in the negative for every question from here on out.

"Malik," Agent Dorsey said softly, "do you remember that farmer's stand you stopped at prior to driving by the President's house?"

Al-Mutallab gave no response, but his mind was racing back to that day. He remembered driving by the President's house and the helicopter that chased him to the parking lot of the McDonald's. But a farmer's stand? After another ten seconds, he remembered he had been late and, to make matters worse, he had been lost. He had stopped to ask for directions. He now knew he had been caught.

"Do you remember walking in the front door and buying a pint of strawberries? You told the woman behind the counter you were a doctor returning to Indianapolis."

How did they know this? Al-Mutallab wondered to himself. He shrugged in response to the statement then added, "It wasn't me."

"We have your fingerprints on the doorknob and on the five-dollar bill you used to pay for the strawberries. Those fingerprints matched those taken when you entered the country five years ago on a student visa." Agent Dorsey leaned in a little closer with his hands folded again. "Malik, guilty people don't lie to us. Who you do work for?"

Al-Mutallab's eyes narrowed. He knew he could say no more. "Screw you, you prick. I want my lawyer."

Agent Dorsey gave him one last chance. "You realize your F-1 non-immigrant visa expires at the end of the month, don't you? Do you want to help yourself out?"

Al-Mutallab looked him straight in the eye. "I have nothing to say to you. I want my lawyer now."

CHAPTER 12

The Supreme Court of the United States – Washington, D.C.

The Supreme Court's term begins on the first Monday in October. The Justices and their law clerks had been hard at work for the last several weeks preparing for the upcoming oral arguments – reading briefs, preparing questions to ask of the attorneys, and drafting memos to pass back and forth once the arguments concluded and the decision whether to affirm or reverse had to be made by the "Highest Court in the Land."

But one Justice had put his legal briefs aside and sat in his office on a blustery Saturday afternoon waiting for something more pressing to come in. It would be his first official and public act as a member of the United States Supreme Court.

Originally set at six justices in 1789, the current nine-member Supreme Court has been firmly in place since 1869, despite President Franklin Roosevelt's plan to pack the bench with as many as fifteen in 1937. Associate Justice John A. Lincoln had been appointed by President Schumacher, confirmed by the U.S. Senate, and took the two required oaths in late July. When then Justice Ali Hussein tried to detonate his suicide vest in the House Chamber, Justice Lincoln and the rest of his new colleagues had a front-row seat of the spectacle. Since that time, Justice Lincoln went from the low-man on the totem pole to number eight in seniority.

President Schumacher replaced Justice Hussein with Janelle Robinson, the first African-American woman on the Court. She was also the first conservative black woman, and she had endured a bruising late-summer nomination battle from the Democrats in the Senate. With a six to three conservative majority on the Court, the Democrats were already starting to take their shots before the new term even began. Justice Lincoln, however, was hoping for calmer days once he and his colleagues took the bench.

Since the Court's term did not start until October seventh, Justice Lincoln had not heard oral arguments on any cases. But that did not mean he was not a functioning member of the High Court. As one of the nine justices, he was assigned to preside over one of the federal circuits of the United States once he came on to the Court. Chief Justice Raymond J. Shannon presided over the D.C. Circuit, the Federal Circuit, and the Fifth Circuit, which covered

Louisiana, Mississippi, and his home state of Texas. Justice Lincoln read and ruled on all the emergency petitions from the Seventh Circuit, which includes Illinois, Wisconsin, and his home state of Indiana. The other seven justices split up the remaining nine circuits.

Muqtada Abdulla's petition for stay of execution had worked its way through the federal judiciary and would soon be on the Supreme Court's doorstep. The CLA and Counselor Hurt had come up with a new and novel theory to argue for a stay of execution. Upon further research, Hurt learned the federal government had run low on sodium thiopental – the first stage sedative in the lethal IV cocktail. Instead, the government intended to substitute the drug pentobarbital, a sedative that is often used in physician-assisted suicides and by veterinarians in the euthanasia of animals. Hurt took the latter fact and ran with it for a good twenty-page argument.

Now it was spitting out of Justice Lincoln's fax machine.

Grabbing page after page was Bryan Lockhart, a former clerk to one of the Court's most conservative members, Justice F. Lloyd Rickenbacker. Lockhart agreed to stay on another term as one of the four clerks for "the rookie" Justice Lincoln. Rickenbacker often stated he was trading the hardworking Lockhart to Lincoln for a clerk to be named later. Or possibly cash considerations. Lockhart had taken it upon himself to get Lincoln's office up to speed and show the Supreme Court ropes to the three other "ghostwriters of the judiciary."

And now he was right in the thick of it.

"Here's the petition for stay of execution," Lockhart said as he handed a copy to Justice Lincoln. Lockhart had made a copy for himself. He took a seat in front of the Justice's desk and started flipping through the pages.

The cable news networks had sent their satellite trucks and legal correspondents to One First Street for a nice shot of the west side of the iconic Supreme Court Building. Banners running across the bottom of the screen indicated everyone was waiting for word on Muqtada Abdulla's motion for stay of execution. Few tourists bothered to stop and ask why the klieg lights, cameras, and primped reporters were taking up space in the plaza. The tourists who did ask had no idea who Abdulla was or that anything of importance was going on at the Supreme Court. They took their pictures and left. One die-hard and committed protester, a woman from a local anti-death penalty organization, had managed to throw on her running shoes and hustle her way from her home in Georgetown to the sidewalk across the street. With her picket calling for the end of capital punishment, she dutifully marched back and forth while chatting on her cell phone.

"The CLA says the lethal-injection drug the government's using is also used on animals," Lockhart blurted out.

"I see that," Justice Lincoln responded. The Justice had his feet resting on the corner of his desk, the top of which could not be seen given the blizzard of papers stacked from end to end. There was enough open space for the telephone and a framed picture of him with his mother Orvetta and the President of the United States after he took the oath of office. He flipped through the pages at a quick pace, skipping the facts, and letting the argument filter through his brain.

"I don't think that's a constitutional violation entitling Abdulla to relief."

"The drug is used to kill dogs, cats, and . . . uh oh." Justice Lincoln stopped in mid-sentence. He sounded like things were going to get dicey.

"What?"

"Dogs, cats, horses and . . . pigs. Page ten." He quoted from the petition. "It would be a violation of the Eighth Amendment's prohibition against cruel and unusual punishment to execute Mr. Abdulla, a man of the Muslim faith, utilizing the same drug used to kill pigs. Also, use of such a drug infringes on Mr. Abdulla's right to practice his religion, a violation of the First Amendment."

"That's preposterous."

Justice Lincoln nodded his head. "You have to hand it to them though. They found another argument that hadn't been made yet."

Lockhart was having none of it. "It's just a bunch of BS if you ask me."

"The consumption of pork is forbidden in Islam."

"But it's not like they are inserting a pig's blood into the IVs," Lockhart huffed. "How can they even make their argument with a straight face? How do they come up with that crap?"

"It's been rumored that General John "Black Jack" Pershing executed Muslim terrorists in the Phillippines in 1911 using hogs' blood."

"I've never heard of that."

"Apparently, he had the terrorists tied to posts prior to their execution and then had U.S. soldiers dip bullets in hogs' blood and fat right in front of their eyes. The Muslims thought they wouldn't go to heaven if they were contaminated with the blood. Either before or after the execution, one of the terrorists was freed and supposedly told his comrades about the Americans' way of doing business. Acts of terrorism were said to have dropped off dramatically."

"So it worked?"

"I'm not sure that it actually happened," Justice Lincoln said. "Some people say it's just an urban legend."

"I think Abdulla is scraping the bottom of the barrel with this alleged violation of the Constitution."

Justice Lincoln leaned back in his chair. "Maybe the argument is being made simply to rile up terrorists around the world. Show them this is how America treats the Muslim believer. At least in their eyes."

Lockhart stopped to think of the politics of the decision, not that politics would have anything to do with it in the end. But part of his job was to think of how the decision would sound in the real world. How it would be interpreted not just by the litigants but by those who might be subject to a similar ruling in the future.

"You might be right," he said. "Denying the stay of execution might not meet much opposition in America, but overseas they'll probably be burning American flags by sunup."

"Probably."

"They might even target you."

Justice Lincoln shrugged, not showing an ounce of concern. "I'm not worried. I get paid $213,900 to put on the fancy black robe and make decisions, some of which might be unpopular to average Americans and even people on the other side of the world. I guess that's why the Constitution grants me lifetime tenure." He stopped before adding. "And it's also why God created U.S. marshals."

"Do you want me to draft the order?"

Before Lockhart could answer, the Justice's secretary buzzed his phone. "Justice Lincoln, Justice Rickenbacker is on line one."

"Okay, I'll take it." Justice Lincoln said. He wondered what Rickenbacker would think of the argument – no doubt frivolous and patently without merit. Justice Lincoln then turned his attention back to Lockhart. "Go ahead and draft the order. Let's make it like the rest of them. Short and sweet. Nothing fancy."

"And then send it to the rest of the Justices?"

"Yes, forward it to them along with the petition."

By 6 p.m. that Saturday evening, the Chief Justice and the rest of the Associate Justices had responded to the petition. Justice Pamela Anders, the other conservative female on the Court, sent her thoughts via e-mail to Justice Lincoln that the petition was "a bunch of hokum" and congratulated him on his baptism by fire. Once the order was typed out, the Clerk of the Supreme Court made Justice Lincoln's ruling available to the public.

16-002 – Certiorari Denied
Abdulla, Muqtada A. v. Armstrong, Warden

The application for stay of execution of the sentence of death presented to Justice Lincoln and by him referred to the Court is denied. The petition for a writ of certiorari is denied.

None of the other Justices indicated they would grant the application for stay of execution. Muqtada Abdulla's final legal prayer was over.

United States Penitentiary – Terre Haute, Indiana

The Bureau of Prisons had specifically picked a Saturday as the day of Abdulla's execution. Nobody wanted a federal office building filled with workers at their desks or young children of the employees playing at the day-care. McVeigh killed 168 Americans on a Wednesday in 1995 when he took down the Murrah Federal Building in Oklahoma City. Nineteen of the victims were innocent children caught in the middle of the homegrown terrorist's war against the federal government. Sunday was out, too. Prison officials had no desire to fulfill the requirements of the law on the Lord's day.

Along with the day of the week, the prison authorities also hoped the innocent date of October the fifth would draw little attention. They made sure the date was not near a holiday for a large gathering of people – the picnics and fireworks on the Fourth of July and the parades of Labor Day being too big of a celebration to allow terrorists to target as an anniversary date for years to come. The Oklahoma City bombing occurred on April 19th, the anniversary of the violent end to the federal government's 1993 siege on the Branch Davidian compound in Waco. In the planning stages of the Columbine massacre, the shooters mentioned Waco and Oklahoma City before unleashing their carnage on April 20th.

The FBI, the United States Marshals Service, the Indiana State Police, and a whole host of law-enforcement agencies were on full alert around the prison. Anyone with business at the penitentiary was screened twice prior to entering the gates. Federal and state offices around the Midwest were being watched and air traffic was being diverted around the blue October skies of Terre Haute.

The special confinement unit was unusually quiet on this Saturday evening. Almost as if the other inmates on death row were sitting in the solitary cells with their ears straining to hear what was going on with the man whose time was up. Their time would soon come.

"You dirty dogs!"

Muqtada Abdulla could not be kept quiet. Even on his last day. Even as he made his way to the execution chamber.

"You dogs will die soon! I promise you that!"

With four guards surrounding him, Abdulla's hands and feet were shackled together and he shuffled down the white painted walls of the special confinement unit. The guards threatened to put a mask over his mouth if he refused to stop spitting on them. Much of the spittle had found its way to the front of his hated lime-green apparel.

Abdulla had spent the last hour with his attorney and his spiritual advisor. There was little else to do. He refused a last meal, saying he wanted his soul cleansed for the virgins he was soon to meet in the afterlife. As they neared the execution chamber, Abdulla became a difficult inmate. He dropped to the floor, his legs seeming to lose their strength. He then refused to move. The guards grabbed him under his arms and by his bound feet and carried him onto the gurney. Once he was strapped down, the guards left and the execution team began their preparations.

Abdulla sat semi-reclined on the gurney. The walls were a gray-blue in color and the curtains covering the windows a dark blue. Behind the curtains in the witness room, seven observers had been chosen to witness the execution. One was a pool reporter from the Associated Press and another a representative from Amnesty International set to observe how executions are carried out by the United States Government. One man seated in the corner had not said a word since he was ushered into the room. The man was a native of Saudi Arabia and a Christian convert after completing his studies in the United States. Upon returning home to visit family, Abdulla had the authorities arrest him for his renunciation of Islam. When the man tried to argue his case, Abdulla had the man's tongue cut out. The man was able to escape with his life and returned to America to live and worship in freedom. He would now watch the butcher enjoy his last breaths.

Once the curtains were pulled back, Abdulla squinted his eyes trying to peer through the one-way windows. Not knowing who was watching but sure someone would remember what he had to say, he spewed forth one last angry tirade against the United States of America promising his brothers would soon invade the country and convert all nonbelievers to Islam.

"Allahu akbar!" he kept yelling.

Once the IV tubes were properly inserted, the execution team exited the chamber and entered the control room. There was no reason to wait any longer. There wasn't going to be a last-minute phone call from the President, the Attorney General, or the Supreme Court. When the pentobarbital dripped in, Abdulla's angry rants against America went mute in short order. Not long thereafter, it was all over.

A half hour later, Warden Armstrong emerged from the main office with the prison information officer in tow and made the hundred-yard long walk to the group of reporters waiting at the front gate for word of Abdulla's demise. Armstrong took no delight in the walk or the statement he would give. He was a man of few words. He was the warden, not some politician who flocked to any camera he could find to say something he thought important. Armstrong had made the same walk on two other occasions. In old-school fashion, he actually pined for the return of the electric chair and the ceremonial but meaningless dimming of the prison lights to announce the switch had been thrown and the inmate had expired courtesy of a twenty-second jolt of 2,000-plus volts.

Warden Armstrong asked the reporters if they were ready and proceeded when hearing they were. He was going to make this quick.

"At 8:07 p.m. this evening, inmate Muqtada Abdulla was pronounced dead as a result of his execution according to the dictates of federal law. The execution was by lethal injection," he said as he looked at the scrap of paper in his hands. "Inmate Abdulla's last words were 'Death to America.'" He then looked up at the reporters and hoped they wouldn't have any questions.

"Was he in any pain?"

"I saw no evidence of him being in any pain."

"Any agitation?"

"He was belligerent to the end, which was not out of the ordinary for Inmate Abdulla. Thank you all." The warden turned on a dime and walked away.

"What will happen to the body!?" one reporter shouted.

The warden acted like he hadn't heard and continued on. The prison information officer was right on his tail. They both wanted this night to be over.

CHAPTER 13

Chicago, Illinois

Mohammed Akbar had been sitting on a bench on the southeast side of Buckingham Fountain for the last twenty minutes. Grant Park was packed with people on that sunny Sunday afternoon – families, tourists, locals with their Frisbees and footballs. At this time next week, runners from all fifty states and eleven different countries would be sprawled out on the ground after a long hard 26.2 miles. A nice collection of runners jogged through the park, some making their last long tuneup for the marathon and others just out for a Sunday afternoon of exercise.

Akbar sat still, his right leg crossed over his left, and a lit Dutch Masters grape cigarillo burning near the end of his right knee. He had smoked for twenty years, and believed that since the Koran didn't specifically forbid it he could allow himself this one vice. Usually, it helped calm his nerves, but it was of little help today. His mind had been racing since the night before. He had failed to stop the execution of Muqtada Abdulla, and Sheik Abdulla was not pleased. Abdulla cursed him on the phone after the execution and made it clear in vulgar terms that he had failed Allah and was a disgrace to the Muslim world. He was worse than one of those godless Americans, a huge insult to any Muslim. Akbar, however, didn't need to be berated to know he failed. He had been working on his grand plan for jihad for over a decade now and he was growing impatient.

And just as Sheik Abdulla had dressed him down, Akbar had done the same to al-Mutallab. When al-Mutallab drove back to Chicago to report on his excursions to Silver Creek and the interrogation by the Secret Service, Akbar slapped him across the face and called him a fool – in part because Akbar knew he would get the same tongue-lashing from Abdulla. Akbar instructed al-Mutallab to pack up his things in West Lafayette and leave the country lest he screw up the plan yet again. Although Abdulla's execution ended the need to free him from prison, Akbar still wanted to kill the President. It would be his singular goal now.

Now Akbar had to come up with a new idea to carry out his assassination plot with or without Saudi assistance.

"Mr. Akbar?"

The question came from behind and to the right. Akbar's sunglasses hid his face such that the man he was meeting was unsure of who was sitting on the bench. Akbar nodded at the young man and motioned for him to have a seat next to him.

"I'm sorry I'm late," the man said. "But I was cautious like you told me."

"Good," Akbar said softly.

The young man had left his apartment on the campus of Northwestern University and taken the El train down to Roosevelt Street and then hoofed it back east to Grant Park. He was told to walk to Buckingham Fountain and call Akbar for directions on where they would meet. Assan Habib had been teaching chemistry at Northwestern for five years now and had been a casual acquaintance of Akbar for two of those. Now it was his turn to use his expertise to wage war on America.

"I'm sorry to hear about Mr. Abdulla," Habib said with sincerity.

Akbar shook his head, like the dearly departed was a forgotten matter. "He was meaningless."

"Meaningless?"

Akbar dropped a line of ash onto the ground. "Sheik Abdulla only wanted to get his son out of prison. That was his sole objective. Maybe now he will be serious about bringing America to its knees."

"He called for a holy war against the United States this morning," Habib reported.

Akbar nodded with little joy. "We don't need another fatwa," he said. "We need money, we need soldiers, we need instruments of death."

Habib looked out over the long line of cars on Lake Shore Drive to the boats on Lake Michigan. "The election is less than a month away."

Akbar lowered his voice and leaned over to Habib. "I'm beginning to wonder if we are running out of opportunities to get the President."

"Your men thought of the river?"

"Yes. The Secret Service patrols the Wabash with large weapons. We would need a small army to take them out."

The initial plan was to send a wave of boats down the Wabash with enough AK-47s and rocket-propelled grenades to overpower any resisting force. The terrorist assault would then proceed up the hill and into the President's house. But the reconnaissance mission already showed the Secret Service would not be caught off guard by a river attack.

Habib looked down at his fingernails, trying to think of something.

"Airspace above the compound is restricted, too," Akbar said.

Habib looked over at him. "Maybe we should just bomb Newport."

Akbar let the statement sink in, like he wasn't sure what Habib was talking about.

"Newport?" he asked, looking over at the young man. "What the hell is that?"

"It's a chemical depot, probably less than twenty miles south of where the President lives." Habib had done his research. He pulled out his iPhone and searched for the town of Newport on his map function. Once the screen showed the red dot on the map of west-central Indiana, he showed it to Akbar. He then used his finger to show where the President lived. The gap wasn't very far. Habib could see the wheels spinning in Akbar's head.

"That's where the U.S. Government stores and destroys VX nerve gas."

Newport, Indiana is home to the U.S. Army's Newport Chemical Depot, formerly known as the Newport Army Ammunition Plant and the Wabash River Ordinance Works. Situated thirty miles north of Terre Haute, the facility produced VX nerve gas until 2008. Now, it is used to store America's, and hopefully most of the rest of the world's, remaining VX and then over time destroy it before it gets into the hands of those who actually want to use it.

When Habib mentioned "VX," Akbar's eyes lit up like a child on Christmas morning. Akbar had obviously heard of VX nerve gas. Every terrorist had, just like they heard all about Saddam's deadly use of mustard gas against the Kurds in the late '80s and the Aum Shinrikyo sect's release of sarin gas in the Tokyo subway in 1995. But Akbar suddenly had the desire to learn more about the possibilities of VX.

"Tell me about the VX."

Habib put his chemistry education to good use. "It's a nerve agent, and one of the most toxic substances man has ever created. Its original use was in pesticides. Now its only use is in chemical warfare, and like a nuclear weapon, it has been classified as a weapon of mass destruction."

Akbar's eyes widened some more. So much so that Habib could almost see them bulging out from behind Akbar's sunglasses.

"It's a WMD?" Akbar asked. The possibilities were running through his head so fast he couldn't comprehend all of them.

"Yes," Habib said. "It has no odor and it is tasteless. It distributed mostly as a liquid but can be made into an aerosol."

"What does it do?"

"It's nasty stuff. Large exposure to VX will cause your muscles to start twitching, then comes the vomiting, and then your chest will constrict until you'll slowly lose the ability to breathe. You'll asphyxiate in a matter of minutes."

Akbar was beginning to think his chances of killing the President had dramatically improved. Terrorists would not even have to get in close proximity if the delivery method was good enough.

"How would we get it?" Akbar asked.

"That would be very difficult. Almost impossible."

"Could you get it? For experiments?"

Habib shook his head. "There's no chance of that happening. Nobody's going to be doing any research on VX nerve gas in this day and age, and the authorities would never allow for it outside of government research labs."

"Would we bomb Newport?" Akbar asked. The question wasn't far-fetched. Habib had been the one to suggest it.

Habib, however, had been half joking. "It would probably do little good. The VX would be secured and heavily guarded. Plus, the Secret Service would have the President on the move to safety before a plume of VX gas could even reach Silver Creek."

Akbar looked away from Habib and back to the boats on the lake. He was beginning to lose hope.

"We'd first have to obtain the VX and then smuggle it into the United States," Habib said, hoping to keep Akbar's spirits up.

"Who would still have VX?"

"Russia and the United States are the only countries known to possess it. Iran might have purchased some on the black market. Iraq had it before the fall of Saddam. The U.S. has been trying to gobble it up to keep it out of the hands of terrorists. It's possible you might be able to find a small amount hidden away in a bunker somewhere. Maybe someone who squirreled it away until the time or the price was right. But you'd have to know who to ask."

Akbar nodded his head. He knew people he could ask, and they would likely know where to get it. He knew he had a lot of work to do and not a lot of time to do it. He held out his hand. "Thanks for meeting with me. I am going to go call Sheik Abdulla and offer my condolences once again."

Habib shook Akbar's and smiled. "Let me know if you need anything else."

Less than one hundred yards to the north of the get-together between Akbar and Habib, another meeting was about to take place. And that man's mission was little different from that of his unknown Muslim brothers sitting on a bench to the south.

Mohammed Hamda could barely sit still on the bench on the northeast side of Buckingham Fountain. His head was going round and round more times than the Ferris wheel at Navy Pier. He was nervous by nature, but the last month of his life had been nothing but a whirlwind of preparation and planning. And today was the last meeting he was going to have before becoming a hero to Muslim terrorists around the world.

In less than a week, he would be the FBI's most wanted man.

He had agreed to meet his bomb maker at 3 p.m. Fayez Harraj had called Hamda and let him know about a guy who could help him pull off the bombing. The man was said to have once met bin-Laden and supposedly spent a year making car bombs in Iraq after the U.S. invasion. Harraj said the man knew what he was doing.

Growing increasingly paranoid by the day, Hamda demanded his terrorist cohort dress in running clothes and come alone. He was making sure to cover all his bases, not wanting to be like those other dolts who had fallen into the trap of an undercover agent only to be arrested before the fake bomb was set to go off. No sir, he was too smart to fall for it. He was going to be the grand mastermind that would pull it off.

"Martin?"

Hamda had instructed the man he was meeting to call him Martin. He didn't want to use the man's real name and make some innocent passerby suspicious.

"Mike!" Hamda said too loudly. He looked around. Control yourself, his mind scolded. Act like you know what you're doing.

"Martin, my friend."

Hamda shook Mike's hand and looked over his shoulders. "Did you come alone?" He knew he had to ask. That was the way they did it in the movies. He was no dupe.

The man's name was Moshie Masahn. Hamda, however, demanded the man be called Mike, again one of his brilliant ideas so as not to raise suspicions if out in public. Moshie, however, went along with it. He didn't mind being called Mike so long as jihad was the name of the game.

"Yes," Mike said. "I came alone just like you told me."

Hamda kept glancing over Mike's shoulders. He was unable to stand still and made a 360-degree circle around him. His paranoid sensibilities made him question everyone and everything he encountered. Anything less than paranoia risked blowing the whole operation.

"Take your shirt off," Hamda said with some hesitation. He had not done this with Harraj at the ballpark. But now that things were getting hot and heavy, he was not going to take any chances.

"What?" Mike was not prepared for this.

"Are you a cop?"

"Martin," Mike said, seemingly offended. "It's me. I am a friend of Fayez as are you."

"If you're a cop, you'd be wearing a wire." Hamda had seen that too in the movies. The cops always got their man with a wire hidden under their shirt. Hamda had picked the spot because of its wide open air around the fountain. He wasn't going to meet his bomb maker in a restaurant or coffee shop where cameras and microphones could easily pick up their conversations. Plus, he wanted to look at the scene of the crime, not just envision it on some map. To blend in and to throw off the authorities, he wore his running clothes like his friend and most of the rest of the patrons of the park.

Mike whipped off his Nike running shirt without further protest. The only thing it showed was a nice pack of abs and some finely shaped pecs. He moved in closer to Hamda and pulled his shorts an inch away from his waist revealing nothing that God hadn't provided him at birth. He also took off his hat and flapped it around in the air for good measure. Nothing.

"Good," Hamda said. That's the way he ran the show. People did what he said for fear of the consequences.

Mike looked at Hamda with wide eyes. As if wondering what Hamda wanted to do now. He was supposedly the brains behind the operation. Maybe Fayez didn't know who he was dealing with. Hamda, however, recovered quickly and told Mike to sit down on the bench. They had communicated over the Internet on three other occasions. Two weeks ago, Hamda had praised a radical cleric's call for jihad on his Facebook page, and hundreds of angry Muslims around the world indicated they "liked" Hamda's virulent writings. He was definitely gaining a following. After a call from Fayez, Hamda had a new partner in crime.

Hamda took a few seconds to tie his running shoes, like he was lacing up for a quick trot around the park with his running buddy. He then sat down at an angle so he could keep an eye on the surroundings.

"How are things for next weekend?" Hamda asked with great excitement in his quiet voice.

Mike leaned in closer and spoke barely above a whisper. "The van will be parked down there at the corner of Monroe and Columbus." He pointed his finger to the northwest to show Hamda the spot. "I painted a sign on the side of the truck that says it's an official marathon vehicle. Just like you told me."

"The cops won't even think twice about it."

"It's brilliant," Mike gushed. He could see Hamda's pride swelling.

"And the explosives?"

"The van will be filled with six drums of diesel fuel and ammonium nitrate."

"The same stuff we used last week?"

"Yes, just more of it," Mike said. He and Hamda had traveled to a wooded area north of Kankakee and set off a smaller size bomb as a trial run. Hamda had practically jumped for joy when he pushed in the number on the cell phone and watched the ball of fire scorch the earth from a safe distance away.

"What about the second truck?"

Mike had it ready too. "It's painted the same way and will be carrying the same amount of goods." Mike gave Hamda a quick wink. "I'll have the detonation cords ready to go by Saturday night. On Sunday morning, you'll have to drive it to the corner of Columbus and Balbo and leave it there." He threw his thumb over his left shoulder to note the spot. "As long as we are there early enough, the cops won't be around to tell us we can't be there."

"And all I have to do is call the first number and the north truck with explode?"

"Yeah."

"And then all the runners who weren't killed will run south toward the second truck?"

Mike nodded. "They won't know what hit them."

Hamda was practically giddy. He could not wait for next Sunday. He became lost in his jihadist dreams – the acrid smoke, the dead bodies, the crying bloodied Americans. He thought it would be a magnificent day.

Marathon Sunday would indeed be a magnificent day.

CHAPTER 14

Tangier, Morocco

Rex Atlas had lived in Africa going on twenty years now. As the CIA's resident expert on the continent, he was the only one the higher-ups at Langley trusted to gather intel and vanish without a trace. At forty-one years of age, the single Atlas had initially been stationed in Egypt for ten years where he spied on the Mubarak regime and warned his bosses that Africa was becoming a hotbed of terrorist training activity. After two years in Somalia, he moved to his current station on Africa's northwest coast in Morocco.

Morocco was no stranger nation to the United States of America. While the United States struggled in its infancy following its independence from England, the Kingdom of Morocco recognized the U.S. as an independent nation in 1787, one of the first nations to do so. The American Legation in Tangier was one of the first property purchases made by the United States. To this day, the Moroccan-American Treaty of Friendship remains the longest-standing friendship bond America has held with another country. During this period of friendship, Morocco was of great use to the United States. In 1943, Roosevelt and Churchill conferred in Casablanca, the city where the American military staged its aircraft for use in the European Theater during World War II.

Atlas's father, a former career military man who himself had launched sorties from North Africa, had married an Indian chemist he met in Germany after the War. Their collaboration resulted in Rex Atlas, their only child, and his sandy brown complexion and love of faraway lands destined him for duty in the foreign service. Rex decided against a tour of duty in the State Department finding a career behind a desk in Foggy Bottom unappealing. Instead, he signed up for the secretive world offered by the Central Intelligence Agency.

And things were starting to pick up.

Just the night before, Atlas took a call on his secure satellite phone from the CIA Director himself who briefed him on the concerns of a possible connection between al-Qaeda terrorists and Mexican drug cartels. It was the potential beginning of an unlikely and most deadly alliance. Intelligence analysts picked up conversations that both groups were setting up a meeting in Tangier. And Atlas was the man the CIA needed.

Tangier, Morocco had become a magnet for tourists looking to quickly make their way south from Europe to step foot on the Dark Continent. For those not wanting to travel to Rabat, the capital, or Casablanca, Morocco's largest city, ferries from Spain crossed the Strait of Gibraltar to Tangier bringing tourists looking to eat the spicy African fare, buy the hand-made goods its markets had to offer, and then scurry back to their home continents with the fervent desire to miss out on the warlords, pirates, and pestilence certain other parts of Africa had to offer. Given the hustle and bustle of tourist traffic, Tangier offered a quiet place for terrorists and their network of friends to meet and blend into the surroundings and then be on their way without raising the suspicion that would follow them in the camera-shrouded streets of London, Paris, and Rome.

In his single-level stucco, Rex Atlas lived a simple life. A single bed and a lounge chair were his only furnishings. He had plenty of books to keep him occupied, but he had little time to read. His job was to observe, to immerse himself in the community, to blend in and become a part of the fabric of Moroccan life. His kitchen was mostly bare since he bought his daily meals from the markets three blocks away. A transistor radio played African music only when he was making a secure call to the United States. While his furnishings were sparse, the inner walls of his humble abode were lined with some of the best technological equipment the CIA could offer its spies. Behind the painting of two camels crossing the Sahara, Atlas kept his two Nikon D3X Digital Masterpiece cameras, three encrypted cell phones, and the secure satellite phone/fax that he used when secrecy was at a premium. If he ever needed to make a more secretive drop, Atlas had been known to travel to Rabat to meet the butler to the U.S. Ambassador in the dark of night. His only weapon consisted of a short snub-nosed revolver he kept strapped to his ankle. He bought it off a local three years ago – for protection from the feral dogs roaming around, he said. Atlas was not an assassin, but if someone decided to break down his door at night, his rusty but trusty revolver would do the trick. At least against one intruder at close range. If a band of machete-wielding marauders happened to show up, he'd be in trouble.

The knock of his door came a little after noon. It was his friend Abbas, the teenage son of a man who owned Tangier's finest limousine service just up the street. If anyone of importance or wealth needed transportation, Abbas's father could provide a Mercedes, a Rolls, or even an armored SUV at a moment's notice. Atlas used Abbas as his local gossip, paying him a small amount for all the good dirt around the city. Atlas learned a lot about who was cheating whom at the markets and whose camels were being sold even though past their prime. In America, the used-car lemons might find a final resting place in the salvage yard. In Morocco, the used-camel lemons are usually buried out on the outskirts of the desert. Most importantly though, Abbas knew his father's customers, and Atlas was always interested in knowing who was stopping in Tangier and where they were headed. Today, Abbas said a plane from Mexico was arriving in twenty minutes, and an understated white SUV would pick up a male passenger and the two men he was meeting and take them to the hotel. Atlas paid the fee and Abbas was off with open ears in hopes of padding his bank account.

Atlas put on his walking garb, a pair of beige pants and a white dress shirt with the top three buttons undone. A wide brimmed straw hat and a pair of sunglasses completed the ensemble. He grabbed his walking stick and headed out the door.

Ibn Batouta International Airport offered a quick in and out for small business class jets looking for fuel as well as passenger flights from Madrid and Paris. The locals would often come out and look at the shiny planes and marvel as they shot back into the sky. Right along with the crowd in the terminal was Rex Atlas.

The door to the Lear jet opened and settled in place on the tarmac. Three seconds later, out stepped a Hispanic looking man wearing blue jeans and a white dress shirt. Atlas put one hand on top of the head of a rambunctious kid gazing at the aircraft and the right thumb of his other hand on top of his walking stick. A click of the ball on top of the stick captured a picture of Raul Camacho, Jr. now descending the stairs. Atlas watched as the man approached two greeters on the tarmac. The man approached cautiously, looking in both directions. He obviously had never been there before. When the two greeters turned to the left, Atlas clicked off another picture from his walking stick camera. He recognized them – Abdi Rumallah and Khalid Mullab. The men matched the pictures faxed over from CIA operatives in Yemen. Both men were affiliated with al-Qaeda. They were full-fledged terrorists who could rustle up trouble with a quick phone call. After a quick picture of the plane and its tail number, Atlas patted the boy on the head and walked outside.

Atlas hustled down the sidewalk, losing sight of the SUV but showing no concern. He knew where it was headed. He entered the side door of the hotel, left his hat on the rack, and walked to the bar. Without any windows, the dimly lit place was a great spot for those wanting to keep meetings as low key as possible. Atlas headed for the left side of the bar.

"Bonjour, Monsieur," the bartender said. The language was French, one of the four that Atlas spoke. Given that Morocco was a colony of France until 1956, the French language was not foreign to the locals' ears. Atlas was a regular at the bar, another place where he could watch the people and hear what was going on.

"Café noir," Atlas said.

When the bartender placed the cup of black coffee on the counter, Atlas tipped him generously with ten dirhams and a wink before heading to the far corner. From what he could see after surreptitious glances out the corner of his eye, the interior of the joint looked like the *Star Wars* bar scene. A violent assortment of reprobates, butchers, thugs, and murderers huddled around the tables near the far wall. Some of the most detestable human beings ever to have inhabited the earth were in town to offer their services for the right cause and the right price. Their mode of operation included raping, maiming, torturing, and bombing their victims into submission. Most of the men were wanted by multiple governments but their violent streaks and carefully placed bribes often led authorities to look the other direction.

Atlas could see Camacho, Rumallah and Mullab seated in the corner. They appeared to be saying little to each other, no one in the mood to discuss the weather or each other's family. Less than five minutes later, the darkened bar seemed to dim at the appearance of a fat man who stood at the door blocking the light from the hotel lobby. The man was dressed in green military fatigues, had an empty holster on his bulging hip, and a black beret on his head. After Rumallah raised his hand and motioned the fat man over to the table, the man waddled through with all eyes in the place following right along with him. The man pulled out a chair and plopped down facing the three men. His large rear end fell over the edges of the seat, the legs of the chair almost straining under the weight.

Rumallah introduced his guests to the fat man, who was quietly known in terrorist circles as one of Saddam Hussein's former henchmen. Tariq Taseer had managed to slip out of Iraq just prior to the U.S. invasion to oust Saddam in 2003. He had been the head of weapons security with the Iraqi Republican Guard during its glory days of mayhem and brutality. His girth was a product of Saddam requiring Taseer to constantly travel to weapons sites and hideaways to evade capture from U.N. inspectors and U.S. spy satellites. For most of the twenty years under Saddam, Taseer sat in a car, eating whatever he could get his hands on, and shouting orders out the window to his underlings before he moved on to the next site. After his escape, Taseer hid under the radar in Morocco and gorged himself with the finest African foods purchased from his hidden stash of money. Given his current fat self, he bore little resemblance to his wanted posters of the past.

"You have come a long way," Taseer said to Camacho. Taseer had heard of the Mexican's name through various channels. Camacho's name was in the headlines enough that it crossed the ocean every so often.

"Yes, I have." Camacho tried to take in the view of Taseer, his big jowls and double chin a sight to behold. Taseer's obesity caused many who met him to really wonder whether his past included safeguarding Saddam's instruments of death. "I am led to believe you used to work for Saddam."

Taseer nodded with no showing of pride or sorrow for his years in the regime.

"I was also under the impression that you were dead."

Taseer laughed, his fat jiggling up and down. "The U.S. tried to kill me but I was too quick for those fools," he said winking.

The United States had tried to kill him and three other Iraqi military leaders during Desert Storm, and U.S. intelligence agents believed Taseer had been killed in a missile strike north of Baghdad. Although the intelligence proved to be erroneous, Taseer got the hint that the U.S. was on to him and started working on his exit from Iraq and squirreling away what he would need to survive a life in exile.

Rumallah spoke up to make sure everyone was on the same page. "I have been asked by my clients if you still have some five-ten for sale." Five-ten was code for VX.

Taseer leaned back in his chair and rested his large arms on his fat rolls. "That depends," he said.

"On what?"

"Only if the price is right." Taseer's stockpile once included a dizzying array of chemical, nerve, and blister agents. Two years ago, he sold his last amounts of the sarin and mustard gas that he and Saddam had unleashed on a Kurdish village killing five thousand. And his supply of VX was slowly dwindling. Considering it was in essence his retirement plan, he had to make sure he received enough to last him through his golden years.

"How much five-ten do you have?"

"That's for me to know," Taseer said. "How much do you need? Do you want to kill a thousand people? Ten thousand?" His tone insinuated he had enough to do whatever amount of carnage the men had in mind.

Rumallah shook his head. "No," he said. "Just one person."

Taseer could not hide his shock. One person! Hell, that wouldn't make him any money at all. You could kill one person with a cup of VX. And he had drums of the stuff that, quite frankly, he wanted to get rid of. With the appearance of a few specks of rust, he was worried the drums would start leaking. The skull and crossbones painted on the outside scared him every time he went to check on them.

"Just one person?" he asked, wanting to make sure he heard over the noise of the bar.

"Yes."

"May I ask whom?"

Rumallah and Camacho looked at each other. One was a Muslim terrorist and the other a leader of one of Mexico's biggest and most ruthless drug cartels. It didn't take a genius to know who the two men had a problem with.

"Let's just say he lives in a country that might have given you some troubles in the past," Camacho said.

Taseer nodded. He didn't need to know any more. He wasn't worried about what the two men in front of him would do with his stockpile. He just wanted their money, and now it was time for some salesmanship. "You'll need at least five drums to make sure you get it right."

"How much?" Rumallah asked.

"You might also want a second set of five drums just in case you run into problems transporting them to their destination." Taseer had ten drums of VX hidden on the outskirts of Tangier and thought he might be able to sell every last drop – get rid of it once and for all.

Rumallah leaned in and grumbled louder. "How much?"

Taseer leaned his fat self closer to the table. He had a number in his mind but doubled it in case Rumallah wanted to dicker. "One million dollars."

"Done," Rumallah said without hesitation.

"That's one million U.S.," Taseer said just to make sure.

"That's not a problem."

Taseer silently cursed himself, thinking he should have asked to be paid in gold rather than greenbacks. But he did not press the matter. After further negotiations on how the VX would be scurried out of Morocco and to which bank accounts the money was to be deposited, Taseer did have a few more questions.

"How are you going to get the five-ten into the United States?"

Rumallah pointed at Camacho. "That's his job."

Camacho nodded. "That's my territory."

"How are you going to distribute it?"

Rumallah and Camacho looked at each other. Neither had thought that far ahead. "You'll just have to watch the news," Camacho said.

Taseer nodded and used his large forearms to push himself out of his seat. The group said their goodbyes and walked out of the bar.

Rex Atlas got good head shots of every one with his walking stick camera. Now it was time to send the pictures to Rabat.

CHAPTER 15

Beverly Hills – California

General Graham was ushered to his table at the Circa 55 restaurant at the Beverly Hilton on a warm Saturday in southern California. His table overlooked the pool, which was still empty at this early lunch hour. He had spent the previous evening with Congresswoman Sanchez, wining and dining with $10,000 contributors until the wee hours of the morning.

Graham, however, was on his own today, as his running mate had jetted off to New York and Massachusetts to stump for votes and attend yet another round of black-tie fundraisers. Graham had stepped in it big time three nights before and hadn't heard the end of it. At the debate between Vice-Presidential hopefuls, General Graham twice referred to Vice President Brenda Jackson as "sweetheart" and made a host of other statements that independent fact checkers blasted for their utter falsity. Republicans excoriated him for his lack of respect for the sitting Vice President along with his ready use of made-up figures that were not even close to reality.

The Sanchez campaign simply responded that General Graham was being General Graham and his outspoken candor was a refreshing change to the tight-lipped and holier-than-thou attitude of the Republicans. Liberal women's groups were noticeably silent, not feeling the need to stand up to support the first female Vice President of the United States since she was of the conservative persuasion.

General Graham, however, was not knocked off track a bit. He charged forward like he had won the debates hands-down. He also pointed out to worried staffers that he had been the talk of the morning news shows for days now.

"And any publicity is good publicity," he told them.

About the only thing that could push General Graham to the back pages of the newspapers and talk shows was one of the guests he was about to meet. Hollywood starlet Rebecca Morrison had been stopped for speeding two days ago and during the stop police found two grams of marijuana in her very expensive designer purse. She was arrested, handcuffed, fingerprinted, and spent three hours in jail. Her starry eyed mug shot was plastered on every tabloid from L.A. to the Big Apple and a grainy video of her arrest on

Hollywood Boulevard was played on every gossip web site and entertainment show.

General Graham's meeting with Morrison had been on the schedule for weeks. Along with the leggy blonde, a woman no man would cancel on regardless of her legal troubles, Graham was to meet with several Hollywood big shots – actors, producers, the mega high rollers that could not only bring millions of dollars to the table but also provide free campaign buzz through glitzy TV appearances and red-carpet parades. A well-timed tweet or Facebook posting from Morrison that Sanchez and Graham were going to end all wars, and save the planet while they're at it, could reach millions of followers and indoctrinate a new generation of young adults on the liberal agenda.

Academy award nominee Chris Allen, also a devoted liberal, had wowed audiences with his epic on saving the world from the melting glaciers caused by man-made global warming. He and Morrison had engaged in a much-publicized liplock in the climactic scene of the movie after saving Mother Earth from the evil corporate polluters. He was a huge proponent of federal tax subsidies for wind and solar power and showed up to the meeting with General Graham in his battery-powered car. Whether he would be able to make it back home without charging was unknown.

When Morrison walked in the restaurant at noon, all eyes watched her glide to the General's table. Her blonde hair seemed to be flowing elegantly behind her. The red dress was expensive, notwithstanding the seeming lack of material that was wrapped around her curvaceous six-foot frame. She was on time, a rarity, and had waded through the paparazzi staked out at the front entrance with a bright sober smile. When she made it to the table, all the seated men rose.

"General," Morrison said with a kiss on Graham's cheek. "It is so nice to see you again."

"It's always nice to see you too," Graham said, holding the light hug long enough to take in a whiff of Morrison's coconut-scented conditioner. Up and down her back his hand went, finding bare skin on every glorious swipe. "Please sit down and join us."

Morrison sat in between General Graham and Allen, her celluloid colleague on the glacier epic.

"We haven't ordered yet," the General said. "What would you like?"

Morrison didn't need to look at the menu. She had stayed at the Beverly Hilton on a number of occasions, most of the time when she was too drunk to make it back to her Hollywood Hills home. The paparazzi had once photographed her topless in the pool making out with some rock star after the Golden Globe Awards show. She looked up to the waiter. "I'll have the Caesar salad."

"With or without anchovies?" the waiter asked.

Morrison made a face, just the thought of it made her wince. "Without. And an ice water with lemon."

"And General Graham, what can I get you?"

"Santa Barbara rock cod," he said without a second thought. It was thirty bucks a plate but what the hell, the campaign was paying for it. "And an iced tea, please."

"Very good, sir."

The rest of the table ordered, but General Graham heard none it. It was all about the woman of every man's dream sitting next to him. This surely had to be one of the best perks of running for high office. If he didn't have to head to Phoenix for a rally after lunch, he thought he might just reserve the Governors Suite and ask Morrison to join him.

"I hear you have had some excitement in the last few days," Graham said.

"Excitement I didn't need," she said rolling her eyes. She brushed her blonde hair away from her tanned face. "I hope I won't be causing you any bad press by being here."

General Graham scoffed at such a remark. He'd swim through two miles of crap just to take another whiff of her. "Nonsense, I'm glad you came. And don't forget, any publicity is good publicity."

Along with her fight to end global warming, Morrison had been a low-key proponent of legalizing marijuana for several years now. Given her legal troubles, she now hoped more than ever that legalization would occur and her little miscue would fall under the heading of "everyone was doing it." She would be right on that. Hollywood's young stars spent most of their down time trolling the clubs, swilling their high-end liquor, and lighting up the pipes whenever they got the chance. Word spread quickly on who was the dealer to the stars, and home delivery was a convenient way for actors and actresses to get their high without searching the back alleys for drugs.

The chivalrous General Graham felt the need to comfort his damsel in distress. He reached over and grabbed her hand. "Don't you worry about a thing, sweetheart," he comforted her. "When Congresswoman Sanchez and I are sworn into office in January, I'll make sure that any crusade against marijuana will be pushed to the back burner."

Chris Allen, much more of a political junkie than the blonde bombshell to his right, wanted to know how General Graham was going to get marijuana legislation passed in a Congress that was most likely going to be controlled by Republicans. He sounded skeptical, although it might have had something to do with the horny Graham practically groping Allen's one-time leading lady and part-time lover.

"Chris, you're probably right about the Republicans keeping the House and the Senate," General Graham said. "But the real power will come from the Department of Justice. We'll just tell the Attorney General that we want federal authorities to spend their time on other matters and leave small-time marijuana users alone. Plus, we'll leave it up to the states to determine whether they want to police marijuana use. Republicans will have a hard time voting against giving power to the states."

"You sound very sure of yourself, General," Allen said. Morrison gave Graham a look that indicated she was inspired by his manly confidence.

Graham did not hold back. "We are going to win, Chris. We have a great campaign. We are going to carry the Hispanic and African-American vote. We are going to win California, Texas, Florida, New York, Illinois, Pennsylvania – all the big electoral vote states." Graham stole a glance at Morrison. He thought she might be getting turned on by his bravado. Or maybe it was his dashing good looks, as good looking as his comb-over and stratospheric ego would allow him to imagine. He reached over and touched her hand again. He added a wink while he was at it. "We are going to win the presidency and you are going to come right along with us."

Chicago, Illinois

"Welcome runners to the Chicago Marathon!"

The sound system speakers blared their welcome along with the race instructions to the tens of thousands of runners huddled together in a mass of athletic humanity on a single strip of pavement on the west side of Grant Park. It was seventy-five degrees outside at thirty minutes til eight, and the forecast called for slowly rising temperatures and lots of sun. There were no long pants or stocking caps on today, no throwaway sweatshirts used for pre-race warmth and then discarded in an amusing ritual of flying clothes when the starting gun goes off.

Safety pins affixed the bib numbers on every runner from front to back. Toeing the starting line, the defending champion, a diminutive Kenyan favored to win again this year, wore bib #1. A two-hundred-forty pound accountant, who just hoped to finish before sundown, wore bib #35750 and was ready to pull up the rear in the back of the pack. As the time grew closer to the start, the starting corrals squeezed tight, the sea of people – a mix of elite Olympic-caliber marathoners in front, the semi-serious runners, who actually had real jobs Monday through Friday, in the middle, and the waddlers and the shufflers intent on proving a point or checking off an item on their bucket list in the back. The smell of pre-race sweat, jitters, and a healthy amount of Ben-Gay filled the humid and windless Chicago air.

Mohammed Hamda had driven his bomb-laden van to his designated corner an hour before the runners had started lining up. He had been up since three a.m., ate nothing for breakfast, and paced the floor of his hotel room until he got the call from Moshie "Mike" Masahn. Once it came in, he took the El south to 35th Street. He walked three blocks west and found Masahn under a darkened railroad overpass. They walked another block and found the two moving vans. Hamda inspected them both – each with their drums of diesel fuel and ammonium nitrate. The smell of the contents was almost overpowering. Hamda didn't dare open up the drums for fear of causing a spark and setting off an explosion.

Hamda took the lead on the Dan Ryan Expressway and found his spot just off Michigan Avenue. He parked the van with the cab facing west and the rear facing the athletes who would be streaking past at the start of the race. He locked the door and went to meet with Masahn, who parked his identical van a quarter of a mile south of Hamda's van.

"Did you park it where I told you?" Hamda asked Mike as he found him on the sidewalk in front of the Congress Plaza Hotel.

"Yes," Mike said. He then pointed through the trees to the corner of Columbus and Balbo. "See it?"

Hamda moved his head up and down before finally finding the van on the other side of the trees and amongst the thousands of spectators.

"I did not know there would be this many people," Hamda said. He was almost overwhelmed by the enormity of the crowd.

Mike stood next to Hamda without saying a word. There were indeed a lot of people milling about – runners, their families, volunteers, cops. Mike could see out of the corner of his eye that Hamda was looking up and down the sea of people between him and Grant Park. Mike couldn't tell whether Hamda was having second thoughts or not. Maybe he was scared. Or maybe he was dreaming of the body bags that would be needed in a short while. Terrorists were known to be giddy with anticipation at the thought of the carnage they were about to unleash. It was the thirst for jihad that pushed them forward.

"There are a lot of people," Hamda said again.

"We can call it off if you want and get out of town before the authorities even realize what they're dealing with."

Given the enormous crowd and hubbub leading up to the race, Hamda had forgotten all about the possibility of cops and law-enforcement agencies lurking about. He didn't even ask Mike to take off his shirt. He told himself to snap out of it. This was the moment he had been waiting for all his life, the moment he had prayed about and dreamt of every night. Today was the day he became a legend in the Muslim world.

"How much time do we have until the race starts?"

Mike looked at his watch. "About twenty minutes." He then looked at Hamda. It was Hamda's call. Mike was just the bomb maker.

Hamda took one last look and a deep breath. He was ready to kill. "Let's go get into position."

Hamda and Mike had considered where they would go to set off the bomb and then watch the carnage. Mike had thought about docking a boat on Lake

Michigan, making the cell phone call to set off the bombs, and then sail away to safety. The last place the authorities would look for the perpetrators would be on the water.

But Hamda wanted to stay on dry land and at a vantage point from where he could watch the chaos. Hamda suggested the Congress Plaza Hotel with its view of Grant Park. He was able to get a reservation within the last two weeks but only at a steep price given the marathon crowd. Upon entering his room the night before, he was dismayed to learn the view only included a small edge of the southern portion of the Park across the street. He wouldn't even be able to see the truck on the corner. He thought about raising hell at the front desk but thought better of it.

Hamda and Mike entered the suite on the twelfth floor. Mike saw Hamda's prayer rug on the floor. The bed was made and Hamda's bags were packed. A video camera on top of the TV had the previous evening captured Hamda's statement to the world – claiming responsibility for the Chi-town slaughter and promising more attacks across the U.S. in the future unless America ended its occupation of Iraq and Afghanistan.

"Five minutes until the start," Mike announced.

Hamda knelt down on his prayer rug and asked again for Allah's guidance. He imagined the glorified status he would soon take – with Muslims around the world taking to the streets and chanting his name in jubilation. After several minutes, he stretched his arms out to the floor. He had made his decision.

"Allah says I must bring destruction to America today," he said solemnly.

Mike walked over to him and put his hand on Hamda's shoulder. "Are you sure?"

"Yes, they must die today."

Mike looked at his watch and then nodded. "All you have to do is call the number."

Hamda took the piece of paper containing the numbers Mike had given him last week. He had memorized them but gave the paper one last look. He walked over to the nightstand and picked up the hotel phone. He knelt on the floor and picked up the receiver.

"Allahu akbar," he said twice. He then pressed nine, listened for the dial tone, and dialed in the number. After a couple of seconds, the line started ringing. "Allahu Akbar."

Hamda looked at Mike, his eyes wondering when it would happen. Shouldn't they have heard the blast by now?

"Maybe you should try your cell phone," Mike suggested.

Hamda stood up and hurried to his bag on the bed. He grabbed his cell phone and carefully punched in the numbers. He then hit "send."

The walls of the hotel room shook. Hamda could even feel the floor of the room rumbling underneath him. He looked out the southern window. Still unable to see out toward the north where the van had been parked, he noticed wispy gray smoke floating past the window.

A female in the room next door let out a blood curdling scream of terror. "Oh my God! Oh my God!"

Hamda began jumping up and down. He had done it. He now had the confirmation he needed. "Death to America! Death to America! Allahu akbar! I have done it! I have done it!"

He kept looking out the window hoping to see thousands of frightened runners fleeing in terror so he could make the second call. He saw a smattering of people but they weren't running away. Maybe they were so stunned they didn't know what was going on.

"Should I set the second truck bomb off now!?" he asked Mike, who was also peering out the window.

"Whenever you want! Allahu akbar!"

Hamda's hands were shaking when he punched in the second number. "Allahu akbar," he said as he hit "send." Nothing happened. He tried the number again. Nothing.

"Why isn't it working?"

Mike shrugged as he took a look at the phone. "Maybe the first bomb took out cellular service. Maybe you need to get outside to get a signal."

Hamda agreed and grabbed his bag. He ran to the door hoping to get downstairs in time to unleash his second round of carnage before the frightened Americans had found safety. He also wanted to get outside to see the mayhem he had already caused. "Let's go!"

Mike was right on his tail.

Until he reached the door. Once Hamda was in the hall, Mike closed himself in the room. The only people that saw Hamda running down the hall were the FBI agents in the adjacent room aiming to take him down. The leader of the FBI SWAT team watched through the peephole for Hamda to make his way past the room. Hamda was halfway down the hall when he looked back to see Mike wasn't behind him.

"Get down on the ground! Get down on the ground!"

Hamda turned back around just in time to see a line of heavily armed men filing toward him from the other direction. "Get down on the ground! Get down on the ground!"

He struggled slightly when the agents slapped the cuffs on him. "I have caused blood to run in the streets of America!" he yelled. "Death to America!"

He, however, had caused no death to America. He had been under FBI surveillance for the past month, and Moshie Masahn was also known by his colleagues as Special Agent Mike Hasra. After learning of Hamda's desire to set off a bomb at the Chicago Marathon, the FBI set up the sting operation.

Hasra befriended Hamda, showed him how the bombs would be made, and even made a dry run in a wooded area an hour south of Chicago. And the FBI was watching them all the way – in the forest, at the Grant Park meeting, and in the hotel room. Surveillance cameras kept an eye on Hamda throughout the night and morning. Once Hamda punched in the phone number, the call went to an assortment of enterprising FBI agents who proceeded to barrage the walls, the floor, and the ceiling with the room furniture and a couple of battering rams. One female agent let out a scream good enough for a horror movie. The smoke wafting by the window – just a smoke bomb attached to a pole that was lowered from the roof. All in a day's work for the FBI.

The agents escorted Hamda to the basement of the hotel where he was promptly put into an armored van and taken to the federal lockup. Two other agents entered the vans with the dummy bombs and drove them back to the FBI field office. Agent Michael Hasra, aka Moshie "Mike" Masahn sat on the bed, grabbed the remote control, and turned on the local NBC broadcast. A knock on the door was followed by the entry of Fayez Harraj, also a special agent with the FBI. They had spent the last two months in the world of a wannabe but committed terrorist. And now they could relax.

"You feel like running twenty-six miles?" Harraj asked.

Hasra shook his head. "Maybe next year."

The Kenyan with the #1 bib was already four miles into the marathon and two steps ahead of the lead pack of runners. The accountant in the back hadn't even crossed the starting line yet. In less than two hours, the Kenyan would cross the finish line and receive the adulation and financial awards that one of America's largest marathons had to offer.

At the same time two miles away, Mohammed Hamda would receive the lawyer that America's Constitution offered its citizens.

CHAPTER 16

FBI Headquarters – Washington, D.C.

Director Stubblefield strode to the microphones with a sense of purpose. Today he would praise his agents for their hard work and dedication and warn the American people that the fight against terrorism must roll on. Behind him stood the Attorney General, the Director of Homeland Security, and the Deputy Director of the FBI.

"Good afternoon," Stubblefield said. "Today, I want to announce that Mohammed Hamda, a Yemeni-born and naturalized U.S. citizen and resident of Chicago, Illinois, has been arrested on charges of attempting to use a weapon of mass destruction in connection with a plot to detonate two truck bombs during the running of yesterday's Chicago Marathon."

The FBI had on multiple occasions engaged in sting operations where would-be terrorists let it be known they wanted to cause great harm to America. Undercover agents posing as like-minded American haters would then provide the terrorist with a fake bomb and allow him to push the proverbial button before being arrested. Operations had been conducted across the country – Oregon, Illinois, and Maryland – and FBI brass wondered how many more operations would prove similarly successful. At some point, even the most committed terrorist would have to have reservations about dealing with anyone offering their assistance, maybe ask a question or two to make sure the helpful fellow terrorist was actually who he said he was. But, then again, the lone wolf was not always the sharpest tool in the drawer.

"Mr. Hamda was arrested by FBI agents at approximately 8:20 a.m. yesterday morning after he attempted to detonate two moving vans with what he believed to be laden with explosives and parked in and around the start of the Chicago Marathon. The devices were, however, inert and posed no danger to the participants, spectators, or the general public.

"The arrest was made after a month's long effort during which Mr. Hamda was monitored via hidden surveillance when he contacted multiple undercover operatives. Mr. Hamda often expressed his hatred for the United States and desire to bring death and destruction to America. The hard work of the FBI Field Office in Chicago, the Illinois State Police, and the Chicago Police Department, thwarted Mr. Hamda's plans. He is expected to make his initial appearance in federal district court this afternoon. He faces a maximum sentence of life in prison. The prosecution will be handled by the U.S. Attorney's Office for the Northern District of Illinois in Chicago."

Since his nomination as the Director of the FBI by President Schumacher, Ty Stubblefield had been one of the most recognizable faces on the war on terror. He was a straight-laced law man who did not mind spreading around the credit when law-enforcement agencies besides his own had acted admirably in the collective effort to stop terrorists from waging war on America. Given his notoriety, his name was also becoming a matter of virulent scorn among the terrorists around the world.

He, however, was more determined than ever to keep fighting.

"While we celebrate our successes," he said, "we must also remain vigilant in these very dangerous times. Federal, state, and local authorities continue to work in concert to prevent an attack on this country and bring to justice those who seek to harm America. And we will continue to do so. I'll now take a few questions."

"Director, are you concerned with the rights of the arrestees?" the woman in the front row shouted above the voices of the other reporters. Her snarky tone made it obvious she was from some liberal wire service. "This is the fourth arrest in the last year where the suspects have been enticed . . ., entrapped . . ., cajoled . . ., what have you, by undercover FBI agents to commit crimes?"

Director Stubblefield was almost taken aback by the tone of the reporter's question but he didn't show it.

"First of all, I disagree with your assessment that the suspects that have been arrested were enticed or entrapped to commit these crimes. All the suspects you are referring to made the initial outreach to find someone to help them implement their plan of attack. And I also want to add that the FBI is committed to respecting the rights of all citizens and our agents conduct themselves in accordance with the Constitution and the laws of the United States." He had no desire to ask if she had a follow-up and pointed to the reporter sitting beside her.

"Director, has your investigation uncovered whether Mr. Hamda was working in connection with any other groups intent on committing terrorism? Or was this simply a lone wolf?"

"I'm not going to comment on any possible connections Mr. Hamda might have had with terrorist organizations. I will tell you, however, that the investigation is ongoing."

"Director, given the attempted attack by alleged Muslim extremists in Portland, Chicago, Maryland, New York, and Washington, D.C., do the American people have reason to fear the Muslim communities in these large cities?"

"The FBI has been working with members of the Muslim community to bridge any gaps there might be in community relations. I have spoken with many Muslim leaders who are outraged with the acts of terror committed by a militant wing of their religion. These leaders have also reiterated their commitment to fostering peaceful relations with non-Muslims in their communities. Any other questions?"

"Director, did the President sign off on this operation?"

"The President is not required to sign off on this type of operation, but I can tell you I personally briefed him throughout the investigation."

"Director, can you confirm the reports that an alleged plot to assassinate President Schumacher has been thwarted in his hometown of Silver Creek, Indiana?"

Director Stubblefield stopped ever so briefly before answering the question. "I can neither confirm nor deny that. I'm not sure where you are getting your information."

"We have received several reports from high-level government sources saying the Secret Service and the FBI have disrupted an attempted al-Qaeda-style attack on the President's compound."

"It would not be prudent for me to comment on any ongoing investigations," Director Stubblefield said. "Any questions involving the President's personal security should be addressed to Director Defoe at the Secret Service. Thank you all very much."

Ciudad Juarez, Mexico

The container ship carrying ten drums of Saddam Hussein's former stockpile of VX nerve agent arrived early that morning at the port in Veracruz, which sits east of Mexico City on the coast of the Gulf of Mexico. From there it traveled northwest through Mexico under the armed guard of Raul Camacho's Sons of the Devil drug cartel. Given that the cartel controlled the roads in the northern part of Mexico, the shipment reached its destination without a hitch and with nary a look from the Mexican authorities.

Raul Camacho plopped down in the leather chair in his office and invited Abdi Rumallah to have a seat. Camacho had had a bad evening. Although the VX had arrived intact, he now had to come up with a plan to smuggle it across the border.

And he would have to do it with ten less members of his cartel.

The day before, members of the Sonoran drug cartel had entered into a deadly firefight, claiming the Sons of the Devil had encroached too far into their territory. The cartels, like even the most juvenile of urban gangs, protected their territory with ruthless precision. As a sort of unwritten treaty, the Sonoran cartel was to control the area from Tijuana on the Pacific Ocean to Nogales, Mexico, a region consisting of about halfway through the state of

Arizona. East of Nogales through the Chihuahuan Desert to Nuevo Laredo, the Sons of the Devil were believed to be in charge.

Perhaps it was Camacho's increasing notoriety or maybe the successful transport of some of the most lethal weapons in the world into his arsenal, Camacho decided he wanted the Sons of the Devil empire to include the Nogales area controlled by the Sonoran cartel. Armed with rocket-propelled grenades and AK-47s, fifty members of the Sons of the Devil rolled into the outskirts of the Sonoran's territory and unleashed a small war. The battle raged for ten hours south of Nogales. Ten members of Camacho's cartel were killed and thirty Sonoran members were gunned down. Unfortunately for both sides, sixty-three Mexican citizens were killed in the crossfire, including four five-year-old girls in their white dresses as they walked to school for their kindergarten class.

Although Camacho was cold-hearted and loved violence when it helped his cartel, the images of the slain girls along with their dolls and lunch boxes splattered with blood caused him great angst. Not so much at the loss of life but the bad press for his cartel. Governments around the world condemned the violence and called for the United Nations to intervene. Had the only casualties been cartel members, few would have given it a second look.

Camacho looked like a business man whose corporation just found out its best-selling product was full of lead. He would have to work on damage control. But first things first, the VX matter was tops on the list.

"I see you have had a tough night," Rumallah said. He took some joy in Camacho's uncomfortable state. Rumallah was no stranger to the collateral damage that comes with warfare. As an al-Qaeda terrorist, he had learned to believe that innocent men, women, and even children were his enemies. If the enemy did not kill him now, he might do so in the future. Thus, Rumallah envisioned every innocent civilian in military fatigues. It made the slaughter in the name of Allah much more palatable.

Camacho reached into the drawer and grabbed a bottle of aspirin. He had a pounding headache and was not in the mood for Rumallah's good-natured ribbing. He downed two pills with a bottle of water and cleared his throat.

"Did you make it into the country without detection?"

"Yes, I came with your men," Rumallah said. He had stowed away on a freighter full of Saudi Arabian oil bound for Mexico.

"And you have seen the shipment of five-ten?"

"Yes. I think your men have stored it satisfactorily for the time being."

Camacho shook his aching head. The last thing he needed was a load of VX seeping into his compound and killing off his cartel. "What is your plan for delivering the five-ten once I get it into the United States?"

"Some sort of spraying device, whether that be from an airplane or a tanker truck."

"And where are you going to want me to deliver it?"

"I just want you to get it across the border."

Camacho didn't mind hearing that request. "Just across the border?"

"Yes. My men will take it from there."

"By when?"

"Before the election."

Camacho winced. A day ago he would have said no problem, so sure of himself and his cartel's ability that a two-week deadline would be nothing. But now, he had a lot on his plate. "That's asking a lot."

Rumallah nodded. "And I am paying a lot."

"I just lost ten men last night."

Rumallah was, however, not concerned with Camacho's losses. "That's your problem, not mine."

"I don't think I can get the five-ten up there before the election."

"I think you will, you son of a bitch," Rumallah said angrily. He was getting impatient. He wanted President Schumacher dead. Assassinating the President days before the election would throw the world into chaos, stock markets would crash, transportation would grind to a halt, and Americans would be scared to walk the streets for fear of the second and third waves of al-Qaeda's assault.

"Don't you talk that way to me!" Camacho shot back, jumping out of his seat and getting into Rumallah's face. "You've got a lot of nerve talking to me like that!" He then grabbed Rumallah by the shirt with both of his hands. "I could kill you right now!"

Rumallah shot his left hand up to Camacho's throat and took a step forward. As he squeezed his hand ever so slightly, he managed a low growl. "Let me tell you something, Mr. Camacho. If you don't get the five-ten to the U.S. before the election, you don't get the money. The delivery date is non-negotiable."

"Don't you threaten me," Camacho said, wrangling out of Rumallah's grasp on his throat. "I don't need your money."

Rumallah wagged a finger at him. "You might not need the money," he said. "But if you don't get the five-ten to its destination, I might have to let it leak to your Sonoran friends that you are holding some of the world's deadliest toxins a couple of miles south of the U.S. border. Maybe I'll let it slip to CNN. Then you'll have a lot more to worry about than me."

"Get the fuck out of here!" Camacho fired back. He didn't want to deal with the terrorist's threat right now.

Rumallah straightened his shirt and headed for the door. "I will be waiting for your call notifying me of the delivery."

"Get the hell out!"

Camacho fell back into his chair and muttered profanities at the man who just left. He closed his eyes and felt the hammer pounding on the inside of his head. He picked up the phone and waited for his delivery man to pick up on the other end.

"Yeah, it's me. Get the five-ten ready. We're heading to Nogales."

CHAPTER 17

The White House – Washington, D.C.

The President and the First Lady welcomed Director Stubblefield and his wife Tina over to the White House for a dinner between two of the most powerful couples in all of Washington. The President had known Mrs. Stubblefield since his early days in the FBI, and she was a trusted friend.

Tina Stubblefield, a former USC cheerleader, first met Ty during a Southern Cal media day when the university was heralding the upcoming football season and their star linebacker. The editor of the media guide thought it would be fun to have the six-six, 240-pound Ty holding two diminutive and peppy cheerleaders in the palms of his hands. One of those cheerleaders happened to be the former Tina Robinson. They married following their graduation. Tina worked as an accountant while Ty spent four years with the NFL's Oakland Raiders. She continued to work after he retired from football and while he returned to school to get his law degree. As a newly minted lawyer, he applied to the FBI and became the roommate of a young lawyer named Anthony Schumacher. Their careers sent them to San Diego, where the then-bachelor Schumacher would often eat dinner at the Stubblefield residence along with their two children, David and Tisha.

Tina no longer worked as an accountant but spent a great deal of her time doing charity work with the First Lady. Like Danielle, a part of her wanted to return to California and their peaceful home of San Diego.

"You ladies sure are quiet this evening," the President said. The meal was lasagna, the White House chef's specialty, to go along with his award-winning bread.

"They don't like it when we talk shop after hours," Ty said.

The President looked at the two women, who weren't disagreeing with the Director's assessment. "Unfortunately, we don't have after hours."

"We're always on the job."

The President looked over at Tina Stubblefield. "Tina, you look like you have something that you want to get off your mind." He had known her long enough to see it.

Tina stole a glance with the First Lady. They had talked nearly everyday since the Schumachers moved to Washington back in the President's early days in Congress and lately there had been a lot of crying going on. Tina and Danielle lived in constant fear that something was going to happen to their husbands, notwithstanding the teams of bodyguards that surrounded both of them. The First Lady had to endure multiple attempts on her husband's life. Terrorists even tried to kill their daughter in the National Archives attack. A small but growing part of her wanted her husband to leave politics and retire to the safety and security of Indiana.

"We were listening to Ty's press conference the other day," Tina started quietly.

The President interrupted. "Didn't he look good on TV?" he gushed. "He was striking fear into the hearts and mind of terrorists around the world. Americans are sure lucky to have him on their side."

Tina nodded, appreciative of the President's kind words about her husband.

"He looked just about as good as that time he took on Congresswoman Robinson up on the Hill."

The Director smiled at the trip down memory lane.

The President then laid it on thick. "He's going to make a great President some day, isn't he?"

The Director shook his head with a little more emphasis on that one. He had no political aspirations, and Tina was thankful for that. But there was something else she wanted to talk about.

"At the press conference, Ty was asked about an assassination plot in your hometown." Tina looked at Danielle, who looked like she might start crying. The President hadn't discussed any thwarted plots with her.

The President looked at Director Stubblefield. "You want to handle this one?"

"Sure, Mr. President," Ty said. "Let me start out by saying there is no credible threat that the President, your house, or anything in Silver Creek is a target at this time. The Secret Service confronted a young Middle Eastern engineering student who had visited Silver Creek twice within a week. The man was questioned, determined not to be a threat, and released. The man has since left the country."

"That's it?" Danielle asked. She sounded relieved.

"That's all it was," Ty responded. "And as I have said before, I have the utmost confidence in the Secret Service. They are the best at what they do."

"That's the story I was led to believe as well," the President said.

"Since it wasn't a big deal, the matter slipped my mind. I was surprised when the reporter asked me the question."

The President then remembered he had a question. "You wouldn't happen to know this high-level source that supposedly leaked the information, do you?"

Director Stubblefield thought for a second. "Actually, I thought it might have been ol' Wiley Cogdon himself. Maybe he was letting it be known that a threat still exists and we need you to be in charge in the White House."

"I don't think it was Wiley. Although he wouldn't have told me if he had leaked it. He's worried the voters are going to think I attract too much attention from the terrorists and the voters should choose someone a little more safe." The President then looked at his watch. "Hey, if we're going to watch that movie before my bedtime maybe we should head down to the theater."

The women, their spirits buoyed by the apparent good news for the time being, thought it was a good idea. A night at the White House movie theater was the closest they would get to having a double date out on the town with their husbands. They grabbed their drinks and asked the butler to rustle up some popcorn.

"You two go ahead," Stubblefield said to them. "I want to talk to the President about a couple of other matters." He gave them a wink, acting like it was nothing that would worry them. "Highly classified. Very hush-hush."

The women took the elevator down first while the President and the Director waited in the center hall.

"I talked with Director Parker this afternoon," Stubblefield said, recalling the details of his call with the CIA Director. "The NSA has been picking up several mentions by some unsavory individuals of something called 'five-ten.'"

"Five-ten," the President said, letting the words rattle around in his brain. "Five-ten."

"We don't know whether it's a thing or a date or . . . maybe it's nothing."

"I guess it could be May 10th," the President offered. "Maybe they are looking at the Indianapolis 500 in late May since they know I attend every year. What was it that the 9/11 hijackers used as code words?"

"I remember they used the words 'commerce' and 'marriage' in some of their coded messages."

"What about the specific date of September 11th?"

"It was two branches, a slash, and a lollipop," Stubblefield said.

"Eleven slash nine?" the President asked.

"Most foreigners would read that as eleven September."

"Muqtada Abdulla was executed on the fifth of October," the President said. "But we're beyond that. You say that the NSA has picked up the usage of 'five-ten' recently?"

"Yes, within the last week."

The President shook his head. "I've got no clue what 'five-ten' could mean." He then put a hand on his friend's shoulder. "And doggone it, now I'm going to be thinking about it all through the movie."

"I have one other thing," Stubblefield said, reaching inside his suit jacket. "Director Parker faxed this photo over to me this afternoon."

The President looked at the grainy picture showing a fat man in fatigues and low light. "Who is it?"

"That is Tariq Taseer, taken during a recent meeting in Tangier, Morocco. He is a former leader in Saddam's military."

"I've never heard of him."

"He was actually number fifty-eight on our most wanted list after the Iraq invasion," Stubblefield reported. "But since he was so low on the totem poll, he never made it into that deck of cards of Saddam's goons."

"Why should I be worried about him?"

"He was the head of weapons security in Iraq. He was meeting with a known al-Qaeda terrorist and two other individuals in Morocco."

"You think Saddam or his cronies might have hidden some nukes prior to the U.S. invasion?"

"It's possible."

"Just one more thing for me to worry about."

"Yes, sir."

The President felt like he was being constantly bombarded with new information about possible harm to the United States. Sometimes he needed a break to clear his head. "We better get to that movie or the ladies will start worrying that we're discussing something that would make them worry even more."

Phoenix, Arizona

Congresswoman Sanchez and General Graham had reunited on the campaign trail for a rally in the Grand Canyon state. Less than two weeks remained before Americans would go to the polls and cast their vote for President and Vice President of the United States. Sanchez and Graham met with Niles Bongiorno, their campaign strategist, at the Arizona Biltmore. They chose the location for its space but more for its opulence. Presidents had been known to frequent the Jewel of the Desert on various excursions to Arizona. Other political bigwigs made big news there. Senator McCain and Governor Palin conceded defeat on the front lawn. Feeling the need to prepare for their upcoming ascension to the magnificent beauty of the White House, the Sanchez campaign found the upper-class setting fit their tastes quite well.

On the balcony of the Villa suite, with its stunning views of Camelback Mountain and a hefty price tag of $1,200 a night, the Sanchez brain trust sat around the table full of schedules, poll numbers, and generous portions of the homemade butternut squash ravioli.

"We are seeing tossups in all the key states," Bongiorno stated with glee. He had started to allow himself the thought that he might orchestrate an upset and pull out a victory. "We are this close," he said with his thumb and index finger almost touching.

"I'll think we'll win California, New York, and Illinois," Sanchez said. "The Democrat political machine will carry the day."

General Graham took his eyes off the area of the pool, the water sparkling in the sunshine. He had already informed the group twice that Marilyn Monroe used to frequent the pool on many occasions. They could almost see General Graham lost in the moment, envisioning the blonde star in his mind as she sunned herself under the Arizona sun.

"The Northeast looks good," he said, snapping out of it. "But we're going to have to have victories in Florida, Ohio, Pennsylvania, and Michigan plus our reliable strongholds to win it all."

Each person around the table had a two-column chart separating the states and their electoral votes that would likely go to either President Schumacher or Congresswoman Sanchez. At the bottom, Bongiorno had listed the states that were too close to call as well as noting the percent that Sanchez was either up or down in each state. She was minus five in Texas, minus four in Florida, but closer in Ohio and Michigan. All four of those states were within the margin of error.

"I think we can safely put California in our column," Bongiorno said, writing the Golden State in blue ink in Sanchez's column. Utah and Nebraska were solidly typed in President Schumacher's column. Those states hadn't voted for Democrats since LBJ in '64. On the other side, Massachusetts and Connecticut were firmly planted in Sanchez's column. Other states were written in pencil and subject to move from one column to another or the undecided pile depending on the latest round of polling data. "We won't need any campaign appearances there unless the President closes in."

"Texas is so close," Sanchez said, almost tasting a victory in the Lone Star State.

"I think a campaign stop in Houston might be in order," Bongiorno said, tapping his index finger on his chin and then pointing it at Sanchez. "It has a large Hispanic population, and there are a lot of Democratic folks from New Orleans who moved to the Houston area after Hurricane Katrina."

"All right," Sanchez said. "Let's get to Houston this week, and if the race tightens we can make a return trip."

General Graham put down his electoral-vote chart and started rummaging for the morning paper. Above the fold on the front page of the *Arizona Republic*, a large picture showed Sanchez and Graham in downtown Phoenix at yesterday's rally. The streets were packed with people, some carrying homemade signs and others waving flags, the former were not in English and the latter were not of the red-white-and-blue variety. The article noted how Sanchez had promised "comprehensive immigration reform" if she was elected President and the crowd had loudly shouted their approval. She had no specific plan but everyone knew it would include amnesty, free college tuition, a whole host of expanded welfare and healthcare benefits for those who had crossed the border illegally.

"Let me find that article," General Graham said as he flipped open the paper. Once he spread it out in front of him, he pointed his finger at the headline he had circled in red ink earlier that morning at breakfast. "Here it is. 'Mexican drug cartels clash near border; sixty killed, including four girls.'"

"I read that article," Sanchez said. She sounded genuinely concerned about the loss of life. "Tragic."

General Graham put his elbows on the armrest, brought his hands together like a steeple, and rested his chin on the tops of his fingers. "I've got an idea," he said, his eyes showing his belief that the idea was a good one. Of course, all his ideas were good. "I've been thinking about it for a few days, and this article just reinforces my belief that we can do something about it. The Sons of the Devil cartel has been warring with the Sonoran cartel for several years now. Violence has escalated, innocent civilians are being killed, and it doesn't seem to be getting any better."

"We're also seeing some of the violence spilling over the border into the United States," Sanchez added.

"That's right," Graham said. "Now, what if I was to go down to Mexico, meet with President Garza or some high-ranking Mexican official, and see if we can broker a truce between the cartels. Garza's a bit of a leftist and is already worried about losing further control of his northern border. He might appreciate some help."

"A peace mission?" Bongiorno asked.

"You got it. Maybe I can even get the cartel leaders to meet face to face."

Sanchez wasn't sure what to think of the idea. Plenty of Americans had jetted off to hostile territory to meet with thugs and despotic regimes in hopes of bringing about world peace or freedom for the oppressed. Reverend Jackson met with Saddam Hussein to seek the release of hostages being used as human shields. Former President Carter met with the North Koreans on the issue of its nuclear program. Not to be outdone, Bill Richardson met with both Saddam and the North Koreans. So, there was precedent to back such a diplomatic journey.

"What type of deal are you going to broker?" Sanchez asked. "It's not like you're going to get the cartels to stop dealing drugs." She liked General Graham but stopped short of thinking he was a miracle worker.

"No, you're right," Graham said, nodding his head in agreement. He wasn't ready to give up just yet however. "What I would do is just try to get them to stop the violence. Keep the innocent civilians out of it. Hands off the Americans and stay away from the U.S. border. If we can get the Israelis and Palestinians to meet and make peace, why not the cartels?"

"I don't think we have peace in the Middle East," Bongiorno added. He sounded like he needed more convincing. "And I'm not sure what Americans will think when they see you standing in between two drug cartel leaders with a big smile on your face."

General Graham, however, was adamant about his plan. "It's all about peace. Forget the drug part of it. If I go down there and bring about a cease fire into this Mexican war, it will be a gold mine for the campaign. An absolute gold mine. Then all we have to do is put a commercial together saying how the Sanchez Administration will utilize the diplomatic process to bring about peace in the world. As opposed to that warmonger of a President we have in there now."

Once dubious of the General's plan, Sanchez was now on board. She would have little difficulty getting the minority vote – the Hispanics and African-Americans solidly in her corner. But it was the independents and moderates who needed convincing, and the main issue on their minds was the safety and security of the United States. If Sanchez could reassure the undecideds that she could be counted on to keep Americans safe and bring about the possibility of peace, they might cast their votes in her direction. Also, those worried about her leadership and executive skills could rest assured knowing a retired, but most importantly, a respected three-star general was right by her side if the going got tough. "Who would we contact to get this set up?"

"I have some acquaintances in the upper reaches of the Mexican military," General Graham said. "I can put in a call to them and then another one to President Garza. I'll tell them it's in their best interests to help put the meeting together."

"What do you think President Schumacher is going to think about this?" Bongiorno wondered.

"Screw him," Graham snapped. He thought the President was too close-minded to know any better. "I don't care what he thinks anyway."

"He might argue you're butting in on American foreign policy."

"Then we hit him back that he has failed to work the diplomatic front. Too busy dropping bombs on people around the world instead of listening to our enemies and seeking common ground."

Bongiorno looked at Sanchez. He still wasn't sure about the political ramifications of the General's plan. She would have to make the call on this one.

Sanchez started shaking her head. "Let's do it. I fail to see the downside of it. If anything, it will be a mountain of publicity for the campaign." She then smiled at the General. "And any publicity is good publicity."

"That's right."

"And if we can put an end to the violence, we will ride the wave all the way to 1600 Pennsylvania Avenue."

CHAPTER 18

The White House – Washington, D.C.

President Schumacher was sitting at his desk in the Oval Office when a disheveled Wiley walked in and slumped down in a chair next to the President's desk. He looked exhausted. The bags underneath his eyes were getting bigger and darker by the day. He had long since given up putting a tie on in the morning. It would have been long gone by eight-thirty anyway. Although he did put on a suit coat before entering the Oval Office – per the President's orders. Less than two weeks away from the end of his first presidential election campaign, he was living off of Red Bull and adrenaline. The President wondered if his friend would make it to the end.

"You look like hell," President Schumacher said.

Wiley let his head fall back over the chair. He looked like he might pass out right then and there.

"You need to get some rest."

"I'll be able to rest once the election is over," Wiley said, his tired eyes looking at the ceiling.

"Danielle and I are worried about you. You've been running yourself ragged for months now."

Wiley tilted his head down and took a deep breath. With a clear determined voice and the Red Bull finally kicking in, he said, "One more week and then I'll expect you to send me on a nice long vacation to some fancy tropical island where I can pass out on a nice warm beach and sleep for a month."

"Will do," the President said. Seeing his chief strategist ready to go, he started off on the first item of business. "Have you read the draft that the speechwriters have written that I'm going to give on the trip through Illinois?"

"Is that your 'House Divided' speech?"

"Yeah, I'm also going to incorporate some of Lincoln's words from the Gettysburg Address. I think the speech will do a good job of showing our desire to bring the country together and focusing on the government's responsibility of keeping a united America safe and secure."

Wiley thumbed through the President's draft, looking at his notations made in the margins. He then quoted Lincoln verbatim off the top of his head.

"'Under the operation of that policy, that agitation has not only not ceased, but has constantly augmented. In my opinion, it will not cease, until a crisis shall have been reached, and passed – "A house divided against itself cannot stand." I do not expect the Union to be dissolved – I do not expect the house to fall – but I do expect it will cease to be divided.'"

The President had stopped to admire Cogdon's recitation of Lincoln's 1858 speech.

"Man, that Lincoln was something," Cogdon said to him. "I wonder how he thought about using the 'House Divided' as an analogy."

The President turned to the last page of the speech. "Probably from reading the Bible."

Wiley gave a slight grunt. "Yeah, right."

"No, I'm serious. It's in the Gospels."

"Are you making that up?" Was the President pulling his leg?

The President reached over to the corner of his desk for his copy of the Holy Bible, which was right next to his copy of *The Heritage Guide to the Constitution*. Both well-placed tomes were known to roil left-wing Democrats – the two greatest obstacles in liberals' lives often being the Ten Commandments and the Constitution.

"Let me find it here," the President said as he leafed through the Bible. "'Every kingdom divided against itself will be ruined, and every city or household divided against itself will not stand.' That was Jesus in the twelfth chapter of Matthew, verse twenty-five. It's also in Mark, chapter three."

"I did not know that," Wiley announced. He thought he knew everything about Abraham Lincoln.

"I'm sure you knew it but just forgot about it with all the stress you have been under lately."

Wiley reluctantly nodded. He didn't like not knowing. While he scolded himself, his BlackBerry started buzzing on his hip. He grabbed it, blinked his eyes a couple of times, and set to reading the message on the screen.

"Oh, you are not going to believe this," he said.

"What?"

"The AP is reporting that General Graham is going to make a peace mission to Mexico in two days to meet with President Garza in hopes of brokering a truce in the war between the cartels."

"Are you kidding me?" Now it was the President who thought his leg was being pulled.

"No, I'm not," he said before continuing on with the story. "The Sanchez campaign has announced Vice-Presidential hopeful General T.D. Graham will leave the campaign trail on Thursday to meet with Mexican officials in an attempt to stop the deadly violence that has plagued northern Mexico for several years. A Sanchez campaign spokesman says General Graham wants to offer his international expertise to broker an end to the violence that has caught innocent Mexicans and even some Americans in the crossfire. General Graham will then return to the campaign trail on Friday at an event in Houston."

"Is he nuts?" the President wondered. "It's not safe down there."

"No, it's not. I wouldn't even go to Acapulco right now what with all the organized crime and cartel violence going on."

The President picked up the receiver on his phone. "Yes, would you get me the Secretary of State, please."

Wiley now had his political hat firmly atop his bald head. "It could help their campaign if the bloodshed stops."

The President shook his head. "The bloodshed might stop for awhile, but where are the cartels going to direct their energies when they are holding hands and singing Kumbayah with each other. Maybe they'll work together and join forces to bring their cocaine and heroin to the United States on a bipartisan cartel basis." His mood was becoming increasingly sour.

"Mr. President," his secretary said over the speakerphone. "Secretary of State Arnold is on line one."

"Thank you, Carla," the President said. He got right to the point. "Mike, have you read the report about General Graham traveling to Mexico on Thursday?"

"Sir, I learned of it for the first time when I read the story online ten minutes ago," Secretary Arnold said. "They didn't notify me about the trip."

"So nobody at the State Department has cleared it?"

"No, sir. I'm not even sure who he's meeting with."

"Okay, Mike. Let me know if you have any contact with the Sanchez campaign." The President dialed his secretary again. "Carla, get me General Graham."

"Yes, sir."

While he waited, the President slowly started getting hot under the collar. He banged the desk with his left fist. "Can you believe this? I shouldn't have to worry about the Democratic nominee for Vice President leaving the campaign trail to go visit drug cartels in Mexico."

"Do you want me to talk to him?" Wiley asked. "Maybe I should call Bongiorno first and see what's going on."

The President shook his head as his secretary said the General was on the line. They might as well get the information straight from the horse's mouth. He punched the button for the speakerphone. "General, this is Anthony Schumacher, how are you, sir?"

"Mr. President," General Graham said in grand fashion. The enthusiasm was both fake and obvious. "I am fine. What a great honor and pleasure it is to hear from you this blessed morning."

The President rolled his eyes over at Wiley. "General, I hear you are thinking about taking a vacation to Mexico in the next couple of days."

"Yes, sir, I am."

"Shouldn't you wait until after the election is over?"

A few seconds of silence left the Oval Office quiet before the General responded.

"Well, Mr. President, I have the opportunity to bring peace to a small part of the world and I didn't want to put it off until later."

"General, I am concerned about the level of violence in northern Mexico. And, putting our political differences aside, I am concerned about your safety."

"Oh, Mr. President," the General said with confidence, "I have entered far more dangerous dens than the one I'll be visiting later this week. Unlike you, I have seen my fair share of combat, if you remember correctly."

"Yes, General, I do," the President said growing impatient. "But I don't think you should be taking my Secret Service agents down into a war zone for a campaign photo op."

Not only does the Secret Service protect the President of the United States, the Vice President, and the First Families, it also provides temporary protection for the Presidential and Vice-Presidential candidates within three months of the general election. Sanchez and Graham had had the full compliment of security agents, magnetometers, and armored caravans transporting and following them around wherever they went. And the President did not like the thought of agents from the Secret Service, which falls under the executive branch and its Department of Homeland Security, chauffeuring Graham south of the border so he could feed his ego and try to save the world.

"Sir, I won't be taking *your* Secret Service agents," General Graham huffed. "I have a team of security guards that *our* campaign is paying for. We will be in and out before you know it." After a slight pause, he added. "But I don't envision any problems. I come in peace for all mankind."

"Well, General, I hope you realize that you have no authorization to act on behalf of the United States."

"Mr. President, I don't need a lecture from you. I know what I'm doing, and I've been doing it for a hell of a lot longer than you have. Good day to you, sir." He then hung up.

Wiley had left his chair and was prancing around the room like a prize fighter. The Red Bull was now coursing generously through his veins. He was ready to go a few rounds. "You want me to get a statement ready denouncing the trip?"

The President sat back in his chair nodded his head. "Yeah, go ahead. Don't use the word 'denounce' though. Make it clear that the visit is not on behalf of the United States. I don't want those cartels thinking we are going soft on them."

"You know the Democrats will say you don't want peace, that they're taking the bull by the horns and bringing the bad guys to the table without sending in troops and dropping our bombs."

"I don't see the benefit in bringing violent drug cartels to the table. It only makes them want to come together to fight the drug war against us."

"Maybe you should call Ty and fill him in."

The President had a million things to do today, and General Graham and the Democrats just put one more heap of worry on his plate. He hit the call button for his secretary. "Carla, get me Director Parker, please."

Wiley quit shadow boxing when he heard the President's request. "You think the CIA might have some information that would make General Graham rethink his plan?"

"I doubt the General will change his mind no matter who tells him not to go."

Director Parker came on the line. "Good morning, Mr. President."

"Good morning, Bill. Have you heard General Graham is going to travel to Mexico to meet with the cartel leaders?"

"Yes, I am aware of it."

"Do you have any intelligence that would indicate he is a target? Or maybe something that he should be aware of?"

"No, none of our intelligence has ever mentioned General Graham. I'm sure this is just a photo op for him and the cartels."

"I guess."

"What do you want me to do, sir?"

The President wondered if he was overreacting. Maybe it was the campaigner in him. And maybe Wiley was right that it would look good for the General and the Democrats if things went well down in Mexico. It could give them a last-minute bump in the polls. Still, he was the President. And thus he still had some control over the situation.

"Sir?"

"Bill," the President said. "Put a Predator on him."

Nogales, Mexico

Ten drums of VX were sitting on the ground floor of an abandoned restaurant on the eastern outskirts of Nogales, less than a half mile from the U.S./Mexican border. The restaurant hadn't served a meal in ten years but business inside the place was booming, the activity almost nonstop. The Sons of the Devil drug cartel used it as a forward operating base where they could prepare to send their shipment of drugs across the border. Loads of marijuana, cocaine, and heroin could be packed and trucked over, put on rail cars, smuggled in on foot, and even dropped in by ultralight.

But today, Raul Camacho was not taking any chances with his precious cargo. Speed was not a requirement. No sir, Camacho was prepared to take the drums of VX one inch at a time, and that meant utilizing the tunnels his cartel had been working on for the last ten years. In the kitchen of the restaurant, the cartel had dug a five-foot wide tunnel underneath the desert earth of Mexico and the southwestern United States. The walls were lined with concrete blocks, and rails along the floor allowed cargo to be moved quickly. Florescent lighting and a decent ventilation system made the tunnel one to be admired by rival cartels who had their own underground highways. Camacho's tunnel ended behind a collection of Dumpsters used by a gas station on the American side of the border.

Law-enforcement authorities on the U.S. side have utilized ground-penetrating radar and large drills in hopes of locating the tunnels, some of which have been found to exit into large warehouses where truck drivers wait patiently to haul the cartel's illegal goods across America. It was a never-ending battle between the United States and the cartels burrowing underneath the border.

Raul Camacho and Abdi Rumallah watched as one drum of VX was carefully loaded on to a rail car and slowly pushed forward.

"How are you going to get the five-ten through the U.S.?" Camacho asked.

"We have a tractor-trailer truck ready to go," Rumallah said.

"You're just going to put ten drums of an insanely hazardous substance on a truck and hope you don't get stopped?"

"We have contracted with a Mexican company that supplies oil to various chemical companies in Texas. We will most likely get stopped in Texas, but since the VX has no odor, canine units won't be able to detect it. We show our papers and the cargo and they let us move on. As long as we don't break any laws between Texas and Washington we won't have any problems."

Rumallah had a team of individuals working on his terrorist plot, and he had been in contact with Mohammed Akbar in Chicago. Akbar said he would oversee the final phase once a warehouse or storage unit could be secured for delivery of the VX. Rumallah planned to oversee the operation in Mexico and then head north to meet up with Akbar.

Even though the attack was still a ways away, Rumallah had no desire to take a vacation to sun himself on the beaches of Acapulco or take in the rock formations near Cabo San Lucas. He was a trained killer, and when opportunities cropped up that would allow him to exercise his murderous mind, he was not one to let it pass him by.

"I hear your people are meeting with General Graham," Rumallah said. He had read it on the Internet that morning. The liberals in the media were fawning all over the peace mission, like it was the greatest thing since Jimmy Carter's Camp David Accords.

Camacho gave Rumallah a quizzical look, as if trying to find out what angle the terrorist was playing now. "Yes, in fact I am going to meet with him myself."

"And what do you hope to get out of the meeting?"

"I have been getting a lot of bad press lately. Pictures of bloodied kids on the front page of newspapers and the nightly news. No one likes to see young children killed in our turf battles. Unfortunately, collateral damage is a cost of doing business."

"And meeting with General Graham is simply for public relations?"

"You could say that. It will buy us some time, help calm things down a bit, make it look like we're listening to the international community. All the while, we'll be stepping up our shipments right under the Americans' noses."

Rumallah's five Yemeni cohorts were listening intently as they monitored the third drum of VX disappearing into the tunnel. "Where is the meeting going to be held?"

"South of Ciudad Juarez. We have arranged with President Garza a neutral meeting site, actually it's one of my satellite offices."

"President Garza is going to be there as well?"

"No, he is sending one of his top aides."

"So let me get this straight," Rumallah said. "You are going to meet with a leader of the Sonoran drug cartel, a representative of President Garza, and General Graham?"

"Yes," Camacho said, like it was nothing.

"But you hate the Sonorans," Rumallah reminded him. "And your government and that of the U.S. too"

"It's simply a photo op. We sit around a table and look serious, then we smile, shake hands, and promise to stop the violence amongst our brothers and sisters in Mexico."

"How is General Graham getting to the meeting?"

"He is flying in to Ciudad Juarez International Airport. Then my people will take him to the office."

"And you think this will be good for business?" Rumallah asked.

"Absolutely," Camacho said. "And all the attention it will bring will distract those who should be out looking for your five-ten."

"Good."

Rumallah liked what he was hearing.

CHAPTER 19

Lincoln, Illinois

The President's whistlestop tour of Illinois made its second to last stop on its 200-mile journey from Chicago to Springfield prior to the last presidential debate later on that evening in the capital city. With a crowd of thousands spilling out on both sides of the track and around the old train depot, the President's train rumbled to stop in the first and only town named after Abraham Lincoln prior to his death. The presidential railcar was privately owned, festooned with patriotic bunting, and dubbed the "Railsplitter" for good luck. It bore a striking resemblance to the Pullman Company's *Ferdinand Magellan* that Franklin Roosevelt used in the 1930s. Traveling on the "Honest Abe," Gerald Ford was the last President to make a campaign rail stop in Lincoln during the final days of the '76 election – although during his remarks he mistakenly said he was in Pontiac.

The crowd's red-white-and-blue flags and handmade signs, all proudly made in America, were out in full force. One brightly fingerpainted and glitter-encrusted placard read "Sisters Alexa and Norah Welcome Pres. Schumacher." Down the way, twin toddlers, nicely attired in full Lincoln regalia complete with fake beards and top hats, joined in the revelry of the presidential visit.

Looking down on the crowd were teams of Secret Service sharpshooters on the roofs of the Harris-Hodnett Insurance Agency across from the depot and the Blue Dog Inn down the street. There wasn't a parked car within three blocks as the entire area had been cordoned off since early that morning. Up and down the railroad line hugging Old Route 66, crossings in obscure places like Funks Grove, Atlanta, Broadwell, and Sherman had police vehicles stationed on both sides of the tracks to prevent a suicide bomber from ramming into the train when the President rolled through the prairie. Two police helicopters hovered a mile north and south to keep an eye on the tracks.

"Thank you very much Lincoln!" the President said from behind the bulletproof podium on the back of the train. He was wearing a navy blue windbreaker with the presidential seal over the left breast. On that chilly October day, he was warmed by the bulletproof vest he wore underneath the jacket. Agent Craig was standing nearby with a bulletproof rain coat just in case.

Wiley had made the trip with the President. He was seated in the presidential car listening to the speeches at each stop and watching out the windows to gauge the reaction of those in the crowd. He was more worried about the debate tonight and hoped the President wouldn't go on too long lest he lose his voice. But with his eagle eye always on the lookout for political points, Wiley spotted possible winning lines in the faces of people crowding the area and fired off handwritten notes to the President via his press secretary. And, of course, not wanting any Ford-like gaffes from his candidate, he always penciled on top of the note the name of the town they were in and then underlined it twice.

"It is always a pleasure to be in the great State of Illinois and especially here, the heart of the Land of Lincoln."

The President took a quick glance at the note his press secretary surreptitiously handed up onto the podium. He looked in the direction of eleven o'clock and found what he was looking for. "First off, I want to thank Alexa and Norah for welcoming me here to Lincoln today," he said, pointing in their direction.

The shrieks of joy from the two girls indicated they knew their hard work was appreciated and had not gone unnoticed. With their temporary GOP elephant tattoos adorning their rosy cheeks and proudly displaying their party affiliation, they would have been sure-fire Republican voters had they been old enough. Maybe some day.

"It is great to be back in the stomping grounds of our sixteenth President of the United States. As many of you know, I grew up next door in Indiana, where a young Abraham Lincoln spent a good many of his boyhood years before making the trek to central Illinois. It was here, and in Bloomington, Mt. Pulaski, and Danville, where he would ride the Eighth Judicial Circuit practicing law and solidifying his beliefs in right triumphing over wrong. It was here, and in Petersburg, New Salem, and in Springfield, where he would listen to the people and represent their interests during his days in the Illinois state legislature and in the halls of Congress. It is also where he laid the foundations for a presidency of historic proportions, one where he worked to free the slaves and bind up the nation's wounds from the War Between the States.

"Over one hundred and fifty years ago at Gettysburg, President Lincoln noted that we were then 'engaged in a great civil war.' Well, today we are engaged in a great world war – on one side the forces of freedom and democracy and on the other the forces of evil and tyranny. The war against Islamic extremists has been hard fought, but it will not end with hopeful rhetoric and wishful thinking. Since the war on terror began, nearly five thousand of our fellow Americans have lost their lives in the defense of liberty. Let us today and always remember the words of President Lincoln – 'that from these honored dead we take increased devotion to that cause for which they here gave the last full measure of devotion – that we here highly resolve that these dead shall not have died in vain.' So let us go forward, together as a united country, not a house divided; as patriotic Americans, not simply rival political parties, so that future generations of Americans will enjoy the sweet taste of freedom and liberty. Thank you very much!"

Following the short speech, the President made his way off the back of the train where he met the local dignitaries – the mayor, the sheriff, the circuit clerk, the county clerk, and a whole host of Republicans on the ballot. Given the near-unanimous GOP stronghold in the local government, the President was among friends in Logan County. He also met with Barb and Brad Anders, a couple who had been voted "Parents of the Year" in Illinois; Earl Patton, the oldest surviving war veteran of Logan County; and a collection of costumed individuals, including Honest Abe himself, who were waiting for the President to ceremoniously reenact the town christening which Lincoln had done in 1853 by splitting open a watermelon and pouring the juice upon the ground.

President Schumacher obliged and hopped back on board. He said he didn't want to tie up the tracks any longer. The idling Amtrak from Chicago was waiting ten miles north of town. On board was Mohammed Akbar.

And he was not happy about the wait. It made him more determined than ever to see to it that Mr. Schumacher met the same fate as Mr. Lincoln.

Ciudad Juarez, Mexico

General Graham stepped off the private jet at 6 p.m. and took four steps down to the tarmac. Following behind him were his four security guards from a little known outfit in California called Security Specialists, Inc. While the campaign spent lavishly on catering and lodging, it did not feel the need to spend a good deal of money on security for such a short trip. The men had no military or police experience. They hadn't even been Boy Scouts. More suited to the night shift of the corporate world, they usually sat behind their desks watching surveillance monitors and playing solitaire while the cleaning crew emptied the garbage and vacuumed the carpet.

The Secret Service had protested vociferously when the Sanchez campaign said its agents would not be joining the General. His protective detail went so far as to have Director Defoe make a last-ditch effort to have Graham change his mind, maybe remind him how the agents were the best in the business. The plea fell on deaf ears however, the Sanchez campaign too interested in showing off the General in a foreign land unencumbered by security. So the agents in charge of Graham's detail finally relented realizing he didn't want them by his side. General Graham's new security men were unarmed, as they had no license to carry firearms into a foreign country. And they were constantly reminded to stay out of the way of General Graham and the cameras, as the campaign wanted it to look like Graham had gallantly gone down to Mexico all by himself.

"General Graham, welcome to Ciudad Juarez," Guillermo Ruiz said with outstretched hand. Ruiz was President Garza's director of public relations and had been dispatched to Ciudad Juarez to meet the General and take him to the meeting. Ruiz wore a gray suit, the pocket of which contained a white carnation his wife had given to him earlier that morning for good luck. He had a dark head of hair with strands of silver starting to appear. He had only been on the job for two months.

"Thanks for the welcome wagon," General Graham said. "Let's get this show on the road."

Ruiz and General Graham took the backseat in a freshly washed Mercedes Benz S600 L. The General's security detail was relegated to an Econoline van that followed behind them. A second van of reporters, four of whom were from the United States and the other three from Mexico, followed the first van.

"General, I have been told the leaders of the drug cartels are already at the meeting place. Raul Camacho is the leader of the Sons of the Devil cartel, which unfortunately controls a great deal of the northern Mexican territory from Metamoros to Nogales. Also present is Joaquin Salazar, the head of the Sonoran drug cartel." Ruiz opened a folder and showed Graham pictures of the men he would be meeting.

"I take it these guys don't particularly get along?" he said, holding the photos up closer to the dome light illuminating the interior.

"Yes, sir, they hate each other," Ruiz said. "But they probably dislike me and my government more than each other."

President Garza had been making the effort to crack down on the cartel violence as well as improve the Mexican economy so the drug trade would not be looked upon as the preferred lifestyle by a large number of Mexican citizens, especially young males. Many in Mexico received a good deal of money from the drug network, whether directly or indirectly. The high prices received in America trickled down south, and the cartels were known to spread the wealth around. Many in and out of the cartels resisted government intervention.

And the crackdown had not been bloodless. Mexican military were routinely attacked and often outgunned. Mayors in northern Mexican towns had been kidnapped and murdered. Because those contemplating replacing those mayors were threatened with a similar fate, the offices remained vacant. President Garza's last public-relations director had been shot and then decapitated after calling for an end to the violence. That could have been a reason for Ruiz's gray hairs.

"And they dislike my government as well," General Graham added.

"Yes, sir."

The caravan sped through the streets of Ciudad Juarez with two motorcycle policemen leading the way. The car, along with the two vans, had dark tinted windows on all sides and each vehicle included a darkened shield in front of the passengers making it impossible for them to see where they were going. General Graham's security detail had no idea if they were still behind him or not.

"I am convinced that I can bring about some compromise," the General said, not lacking in confidence. He had met with a handful of thugs during his military days, which resulted in varying degrees of mediational success depending on who you talked to. "At least get them to call a truce and stop the bloodshed. The world cannot stand seeing little girls caught in the middle of warring factions."

"I agree, General. I hope you can bring about peace."

"It'll be good for both of us," he said.

After twenty minutes of zigzagging their way from the airport, the General's car made a final right turn before slowing to stop. He could hear people walking on the crushed gravel outside. He looked at Ruiz. "Is this our stop?"

"General," Ruiz said sheepishly, "I don't even know where we are."

The car opened and a man in military fatigues and a dark bushy mustache looked inside. Seeing General Graham, he nodded. "Right this way, sir."

General Graham and Ruiz exited the vehicle, saw that the evening darkness had overtaken them, and noticed the photographers had disembarked first so they could get a picture of Graham heading into the meeting. Camera flashes lit the way as the General gave them a wave and walked inside. His security detail stayed out of camera shot like they were told.

From what Graham could tell in the darkness, the building looked like an old school house. There were children's desks pushed up against the wall and chalkboards on wheels lined up in the corner. The mustachioed man in the military fatigues stopped General Graham outside of the meeting room.

"General," the man said in decent English. "My name is Juan." He did not mention a last name. He also did not give himself a title. He had no stars or bars on his shoulders or any other insignia noting his rank. "I will be your interpreter this evening. Mr. Camacho and Mr. Salazar are currently inside the meeting room. I am to allow a photographer to enter first so you can have a greeting with the men. Then you will have thirty minutes for a private meeting. After that, the reporters will be allowed in to ask questions. Is that acceptable to you, sir?"

"Absolutely." General Graham began to realize that the Mexican Government was not in control of this meet-and-greet. Ruiz wasn't even able to listen to the conversations.

Once Juan received the word, the door was opened and General Graham stepped in with Juan close behind. Someone allowed Ruiz into the room and motioned for him to stand up against the wall. Graham's security detail was kept outside with the reporters.

"Hola," General Graham said as he approached the two drug lords. It would be one of the few attempts at Spanish he would make that night. "General T.D. Graham."

"General Graham," both men said as they took turns shaking his hand.

Graham put on his serious face, not even showing his whitened teeth for the camera. "I want to thank you for meeting with me."

After the pictures were taken and the photographer left, Camacho and Salazar sat on opposing sides of a small card table covered with a white table cloth. Two Mexican flags stood behind the General as he and Juan took seats opposite each other. Camacho wore his usual red checkerboard shirt and a pair of blue jeans. Salazar, on the other hand, was decked out in his drab military green garb that made him look like he shopped at the same clothier as Fidel Castro.

General Graham took the next thirty minutes and implored the drug lords to temper their violence, or at least keep it out of the city streets frequented by kids and innocent civilians. He never once mentioned the drug trade, acting as if the two men on each side of him were simply in a violent dispute over land just like the Israelis and the Palestinians. Neither drug lord said much, both of them content to sit and listen.

"Do you guys like boxing?"

After Juan gave the translation, both men nodded. Camacho even smiled. He put up his dukes to show the General he was a pugilist himself. "I am the greatest of all time," he said in a decent Ali impersonation. Salazar didn't look amused, really wanting to say Camacho was more of a smelly old goat than the greatest.

"You both have heard of neutral corners?"

Again the men nodded after the translation. "That's what we need to do here. Let's go to our neutral corners and cool down for a bit. I'm not saying you guys have to get along, but just stay in your own little piece of the world for the time being. That way the women and children won't get hurt."

Camacho and Salazar agreed to keep their cartels on their own turf. Since there were no documents signed or treaties passed around, whether they would abide by their agreement would depend on the whims of the madmen sitting at the table.

After thirty minutes, the press pool came in. With one drug lord on each side of him, General Graham gave the press a recap of the meeting. "I think we have made real progress here today. Both sides have agreed to stop the senseless violence that has plagued the country of Mexico for far too long. It is my sincere belief that the killing will stop and the Mexican citizens will be able to go about their lives in peace."

He then spread out his arms and tried to bring the two men together. "Shake hands," he whispered. Neither man wanted to touch the other scum's hand. "Por favor," the General pleaded quietly. Camacho reached out first, followed by a reluctant Salazar. The sneers on their faces indicated they would just as soon commit suicide than shake the hand of the enemy. After a couple of pumps, General Graham grabbed the shaking hands with both of his and pumped them a few more times. Then came the smile – the full rows of pearly whites basking in the glow of the camera flashes. The General could almost feel the Nobel committee etching his name on the peace prize.

Once Camacho and Salazar were able to slither out of the General's grasp they headed in opposite directions and out separate doors. After Graham gave a thumbs-up to the cameras, Juan ushered him out of the room followed at a distance by his security detail and walked him out to the idling Mercedes outside.

"Thank you for your hospitality, Juan," Graham said with appreciation.

"Have a good evening, General." Juan closed the passenger door and gave a thumbs-up to the driver.

Once Ruiz got in the back seat and his door closed, General Graham let out a whoop that could have been heard all the way down in Mexico City.

"Congratulations, General," Ruiz said.

General Graham clapped his hands together. He then extended his right hand to Ruiz and gave him a good pat on the back. "My friend, do you mind if I make a call to Congresswoman Sanchez so I can tell her the good news before her debate tonight?"

"By all means." Ruiz looked genuinely relieved, like he had been spared the death penalty that evening. He had no idea how it would turn out. He couldn't believe it went so well. He wiped the nervous sweat off his brow and allowed himself to smile.

General Graham hit the speed dial and Niles Bongiorno picked up. "Niles, it's General Graham!"

"How did it go?" Bongiorno asked, straining to hear over the static.

There were no live cameras at the meeting, so the cable outlets could only show Graham exiting the airplane, a file photo of him, and a map of Mexico in an endless loop as the reporters gave the low-down on the trip. A reporter had videotaped the statement and the handshake after the meeting at the General's request so it could be sent out in time for the post-debate talk heads to discuss and undoubtedly praise to high heaven.

"It went great! I was great!" the General gushed. He could barely contain himself. "It could not have gone any better. Let me talk to Rosita before she goes on."

Congresswoman Sanchez was sitting in a holding room making last-minute preparations for the debate that would take place in twenty minutes. Her makeup artist was applying the last touches to her face. Bongiorno walked in and handed the phone to Sanchez. She was hoping to use something positive from the General's meeting during her opening statement.

"General, tell me good news."

"Rosita, they agreed to stop the violence! I even got them to shake hands! It was like Clinton on the South Lawn with Rabin and Arafat! We have peace!"

Sanchez was overjoyed. She pumped a fist in the air. "Thank you, General. Thank you, thank you, thank you," she gushed. "Diplomacy has carried the day!"

"Good luck tonight, Rosita. I will see you tomorrow in Houston. I probably won't even get a wink of sleep!"

Sanchez ended the call and gave Bongiorno a high-five. She told him she thought they might have won the campaign that night. Now all she had to do was project a calm demeanor and a firm grasp of the issues and she would be well on her way to the White House.

CHAPTER 20

The Old State Capitol – Springfield, Illinois

The Old State Capitol building in Springfield provided one of the more famous venues for a presidential debate. While other sites offered more seating and greater acoustics, few compared to the intimate setting where Abraham Lincoln actually gave his "House Divided" speech to kick off his 1858 campaign for United States Senate. As the seat of Illinois Government from 1839 to 1876, Lincoln had served in the State Capitol as a member of the Illinois House of Representatives and later used the governor's office in preparing to move to Washington, D.C. after winning the 1860 presidential election. He also returned to the Capitol in May of 1865, but only to lie-in-state for the final time before his burial.

After President Schumacher had arrived in the capital city, he made his way around Springfield – out to Oak Ridge Cemetery to rub the nose of Borglum's famous bronze bust of Lincoln for good luck and then to pay his respects with a wreath laying at his predecessor's tomb; then it was over to Eighth and Jackson for a stop at the Lincoln family home; up to the corner of Sixth and Adams where Lincoln and his law partner William Herndon kept their law office; and finally a quick tour of Lincoln's Presidential Library.

Now he stood by himself waiting for the debate to begin in the old governor's office – the same office used by candidate Lincoln as his campaign headquarters. An American flag stood tall in one corner and a bust of Lincoln rested in the other, the latter almost reminding the current President that the "occasion is piled high with difficulty," as Lincoln remarked in his 1862 Annual Message to Congress. For the past five minutes, the President had been softly humming the tune to *Back Home Again in Indiana*, a sure sign of his nervousness. He always felt the song calmed him down.

"Do we have any word on how General Graham's meeting went?" the President asked as he put on his dark suit coat. He straightened his red tie in the mirror and gave his American flag lapel pin one last shine.

Wiley had been pacing the floor for the last half hour. The carpet was blue, and it was getting a workout. Wiley's back and forth actually brought the temperature in the room up a couple of degrees. He was not singing or humming to himself. He was a pacer, a worrier, and it was starting to show.

His suit coat was off and the sweat stains were beginning to show through in his arm pits. His eyes never once left his BlackBerry.

"Nothing is coming in over the wires," he said. He refreshed his screen every fifteen seconds.

"Well, why don't I just take it for granted that everything went well and he got the two sides to call a truce. That way I won't be caught off guard if Sanchez injects a surprise statement into the debate."

Still looking at his BlackBerry, Wiley reluctantly agreed. "Okay. But just remember to shift the focus back to the war on drugs. You might even ask her if he got them to stop shipping illegal contraband into the country."

"If she says yes, I might vote for her," the President said smiling.

Wiley looked up from his BlackBerry with a horrified look on his face, his eyes wide and his mouth open, like a little boy who had just been told there was no Santa Claus.

"Easy there, big fella," the President said, holding out his hands. "Just a little pre-debate joke."

Wiley took a breath. "Try not to joke too much tonight. Your humor doesn't always go over well with the liberals in the media. A bad joke from you is all MSNBC will talk about tomorrow."

"Okay, no jokes."

While they were at it, Wiley thought it prudent to start running down his mental checklist of debate do's and don'ts. Mostly don'ts. "Don't invade her space like that guy did with Hillary. And don't compare yourself to a young Jack Kennedy. Don't look at your watch either. And no heavy sighing like that gasbag Gore."

"Stay away from her, I'm not Jack Kennedy, don't worry about the time, and no heavy sighing," the President said, trying not to laugh at his half-neurotic strategist. "Got it."

"And if you feel any sweat starting to form on your upper lip, make sure to wipe it off when the camera's on Sanchez. I don't want you looking like Tricky Dick Nixon on national television."

"Okay."

"And don't forget to mention Reagan and Lincoln a lot. People in Illinois love 'em."

"What about Obama?"

Wiley looked genuinely peeved, like the President had not been listening to all his insightful instructions he had given him over the past several months. "Let's just stick with Reagan and Lincoln," he said through gritted teeth.

Agent Craig stuck his head in the door. "Two minutes, sir."

President Schumacher headed out into the rotunda and stood outside the south end of Representative Hall, a life-size statue of the five-foot-four Stephen Douglas guarding the door. The President looked it over, mentioning to the balding Wiley that he bore a striking resemblance to the Little Giant with the exception of the full head of hair. Wiley did not find the comparison amusing.

Across the way, Congresswoman Sanchez and her entourage took their place outside the chamber on the north end. The scene reminded some of two prize fighters waiting to be introduced before they entered the ring – minus the verbal taunts and screaming fans. Through the throngs of staff, the President made eye contact with Sanchez and gave her a friendly wave. She smiled, raised her fists, and made a few playful jabs into the air. The President laughed.

Inside the old House chamber were one hundred lucky citizens and various dignitaries, including the First Lady. Some were seated behind the curved rows of replica desks that would have been once used by state legislators known now only by the history books. Quill pens and candle holders were still in place for an authentic touch. The rest of the crowd packed in to the upstairs gallery. It, along with the pillars in the hall, were decorated with patriotic bunting and red-white-and-blue banners. With a large portrait of George Washington looking down on them, the candidates would stand behind their podiums and face the world with the moderator, NBC news anchor Byron Anderson, seated in front of them.

The President could hear Anderson welcoming those watching on television to the third and final debate between the two candidates for President of the United States. The President took a deep breath, cleared his throat, and softly sang his favorite refrain, "How I long for my Indiana home."

Just before the moderator introduced the candidates, a nervous Wiley gave his last-minute instructions.

"Remember, no jokes," he implored of the President.

The President nodded but couldn't resist one last jab at his friend. "No jokes. And I'm Jack Kennedy, right?"

"No, no, no," an exasperated Wiley said. "Please, no jokes. Just remember Lincoln and Reagan. Lincoln and Reagan. Go get 'em!"

He gave the President a good pat on the back as he walked into the chamber to the applause of those now standing inside. Wiley stayed out in the hall to pace the floors beneath the rotunda and watch on the closed-circuit televisions scattered throughout the building.

He felt like he might throw up.

The microphones at the moderator's table picked up the President saying it was nice to see the Congresswoman again. She said the same of him. They each took a spot behind their respective podium with the American flag standing behind the President's right shoulder. The President reached underneath the podium and took a quick sip of water and then fished out a pen from the pocket of his suit coat. A blank note pad had been provided to both candidates.

Each side then made their opening statements – the President focusing on national security and the war on terror, Sanchez wanting to finally stop the wars in Iraq and Afghanistan and try the diplomatic route. Early on in the questioning, she came right at President Schumacher with full force in her answers.

"The President has led us into a police state," she lectured. "Ever since President Schumacher has been in higher office he has been a magnet for terror. And that only leads to a greater loss of freedom for the rest of us. We have to endure long lines at the airports and to get into government buildings. All because of President Schumacher attracting so much attention from the terrorists."

She then played the one card that Bongiorno told her had polled well in some political circles – that the President was making life more difficult for the American people by just being in the Oval Office.

"Let's take today," she said, the tone of her voice growing angry. "To get into this beautiful and historic building, I had to be subjected to a pat down by the President's security agents. To think that a member of Congress would have to be frisked and groped like a common criminal is beyond the pale."

A quiet stillness hung over the crowd, the spectators not knowing what to make of the complaint since they all had to undergo the same security screening. They wondered how the President would respond.

"Mr. President," Anderson said. "would you like to respond to Congresswoman Sanchez's comment?"

The President didn't know she had been searched. Nor did he order it to happen. That was the Secret Service's call. He wanted to laugh off such small potatoes. So, turning to Congresswoman Sanchez, he smiled and did his best. "Did they find anything?"

Out of the corner of his eye and even through the bright stage lights, the President could see Wiley in the doorway slapping his right hand on his bald dome in utter panic. "Didn't he listen to a word I said?" Wiley thought to himself.

A few in the crowd got a chuckle out of the remark. But the scribbling reporters in the back of the room indicated it was making headline news. And probably not the positive kind. The President probably just gave MSNBC a whole day's worth of programming. He tried to recover. "I had a bit of a problem once when not everyone was screened prior to one of my speeches."

He was referring to when Supreme Court Justice Ali Hussein slipped into the House Chamber at the U.S. Capitol without undergoing security screening and then tried to detonate the suicide vest hidden under his black robe. The Secret Service was taking no chances since that assassination attempt and everyone was searched save for the President and the First Lady.

"Mr. President, you are proving my point," Sanchez shot back. "You are a magnet for terrorism and the citizens of this country are the ones who must endure the fallout."

Having now remembered Wiley's admonition not to joke around, he tried to diffuse the situation as best he could. "As a matter of full disclosure, I'll just let the American people know what would have been found if I had to undergo a pat down tonight."

He reached into his left pocket and pulled out a container of ChapStick, the "classic" variety with its black container and white top. He showed it to the cameras for those viewing at home. "I don't leave home without this."

He then reached into his right pocket and out came a plastic card, otherwise known as "the biscuit," that he held up at shoulder level. For those watching on TV, it looked like a credit card or one of those newfangled keys to a hotel room.

"Or this either. This is the card for the President's emergency satchel, also known as the nuclear football, which is present here tonight and wherever I go." He then pointed over to the corner of the hall. "It is currently in the custody of that nicely dressed young man in the uniform of the United States Air Force. Once the card is inserted, it will properly identify me as President of the United States. It will then allow me to direct a retaliatory response if America is under nuclear attack."

The President put the card back in his pocket and looked over at Sanchez.

"This is serious business, Congresswoman. The United States is under assault by militant Islamic terrorists, and we do not have time to worry about certain indignities that you might have suffered when walking into the building tonight. And let me remind you, the brave men and women of the United States Secret Service are ready to put their lives on the line to keep you safe as you travel with them across this great country."

The President had rebounded nicely and now settled in for the rest of the debate.

CHAPTER 21

Ciudad Juarez, Mexico

General Graham was in such a good mood he actually asked Ruiz if it would be possible to stop for a bite to eat. He loved Mexican food, especially chicken and rice. And a large serving of arroz con pollo with an ice cold cerveza would be a nice reward for the day's work. Ruiz politely begged off, telling the General it was best to leave the area and return to the United States as quickly as possible. Outsiders did not linger in these parts. Insiders not wanting to risk their lives didn't dawdle either. Ruiz was himself hoping to get the hell out of there and make it back home to Mexico City before his kids went to bed. The General understood.

"Guillermo, I hope we can do some more business in the future. I am confident today was the beginning of a new personal friendship and a prosperous relationship between our two countries."

Before Ruiz could respond, the driver of the Mercedes hit the brakes, the tires squealing to a sudden stop. Without seat belts on, Ruiz and Graham slammed into the barrier separating them from the driver's compartment. A tractor-trailer had stopped abruptly in the middle of the intersection and blocked their path. The General's driver started yelling at the truck driver in Spanish. "Get that out of the way! Let's go! Let's go!" His gestures were understandable in any language.

General Graham had a fleeting thought that they were lucky they hadn't been rear ended by his security detail.

But you have to have someone behind you to get rear ended.

"Get out of the car! Get out of the car!"

The four masked gunmen had exited out of the trailer of the truck and had their AK-47s pointed at the Mercedes driver.

"Get out of the car!"

The driver refused to budge, knowing full well the car was bulletproof. That didn't stop the gunmen from making an attempt. Gunfire erupted from two sides as the driver covered his head with his hands hoping against hope that the glass would hold. It did.

But it wouldn't stop the hockey-puck-sized bombs being attached to the side windows. Two more magnetized bombs were attached to the roof of the driver's compartment. Two seconds later, the bombs shattered a hole through the windows and another through the roof sending shards of glass and steel through the driver's head.

One of the gunmen reached in and unlocked the doors. The other opened the passenger side door in the back. He looked inside and saw General Graham and Ruiz – white as ghosts. The General had been attempting to dial for help on his phone. With the business end of the AK-47, the gunman knocked the phone out of his hand.

"Get out of the car, General!"

"No!" the General said defiantly. He was waiting for his security detail to open up on the gunmen and rescue him from his current predicament. For most of the last decade, he never had to worry about his safety given his stature. Armed men followed him wherever he went – whether it be the U.S. military, the U.N. peacekeeping force, or the Secret Service. But Graham had completely forgotten his rent-a-guards were unarmed. Much to his current dismay, the Secret Service cavalry wasn't going to be returning fire.

Moreover, the security detail and press vans had fallen prey to the drug cartels' preferred method of attack. Large trucks were used to wall off certain streets, cutting off vehicle traffic from all directions. This then gives the cartels time to rob their victims or shoot them without witnesses and, more importantly, without the federales being able to ride up to the rescue.

"Get out of the car, General!"

"No!"

Ruiz had been involved in such a situation once before. And it didn't do any good to protest. "Do what they say, General," he grunted. His hands were covering his head as he crouched forward. The only thing running through his mind was the sight of his kids that he knew he would never see again.

"Get out or Ruiz dies!" the gunmen yelled, pointing the AK-47 at Ruiz.

Graham looked over at Ruiz, who was trembling with fear. In the time it took Graham to look back at the gunman, the AK-47 spat out two rounds into Ruiz's skull. His body slumped over to the side, blood now running down his cheek and dripping onto the white carnation in his pocket.

"Get out of the car now!"

Another gunman reached in, grabbed Graham by the collar of his shirt, and dragged him out. Once forcibly removed, he saw nothing but a deserted street behind him. The lamp posts along the street were dark, and the buildings were deserted with boards crisscrossing their windows. The only light came from the gunmen's vehicles. There was no sound of sirens, and no pedestrians around to call the police. Graham now realized things were not looking good. Two men tore off his suit coat. They then grabbed Graham's arms and tied his hands behind his back. They put a black hood over his head and stuck a gun in his back.

"Move! Move!"

The two men holding General Graham picked him up and threw him in the back of a van. The tractor-trailer rumbled to life and moved forward, while two gunmen torched the General's Mercedes. Their van then peeled out, and Graham rolled around in the back like a side of beef. The chaotic scene was left behind with the General's car now fully aflame.

Three blocks behind and one street over, the vans carrying General Graham's security detail and the press were seen idling on the roadway. Both were on fire. The bodies of the four Security Specialists would soon be found shot to death, their torsos riddled with bullet holes. The reporters and photographers were all shot in the head, their blood splattered across their notebooks and smartphones. The only things taken were the cameras.

The van carrying General Graham screeched to a halt inside a warehouse somewhere south of Ciudad Juarez. The General was so disoriented, his mind spinning as he rolled around the back of the van, that he couldn't keep track of the twists and turns the hostage takers took before they arrived at their destination. They might have gone into a tunnel on the way there. Or maybe it was a parking garage. The General thought they had been on the move for ten to fifteen minutes. He heard the front doors slam shut and then two more on another vehicle. Then he felt the back doors of the van open. The men hauled Graham out the back by his ankles. Four men stripped the General of his outer clothing and removed his shoes. They then took off his hood.

In the garage lit only by a single florescent bulb above the vehicles, General Graham didn't get much of a look at the men. They were all wearing full face masks and military fatigues. "Who are you guys?" he asked meekly.

One of the gunmen raised his right hand and slapped the General across the face.

Once the General recovered from the blow, he straightened up and said, "I'm General T.D. Graham from the United States of America." As if that would put an immediate stop to the violence.

The man gave him another hard slap, the palm-on-cheek smack echoing throughout the cavernous garage. It felt good – like he was slapping the whole country of America with every swipe. "Hola, General Graham," the man said in a low growl.

General Graham tried to determine the speaker. It didn't sound like Camacho or Salazar, both of whom he had spent the last thirty minutes with. And actually the man's accent didn't sound all that Hispanic.

"Who are you guys?"

The man responded with a hard punch to the General's mouth. The only thing that kept Graham from falling backward were the two men holding him by the arms. Now dazed, crimson red blood began seeping through the gaps of the General's whitened teeth.

"Blindfold him and then put the hood back on him."

The men stuffed a gag in the General's bloody mouth and placed the hood back over his head. They hog-tied him and carried him off to a darkened room where they threw him on the concrete floor. The door shut and locked behind them after they left.

The man who punched General Graham removed his hood and wiped the sweat from his eyes. Step one was complete. Everything was going according to his plan.

The man's name was Abdi Rumallah.

The Yemeni terrorist had made sure his shipment of VX had made it safely onto American soil. But when he learned of General Graham's peace mission he could not simply return home to watch Akbar try to assassinate President Schumacher. Rumallah saw one of the greatest opportunities to strike at America, helped out by General Graham's high-minded insistence to come to Mexico to meet with leaders of two of the most violent drug cartels on the planet. The drug cartels had served up General Graham on a silver platter.

Now it was Rumallah's turn to take terrorism to a new level, and if he worked it right, all the blame would go to the cartels.

He grabbed the phone out of his pocket and hit the send button, the number having already been programmed in. Five seconds later, the ringing started.

"Federal Bureau of Investigation, how may I help you?" The call had gone to FBI Headquarters in Washington, D.C. Rumallah didn't want to waste time with a call to the press, the local cops, or the FBI field office in El Paso. He wanted to go straight to the top.

"I want to speak with FBI Director Tyrone Stubblefield," Rumallah said in a slow and calm voice.

"He is out of the office right now," the lady on the other end said. "Can I take a message?"

"I want to speak with FBI Director Tyrone Stubblefield," Rumallah said again. He knew he wouldn't get through to her on the first try.

"Sir, he's not in right now. May I ask what this is about?"

Rumallah's left cheek raised slightly, a smile starting to form in the corner of his mouth. "Yes, I need to get an urgent message to him."

"Okay, go ahead with your message."

Rumallah took a deep breath.

"We have General Graham."

The FBI secretary took down the message verbatim but she did not grasp the significance of its meaning. "I'm sorry, what was that?"

Before the line went dead, the man repeated what he had said.

"We have General Graham."

CHAPTER 22

The Old State Capitol – Springfield, Illinois

A flustered William Cogdon stepped out of the debate in Representative Hall and started pacing the halls again at an even faster speed than before. The statue of the Democrat Douglas seemed to be laughing at him, mocking him on his every lap around the rotunda. Things were not going well. Congresswoman Sanchez had spent the entire evening telling the country how General Graham had brokered a peace deal between the rival drug cartels. She droned on and on about how even-handed diplomacy can bring about peace and tranquility to the world even amongst people who don't agree with each other and the United States. And, with General Graham at her side, she was confident the war on terror could be won. Americans and all the citizens of the world would finally have peace again, she kept saying. Wiley could see her positive poll numbers going through the roof. He just knew it.

Mumbling to himself and wiping the river of sweat flowing down his bald head, the rumpled Cogdon looked up to see his well-dressed counterpart with a smug look of satisfaction on his face. The dapper Bongiorno had worn his finest Italian suit, a dark blue number with pinstripes and a white pocket square. He looked cool as a cucumber, and he would never let anyone see him sweat in public. He was preparing to head down to makeup for a quick touch-up so he could look good while singing the praises of his candidate on the cable-news roundtables that would follow the debate.

Wiley met Bongiorno in the middle of the hall and poked a chubby finger in his chest. "That was a dirty trick you guys pulled, you prick," Wiley growled.

"What are you talking about, Bill?" he asked, looking down at Cogdon from his six-foot-four frame. Of course, the haughty Bongiorno would look down at people if he was only five-feet tall.

"General Graham," Wiley shot back. "With his peace mission to Mexico." He used air quotes around "peace mission." "That was nothing more than a bullshit photo op and you know it!"

"You are upset that we are working hard to bring peace to the world, Bill?" Bongiorno asked. "Are you a little jealous of our success? Or maybe that it came about so easily?" he waved his index finger in front of Wiley's face.

"You mustn't be so quick to anger. It is not good for your weak heart or your small mind." The arrogance of the man would offend an aristocratic Frenchman.

Wiley had to use every ounce of self-restraint to keep from taking a shot at Bongiorno's glass jaw. "You're crowing about peace between two drug cartels? Did you get them to stop sending their illegal contraband to the streets of the United States!?"

His voice had gone up a couple of octaves and was now reverberating off the walls, so much so two Secret Service agents took a step in his direction to find out what was going on. One of Sanchez's campaign staffers shushed Cogdon, fearing those inside the debate would hear his yelling.

Bongiorno needed to get to makeup. He knew he'd have plenty of time to gloat and needle Cogdon later on. "I look forward to working with you during the transition period, Bill." He turned and high stepped it down the stairs with his nose in the air.

Wiley grumbled some expletives under his breath, something about kicking Frenchy's ass. The armpits of his shirt were now fully drenched, and the outline of his undershirt was clearly visible through his once plastic-wrapped Indonesian cotton and polyester button-down. Thankfully, the Schumacher campaign had more telegenic spokespersons to take to the airwaves later on that evening. Wiley grabbed his buzzing BlackBerry.

"Cogdon," he snapped, wondering what the hell else could go wrong.

"Wiley, it's Ty," Director Stubblefield said, his hurried tone indicating something was up. "Get to a private room now."

"What's up?" Wiley asked as he stepped into the empty holding room, the only other life being the TV muted in the corner showing what was going on in the debate across the hall.

"Are you alone?"

"Yeah, it's just me."

"Am I on speaker?"

"No, it's just me and you. What's the matter?"

"Wiley, the FBI in Washington, D.C. took a call about twenty minutes ago from a man saying he has kidnapped General Graham. The General's security detail and the reporters following him were ambushed and have been murdered on the streets of Ciudad Juarez."

"Holy shit."

"Wiley, I'm watching the President on TV right now. And I . . ."

Wiley silently cursed the General before interrupting Ty. "I have got to get him out of there."

Stubblefield agreed. "I don't know who is behind the kidnapping. I don't know if this is the first wave or just an isolated event. But we need to inform the President because a response might need to be made quickly."

"In a matter of minutes."

"Yes."

"I'm going to get him out of there," Wiley said. "Can I give the phone to Agent Craig so you can let him know we need to move?"

"Yes."

Wiley rumbled down the wood floor in the hallway and stopped outside the door of the old House chamber. The President and Sanchez were still at their podiums going back and forth, something about taxes and spending. Wiley checked his watch. The debate could go on for another thirty minutes. With a wave of his hand, he managed to get the attention of Agent Craig and gave him the phone.

Wiley then grabbed the small notebook out of his back pocket. Inside the battered book were pages and pages of the chicken-scratch musings of William Cogdon, written down at all hours of the day in hopes that they would be of use to the President in a speech or a campaign stop. He flipped to the back and ripped out a clean sheet. He then did his best to scribble something legible on the page. He wrote: "General Graham kidnapped in Mex. Must leave now." Ever the political strategist, he drew two lines underneath the word "now." He then added in all caps: "ACT COOL."

"I'm going to get him out of there," Wiley told Agent Craig. "Be ready to go."

"We're ready."

When Wiley put his notebook back in his pocket, he looked down the front of himself. He realized he wasn't wearing a jacket. He looked slightly better dressed than a homeless man. "Shit," he whispered, trying to shove his white shirt into his gray slacks. "I need a jacket."

"You want me to tell him?" Agent Craig asked.

"No," Wiley said, shaking his head. "I need to do it."

Agent Craig then snapped his fingers twice at the Schumacher campaign's legislative director, a rotund gentlemen who spent most of his day on the phone and in front of a computer and definitely not on the treadmill.

"Give me your jacket."

Being a team player, the man whipped off the brown jacket without protest.

Agent Craig helped put it on Wiley and cinched up his tie. He then pushed him forward and said something into his hand microphone.

Wiley took a deep breath. He suddenly realized that he would soon be on every TV in America. Historians would someday note the time and place political strategist William Cogdon interrupted the presidential debate to give the President a message.

"Wiley, go!" Agent Craig whispered into his ear followed by another push.

With his gray slacks, brown jacket, and red tie for all the world to see,

Wiley stepped from the left side of the gathered crowd and entered the area within the view of the cameras. He walked directly to the President.

"Excuse me, Mr. President," he said loud enough for the microphones to hear. "If I could just interrupt for a moment." He then handed the President the handwritten note.

Moderator Anderson had been in the middle of putting a question to the President and was shocked at the intrusion. So was the audience. And so was Sanchez.

"Mr. President," she huffed, once again on the warpath. "Our campaigns agreed that there would be no notes allowed in this debate. If you can't answer the questions without a TelePrompTer or your staff's help, then . . ."

The President held up his left hand instructing her in no uncertain terms to shut her mouth. She complied. He then looked at Wiley and whispered to him. "Are you serious?"

Wiley nodded.

"Would you turn the microphones off, please." The President pushed his microphone away just in case. He then took a step closer to Wiley, the television cameras showing the two with the American flag in between them. The President covered his mouth with his left hand, and tried to act as nonchalant as possible. "Does her campaign know?" he whispered to Wiley.

"I don't think so," Wiley whispered back. The jacket looked like it was four sizes too big. His eyes kept glancing at the camera, his mind wondering what people must be thinking and how it would effect the President's poll numbers. "Ty just called me." He then leaned in closer. "We need to go now."

A hushed silence filled the room. The only noise was an occasional creak from the hardwood floors caused by audience members leaning forward in their wooden chairs in an attempt to learn what was being said. A collection of suits could be seen lining up behind the pillars ready to escort the President out of the hall. The airman with the tight grip on the nuclear football was the last in line and closest to the exit. Everyone wondered what was going on.

"You want me to make an announcement?"

"No specifics, not until we get all the facts," Wiley whispered back.

The President nodded. He folded Wiley's note in half and placed it in his shirt pocket. He stepped back to the podium, grabbed his microphone, and straightened it back closer to him. "Would you turn the microphone back on, please?" He gave it a couple of taps to make sure it was working.

"Ladies and gentlemen," he said looking around the room and then directly into the camera, "and my fellow Americans, I have just been informed that a matter of national security requires my immediate attention. I can assure the American people that they are not in any known danger at this time, but I will need to return to Washington to get fully briefed on the matter. I would like to thank Mr. Anderson for moderating the debate tonight, those in charge of the

Old State Capitol, and the fine citizens of Springfield for their hospitality."

He then turned to Sanchez.

"Congresswoman, if you would please join me, I will fill you in. Thank you all very much."

CHAPTER 23

Air Force One

"Attention on board the aircraft. The President of the United States is now on board. We are officially Air Force One."

Forty-five seconds earlier, the Secret Service motorcade had roared to a stop on the tarmac of the Abraham Lincoln Capital Airport on the northwest edge of Springfield after a record-setting eight-minute ride from downtown. With cameras set up for the President's arrival and filming his every move, the President had walked confidently up the steps to Air Force One, turned to give a quick yet dignified wave, and stepped inside. He had briefed Congresswoman Sanchez at the Old State Capitol with the information he had available, which wasn't much. She was distraught and couldn't believe what she was hearing. He had also considered inviting her to join him on the trip back to Washington, but he was so pissed off he forgot to ask. He didn't need her anyway.

Radio traffic between Secret Service agents indicated no credible threat had been made against President Schumacher. It looked like General Graham's kidnapping was simply an isolated act, reasons yet to be determined. But the Secret Service was taking no chances, and the safest place for the President, save for the White House bunker, was 35,000 feet over the heartland of the United States. Now climbing fast into the dark night, the President would have full communication capabilities, and the secured video conference among the National Security Council was already being put together.

"Ty, who was General Graham meeting with again?" the President asked.

The flat-screen video monitor on the wall of the President's cabin showed Vice President Jackson, Director Stubblefield, Director Michaelson, and NSA Harnacke.

"One was the leader of the Sonoran drug cartel, Joaquin Salazar, and the other was Raul Camacho of the Sons of the Devil cartel," Ty said.

The President banged his fist on the plane's conference table. "That stupid son of a bitch! I told him not to go down there, but he did it anyway!" he fumed. "You don't sit down at the table with a couple of terrorists! And that's what they are – a couple of narco-terrorists! And now we have to get involved to try and clean up the mess. Did he meet with anybody else?"

"He was supposed to have been escorted by a member of President Garza's staff, and there was a charred body found in the remains of the General's car. We have been in contact with the Mexican authorities trying to find out who the man was."

"Could this be Camacho trying to hold the General for ransom, maybe ask for the release of his father?"

"I had thought about that. We'll just have to wait until the man calls back or until he goes public with any demands."

"Do you have any friends in Mexican law enforcement that you can trust?"

"I put a call into Juan Guerrero, my counterpart in the Mexican Investigations Agency. He seems to be in as much of the dark as we are."

"Okay. We're working on a statement up here. If we get credible information on what happened, I'll make a statement once I get back to the White House. Otherwise we'll wait. I want Director Parker in the Situation Room ASAP."

"Yes, sir."

Ciudad Juarez, Mexico

General Graham was lying on the floor in the pitch-black room where he had been thrown an hour earlier. Given the blindfold over his eyes and the hood covering his face, he couldn't even tell whether there was light coming from underneath the door he had entered or whether the room had any windows. He had managed to spit out the gag that had been stuffed in his mouth, which made breathing somewhat easier in the stifling heat of the room. It smelled of mildew. He tried to take stock of his physical condition. His head hurt like hell, his hands and ankles ached under the tension of the ropes tying them together, and he thought he might have urinated on himself, or maybe there had been water on the floor, he really couldn't tell or remember. He heard nothing but the pounding going on between his ears.

After twenty more minutes of silence, the thud from the locking mechanism caused General Graham to lurch over onto his left side. He could feel the heavy combat boots thumping his way. He turned over on his stomach, hoping he wouldn't take a kick to the nose. None came. Just two men who grabbed him by his elbows and set him down on a folding chair over near the wall. A rope was used to tie the General to the chair.

One man grabbed the hood and yanked it off the General's head. Once the blindfold was removed, Graham blinked his eyes trying to bring the two individuals into focus. The only light was from a solitary bulb in the ceiling. Once the General's vision returned, he recognized one of the men.

"Hola, General," Raul Camacho said.

General Graham said nothing. He didn't like being double-crossed. A part of him wanted to spit in Camacho's face. But his jaw was aching and his mouth was too dry to speak or to spit.

"General, I want you to know that kidnapping you was not my idea," a seemingly sincere Camacho said, folding the hood neatly before tossing it on to another chair.

Graham turned his eyes to the other man and tried to size him up. He looked vaguely familiar. "You?" he croaked.

"That's right, General," Rumallah said. He got within an inch of the General's face. "I am Abdi Rumallah, you American dog." He was so close the General could feel Rumallah's hot breath on his face. "I bring greetings on behalf of my brothers in al-Qaeda."

The clenching of Graham's teeth made his jaw ache.

Rumallah and Camacho had worked so well together on the VX they decided to collaborate on a grander plan – one that would serve both their interests.

Once Rumallah learned Camacho and Salazar had agreed to meet with General Graham, he and Camacho devised a plan to kidnap Graham and hold him as the world's most famous hostage. Camacho had a whole host of reasons for the conspiracy. First and foremost was his bottom line. He knew the election of President Schumacher would slow his drug trafficking operation to a crawl, making it more difficult to make a profit. The thought was that kidnapping General Graham would bring sympathy on the Sanchez campaign and lead voters to cast their ballots in her favor to show their support. Once in office, a President Sanchez would be more focused on nationalized healthcare and amnesty programs than on Camacho's drug cartel. It would be business as usual in his mind. Some in his cartel feared kidnapping Graham would bring down the wrath of President Schumacher and the U.S. military and put a stranglehold on the trafficking of drugs into the United States. Camacho, however, was not worried – he knew American politicians were too worried about the Hispanic vote to take drastic action against Mexico.

Camacho also saw two other opportunities present themselves with the capture of General Graham. He could demand the release of his father from U.S. custody, threatening to kill Graham if his demands weren't met. The kidnapping of such a high-profile American, at such an important time in the American political process, would do nothing but raise Camacho's standing in the drug-cartel community. Finally, it brought him face-to-face with his most hated rival, Joaquin Salazar, under the false pretense of calling a "truce" in their own cartel war. When the meeting was over, Camacho and Salazar went their separate ways. But a surprise ambush by the Sons of the Devil and a few specialists from Rumallah's terrorist network resulted in Salazar's decapitated head in a garbage can on the outskirts of Ciudad Juarez. Thus far, the whole violent situation could not have worked out better for Camacho.

Rumallah's motivation for the kidnapping was to seek retribution for

Muqtada Abdulla's execution by the United States. While Abdulla had already been put to death, General Graham's abduction would be a great opportunity to lash out at the Great Satan for its murderous ways. Rumallah would threaten to do the same to General Graham, maybe even jam a syringe full of pancuronium bromide into the General's neck on live TV. It also gave Rumallah an opportunity to take the eyes of U.S. law enforcement off his shipment of VX, which was currently moving slowly through south-central Texas.

Not only would the kidnapping give him time, it would also give him a giant megaphone to spout his evil to the whole world. But there was one other possibility that he could not put out of his mind. One other possibility was on his wish list. He and Camacho had discussed the possibility and how they could make it happen. Whether Rumallah would get his wish depended on what Graham and Camacho could deliver in the coming days.

Camacho opened a bottle of water and poured it near the General's mouth, some of it wetting his lips but most rolling down his chin and into his lap.

"Raul, I thought we had a deal," the General said weakly. He felt betrayed. Just two hours ago he had been grinning from ear to ear while shaking hands with Camacho and Salazar.

Camacho shook his head, almost disbelieving the General could actually be so naive to think he would abide by such a deal like he was some union boss in a collective bargaining matter. "General," he said, "you and I had no deal."

"You had a deal with Salazar," the General reminded him. "You were going to end the violence. What do you call this?"

Camacho reached into his pocket and pulled out a Polaroid picture. The photo was of a severed head, the blood having been washed off but the Castro-style hat still on. He showed the picture of Joaquin Salazar to Graham. "This is what I think about our little deal with the Sonorans."

Graham squinted his eyes at the picture. Camacho provided a second photo, the one taken during the handshake ceremony between the General and the drug cartels. Graham compared the two. It was clear the decapitated head was that of Salazar.

"What do you want?" Graham asked.

Rumallah leaned in toward the General's bloodied ear. He then grabbed the General's throat with both of his hands. "What do I want? What do I want? I want your country out of Afghanistan. I want your country out of Pakistan. I want your country out of the Middle East." Rumallah's hands squeezed tighter with every request before he released the General from his grasp.

Graham struggled to regain his breath. His eyes then looked left. He didn't turn his head because it hurt too much. "I want my country out of those places too," he said. "That's not going to happen with President Schumacher in the Oval Office. You need me and Congresswoman Sanchez to win this election."

General Graham did not feel like he was selling out his country. He sincerely wanted American forces to leave the Middle East. He thought half of U.S. voters wanted the same. It was a policy difference and nothing else. He was willing to make it happen if Rumallah would listen. "We can work this out."

Instead of hearing the General out, Rumallah slapped him in the face. Graham hadn't been hit in over an hour, and it caused the dull pain in his head to roar back to life.

"That's what I wanted to hear, General," Rumallah said. "We have a lot of things to do in the next twenty-four hours."

Camacho yelled something in Spanish out the door to his men. A minute later, two men brought in a video camera on a tripod and set it in front of General Graham. A couple of painter's lamps and their extension cords were hauled in as well. Once plugged in, the two hundred extra watts brightened the General's battered face.

"Okay, smile General," Camacho mocked as he turned on the camera. "Let's see those pearly whites."

CHAPTER 24

The White House – Washington, D.C.

The President landed on the South Lawn of the White House at roughly 1:30 a.m. He hadn't slept at all on Air Force One, and after a long hard day of campaign stops and the debate, he was getting tired. When he got tired, he got cranky. And General Graham's situation had put him in a foul mood.

The Situation Room sprang to life when the President stomped in followed by the disheveled and bleary-eyed Cogdon. Now standing around the table were Directors Stubblefield, Michaelson and Parker, NSA Harnacke, Secretary of State Arnold, Secretary of Defense Russell Javits, and the Chairman of the Joint Chiefs of Staff, General Huey L. Cummins.

"Take your seats," the President said. "Ty, what do we know?"

"We believe General Graham was kidnapped by Raul Camacho and the Sons of the Devil cartel. Joaquin Salazar, the leader of the Sonoran drug cartel who attended the meeting with the General, was found murdered late last evening. His decapitated head was found in a garbage can outside of Ciudad Juarez. Three of his cohorts were also found murdered. We have the video cued up if you are ready."

"Go ahead."

The flat screen TV on the wall came to life with the push of the remote, and the President watched as a beaten and bloodied General Graham appeared on the screen.

"I am General T.D. Graham of the United States," the General started slowly. His eyes then darted back to the left. "I am the Democratic nominee for Vice President. I am currently being held against my will because of the atrocities committed by the United States and the Schumacher Administration against the people of the world." Back went the eyes to the left. "I came in peace but there can be no peace without the resignation of President Schumacher and the end of his murderous leadership in the world." Left again, and then the eyes squinted ever so slightly as the General leaned forward. "If my captors' demands are not met, I will be executed in twenty-four hours."

The screen then faded to black.

"He's obviously being forced to read it," Secretary Arnold said.

The President nodded. "Has the media gotten hold of the video?"

"No," Ty said. "We haven't seen anything yet on TV or on the web. The video was sent to the FBI."

"Do we know the location from where it was sent?"

"Not yet. We're working on it."

"Bill, did you have a drone on him?"

The others in the room perked up at the question from the President to the CIA Director. Given his penchant for secrecy, Parker had not filled anyone in on what his agency knew.

"Sir, we did have a Predator on him." With its sophisticated camera system, the General Atomics MQ-1 Predator had been aloft at 20,000 feet for the last six hours. "At this time, we are still trying to analyze the video. We believe the kidnappers switched vehicles at least once, maybe twice, during the ride until reaching their final destination. We are trying to determine where all these vehicles went. It's possible they are constantly keeping the General on the move."

The President rested his elbows on the back of one of the leather chairs. He then rubbed his face with his hands trying to clear his head. "Do we know the location of General Graham's meeting?"

Ty grabbed the mouse on the table and clicked his way through several windows until he found the map of Mexico. "The meeting took place south of Ciudad Juarez," he said as he used the cursor's arrow to circle the vicinity. "My contacts in the Mexican Government say the meeting was at an abandoned school house that Camacho uses as an office and a staging area for drug shipments."

"Recommendations?" The President left the floor open.

General Cummins stood, something he always did when speaking with the Commander in Chief. "Mr. President, I think an extraction by military force might be in order. I would like to get started on devising a plan. I can have Special Forces on the ground at Fort Bliss by noon tomorrow." Secretary Javits concurred in the recommendation.

"Thank you, General."

Director Stubblefield was next up. "Sir, I think it would be best if I head down to El Paso as well. I will be better able to coordinate any hostage-rescue effort from down there. I have already put the FBI's Critical Incident Response Group on alert. I can get SWAT and HRT teams ready to go by tomorrow morning and we'll standby until we get further information and await your orders."

The President nodded. "Okay. General, Russ, Ty," he said to all of them. "I want preliminary plans as soon as possible. You'll just have to play it by ear until we get more intel. Mike, you gotta start working your Mexican counterparts to see if we can resolve this peacefully."

"Yes, sir."

"Bill, get that drone video analyzed and let these guys know where they need to go if possible."

"Yes, sir."

"Sir, what about a statement?" Ty asked.

The President looked at Wiley. "Do we want to say anything at this late hour?"

Wiley shook his head. He hadn't slept in two days and looked just slightly better than General Graham did on the video. "We should wait until morning. I'll notify the press that you'll make a statement at 9 a.m."

"Anybody else?" The President looked around the room and saw no takers. "All right, let's go get General Graham back."

Ciudad Juarez, Mexico

Rumallah and Camacho had spent the night videotaping the General in varying degrees of distress and requests. The goal was to have as many videos as possible, each with the General's list of the captives' demands, so they could keep the General on the move and hide him before the American cavalry showed up.

"Are your men ready?" Rumallah asked.

"Yes, we can go at any time," Camacho said. "We have three vans, and each one will stop under cover and switch the cargo to one of two other vans and/or cars. The American satellites will not be able to keep up."

"Good. We must be able to keep General Graham hidden until we can get all the pieces of the puzzle into place."

"How much time do you think we have?" Camacho asked.

"The Americans will be putting their response together right now. The military Special Forces and FBI hostage-rescue teams will be able to move within the next twelve hours. Let's send out another video right now."

Camacho gave a series of instructions to his right-hand man. The cartel had spent a large amount of money to wire the safe houses and offices spread across northern Mexico with some of the best technological capabilities available. Broadband Internet along with cable and satellite TV kept the cartel up to date on world news. Surveillance cameras near the border sent images back to operators who coordinated the shipment and pickup of drugs. With a couple of clicks, the man uploaded another of the General's videos to the FBI.

"I am General T.D. Graham of the United States," he said again. He looked more weary on this video than the last. He had been slapped around some more and forced to stay awake with buckets of ice cold water thrown in his face whenever his eyelids closed.

"If the United States seeks my release, it must offer as a sign of goodwill the release of Raul Camacho, Sr." The General's tone was flat and he started and stopped frequently as he tried to read the words on the cue cards.

"He is currently being held by the U.S. at its inhumane torture chamber in Colorado. He was wrongfully arrested by FBI agents Anthony Schumacher and Tyrone Stubblefield, and he must be released immediately or I will be executed."

The General went on to state that U.S. authorities must bring the elder Camacho to Ciudad Juarez, release him to the custody of the Mexican Government, and then Graham would be released at a later time to complete the prisoner swap.

"Abdi, the FBI has acknowledged receipt of the video."

"Good," Rumallah said. "That will give them something else to think about."

"What is the plan now?"

"You must contact your friend in the Mexican Government. Tell him we are willing to meet with the Americans."

"I will have my men contact him at home as soon as possible."

"Good. Now we must move the General out of here. Then we wait for the FBI to show up."

The White House – Washington, D.C.

The President was out of bed by 5 a.m. He was able to get about three hours of sleep. Wiley had crashed in the Lincoln Bedroom for a couple of hours but now had a Red Bull in both hands. He was pissed. So was the President. Both men started their day in the Situation Room, which was never a good sign for the President or his staff.

Director Stubblefield had just landed in El Paso with two plane loads of FBI agents. The Joint Chiefs had readied his forces at Fort Bliss, and an array of helicopters and military vehicles were fueled and ready to go should a planned extraction go forward.

"Ty, go ahead," the President said on the speakerphone.

"Sir, the captors have sent another video," Stubblefield said from the FBI command post set up inside the gates of Fort Bliss. "They are demanding the release of Raul Camacho, Sr."

The President shook his head. "I guess that's not a surprise."

"Not really."

"Where is Camacho being held?"

"He's serving life in Florence, Colorado."

Florence, Colorado is home to the U.S. Penitentiary Administrative Maximum Facility, the federal government's Supermax prison located ninety miles south of Denver. The worst of the worst, at least those not on death row, are housed in the shadow of the majestic Rockies, which, in one last measure of punishment, the prisoners cannot see. The facility's current residents include the "Unabomber," the "Shoe Bomber," the "Olympic Park Bomber," and a whole host of violent murderers, gang leaders, and terrorist conspirators. Most of them would never again set foot outside its protective barrier.

"What else do they want other than a prisoner swap?"

"The General says in the video that more demands will be forthcoming."

"That buys them some more time."

Stubblefield agreed. "And it lets them see whether we are going to agree to their demands."

The President was trying to think the whole thing through. A lot of it wasn't making sense. "Ty, they have to know we're not going to release Camacho. Even if it is General Graham we're talking about. If we did, terrorists all over the world would be picking Americans off the street and demanding their brothers be released from U.S. custody."

"I agree, sir. They have to know the United States does not and will not negotiate with terrorists. And definitely not you."

"There has to be something else," the President said. "Keep your eyes and ears open. And have the FBI send over that second video."

"Yes, sir, right away."

The President looked over at Wiley. "I don't know what the hell is going on."

"It's almost time," Wiley said. "We need to get up to the Oval Office."

While the President and Wiley walked from the Situation Room to the Oval Office, both perused the President's statement to the nation one last time. A thick layer of tension enveloped the West Wing, everybody on edge but nobody knowing for sure what was going on. No one liked feeling they were not in control of a crisis situation. And right now, General Graham's captors held all the cards.

Wiley looked the President over and even told him to blink his eyes a few times to get rid of the cobwebs. Little could be done now to lessen the bloodshot eyeballs short of a good long nap.

"It's all right to be angry," Wiley told him. "Act tough. Tell 'em the United States is going to cross the border soon to kick some ass."

That was just what the President needed. He took his seat behind his desk and straightened the paper statement in front of him. When the red light on the camera blinked on, he gave his ninety-second address.

"Good morning. As many of my fellow Americans are aware, I was called away during last night's presidential debate with Congresswoman Sanchez to deal with a matter of national security. At approximately 6:30 p.m. Central Time last evening, Congresswoman Sanchez's running mate, General T.D. Graham, was abducted at gunpoint south of Ciudad Juarez, Mexico, following his meeting with Mexican drug cartel leaders.

"To those who have committed this dastardly crime – this act of madness cannot and will not be tolerated in a civilized world. We are a nation, and a world, of laws. Laws that protect the rights of free people, and laws that bring justice to those who seek to further their cowardly agenda with bombs, murders, and kidnappings. These laws must be fully respected and followed just as much as the acts in contravention of these laws must be met with contempt and condemnation.

"To my fellow citizens – General Graham is an American patriot, who has worn the uniform in service of our country for over thirty years. I assure the American people that we will do everything we can to get him back safely. Last night, I directed the Secretary of Defense, the Chairman of the Joint Chiefs of Staff, and the Director of the FBI to coordinate a response to secure the General's release. Secretary of State Arnold has been in consultation with his counterparts in the Mexican Government. I have also talked on the phone this morning with Mexican President Felipe Garza, and he has offered his full support.

"To General Graham – please know that you are in the hearts and minds of your fellow citizens, and I ask them to say a prayer for your safe return."

The President then summed it up the best way he knew how.

"And rest assured, General, the United States of America is on the way."

CHAPTER 25

Fort Bliss – El Paso, Texas

Director Stubblefield had been on the ground at the FBI command post set up inside the perimeter at Fort Bliss for four hours. Two mobile command units had been set up to provide Stubblefield with every type of communication device he needed. A SWAT team and a separate hostage-rescue team were pulling on their gear and loading up. They were ready to go.

"Director," Frank Hancock, the FBI's special agent in charge of the El Paso field office, said as he interrupted Stubblefield's conversation.

"Yes."

"Mr. Guerrero is here."

"Thank you," Stubblefield said. "Send him in."

Director Stubblefield stood to greet his guest, extending a hand to Juan Guerrero, the head of the Agencia Federal de Investigasion, or AFI, the Mexican version of the FBI. A short and stocky man with a closely cropped head of hair, he had been one of Mexico's top law men for the last ten years. But it had not been without scandal. His brother was once a leader in the La Familia drug cartel, and it was determined the best way to stop him from continuing his violent ways was to pay him off under the table. And it took a large amount of Mexican pesos to purchase brother Guerrero's peace. Moreover, in his war on the cartels, Guerrero oftentimes liked to shoot first and ask questions later, something human-rights organizations roundly criticized. His brand of justice could oftentimes be just as violent as the cartel's.

The United States had been working with Mexican law enforcement for the last several years to try and restore law and order to the country. The amount of drugs coming in the U.S. and the amount of guns and cash heading in the opposite direction caused both sides to want to work together to stop the illegal flow. Stubblefield had met with Guerrero on one other occasion at a White House reception welcoming President Garza to the United States. He was cautiously optimistic that Guerrero and his agency were serious about cracking down on crime. So far, Stubblefield believed he could trust him.

"Mr. Guerrero, how are you?"

"I am good," he said, shaking the Director's hand. "I wish we could be meeting under better circumstances."

Stubblefield agreed. He was in part thankful that he had jetted to the front lines. Chaos was breaking out back home in Washington, D.C., and he wanted no part of it. The kidnapping of a Vice-Presidential candidate sent the media into a rabid frenzy – an endless stream of breaking news bulletins and press alerts echoing on every network during the wall-to-wall coverage. Every politician in the capital was searching for a TV camera to pontificate on what it meant as to the war on terror and the upcoming election. Some Democrats called on the President to postpone the vote, others blamed him for the kidnapping.

Stubblefield motioned for his guest to sit down and then got right down to business. "I'm sure you can imagine that President Schumacher is not happy with what happened to General Graham."

"I can understand," Guerrero said, nodding his head. "President Garza is also troubled by the situation. One of his aides was killed during the kidnapping."

"Do you know where General Graham is being held?"

Guerrero looked at Director Stubblefield but stopped short of telling him all he knew. Neither he nor the Mexican Government liked the idea of the United States rumbling into Mexico like it was some long forgotten American territory.

"We received a call from the kidnappers within the last hour."

"Where are they?" Stubblefield's voice indicated he better not have to ask again.

"We think they are on the move to Nogales."

"Nogales?"

"The Sons of the Devil cartel has multiple safe houses along the border all the way to Nogales. They are probably trying to keep your General on the move so they can keep the upper hand."

"I need you to work your sources to find out where they are hiding General Graham," Stubblefield said. He intimated Guerrero should work all his sources, even the unsavory types who rarely did business in the light of day. "Whatever it takes. I've got a team ready to go as soon as we hear something."

No sooner had Stubblefield made the statement that Guerrero's cell phone started vibrating on his hip. He grabbed it, punched a button, and looked at the screen. "Excuse me, Director, I need to take this."

"Sure."

Guerrero walked outside, the phone at his ear. He did not say a word to the man on the other end of the line until just before he hung up. "Yes, I understand. I will tell them."

Guerrero walked back inside. The sweat running down the side of his cheek was barely noticeable. He wasn't used to this type of pressure, especially with the Americans involved. Usually he was the one putting the screws to those he sought to intimidate.

"Everything okay?" Stubblefield asked.

"Yes," Guerrero said. He then cleared his throat. "I know where General Graham is. I can take you there as soon as you and your men are ready."

Stubblefield looked at his Mexican compatriot like he had pulled a rabbit out of a hat. "They are ready to release him?"

"Yes. They know your country is amassing its forces. I think they are scared of the American military coming across the border and shutting down their operations."

"Where is he?"

"General Graham is being held at a Nogales safe house." Guerrero said, looking to the door. He wanted to get out of there and head to Nogales as soon as possible. "They will tell us where they are going to drop General Graham once we get there."

"All right, let's go get him."

Nogales, Mexico

Two hundred fifty miles away from the meeting at Fort Bliss, Camacho and Rumallah entered the safe house across the street from the restaurant where the VX had been shipped underneath the border just last week. General Graham had been taken to the basement. He was provided a musty mattress on the floor and a bottle of water. He still had a pounding headache and at times his vision was blurry. He thought he probably sustained a concussion after being kicked in the head. Although he couldn't make out what was being said, he could hear a lot of yelling coming from upstairs.

"We must demand the release of my father!" Camacho yelled at Rumallah. They had been going at it for the last ten minutes, with most of it being Camacho's list of demands that he wanted from the Americans.

Rumallah, however, was getting sick and tired of Camacho's rants. He did not want to be distracted with the real reason why they had kidnapped General Graham.

"The Americans will not release your father, you idiot," Rumallah snapped.

"We have one of their Vice-Presidential candidates!" Camacho shot back. "He is worth more than you can imagine."

Rumallah shook his head. "You are such a fool," he said. "General Graham is an idiot and means nothing to the Americans. He is not even in a position to matter right now. And don't forget, he wants to make your way of life a lot more legal in the United States."

"So we get nothing for General Graham?"

"How many times do I have to tell you? General Graham is simply a pawn in our plan. And let me remind you, if that plan succeeds it will be a benefit to both of us."

"So do we kill him?"

Rumallah didn't answer him. He wasn't sure of what he was going to do with Graham. He would kill him if necessary, but he was not at that point yet. He headed down to the basement to check on his bargaining chip. Once there, he found General Graham sitting against the wall, his eyelids heavy with the lack of sleep and the beatings.

"General Graham," Rumallah said as he knelt on one knee next to him.

"Yes?" The General thought he might be in line for another punch to the head. He told himself to be strong, just like those POWs of the past that had endured harsher conditions than his present state of affairs.

Rumallah pulled a switchblade out of his pocket, hit the release, and the shiny four-inch blade sprang to life. He then gently ran the tip of the blade from the General's ear down to his neck. No blood was drawn, but it did straighten the General's back.

"You are being released today," Rumallah said. The look in his eyes made it seem he was disappointed he wouldn't be able to gut the General right then and there.

Graham looked at him, almost trying to comprehend what was being said. He thought Rumallah said he was being released. He wondered if the videos that he had been forced to read had caused the United States to give in to the terrorists' demands. He had trouble believing President Schumacher would negotiate with terrorists. Even General Graham would not do it if he was sitting in the Oval Office.

Graham thought he'd better ask to make sure he heard right. "I'm being released today?"

"Yes, your FBI is coming to get you."

Graham nodded. "Okay." He wasn't sure whether he could believe Rumallah or not. A part of him thought he might get kicked in the head again. He kept a close eye on Rumallah's knife.

"We just need you to tell them that you are okay. Then we will take you to a drop-off point."

Graham indicated he understood. "And that's it?"

"That's it."

"What are you getting out of it?"

Rumallah glared at him. He actually restrained himself from slapping the General across the face. "You don't get to ask any more questions," he growled. "You tell them you are okay and that's it."

Rumallah motioned over to Camacho, who pulled out his cell phone and punched in the number. He listened until the person on the other end picked up.

"Guerrero," the man said.

"Juan, it's Raul Camacho. I have General Graham here."

"Is he safe?"

"Yes, he is in good health."

There was a short silence on Guerrero's end. "The Director wants to talk to General Graham," he said. They were in the air, about thirty minutes outside of Nogales.

Camacho held the phone in front of Graham's face. "It's the Americans," he told him. "Tell them you're okay."

"This is General T.D. Graham," he said, his voice hoarse and dry.

Stubblefield strained to hear the General's voice over the rush of the jet engines. "General, this is Ty Stubblefield, can you hear me?"

Graham had never heard such a wonderful voice. The cavalry was indeed on the way. "Director Stubblefield, I can hear you loud and clear, sir."

Stubblefield felt relieved. He worried he would have to tell the President that the cartel had killed General Graham, thereby changing the mission to one of recovery and not rescue.

"How are they treating you?"

Rumallah had his arms crossed, his knife firmly gripped in his right hand. Taking that as a gentle reminder, General Graham did not wish to list the human-rights abuses he had endured at the hands of Rumallah and Camacho. That would wait for another day. "I have been treated fine," he said, with both eyes looking directly at Rumallah and indicating he wasn't going to rat anyone out. "I am in good health."

Camacho took the phone away. "I want to speak with Guerrero."

Director Stubblefield handed over the phone. "This is Juan."

Rumallah and Camacho left the room with General Graham and conferred out in the hall. On a map of Nogales taped to the wall, Rumullah pointed his finger at the end of a street.

"We will release General Graham in one hour," Camacho said. "He will be dropped off on the street Calle San Jose just south of the U.S. Consulate."

Guerrero held his hand over the phone and told Stubblefield what Camacho had said. He then told Camacho they would be there soon. After final instructions from Camacho, Guerrero swallowed hard.   "Yes, I understand." He then hung up the phone.

CHAPTER 26

Nogales, Arizona

Director Stubblefield's jet landed in Nogales, Arizona, just across the border from its sister city in Mexico. From there, he could coordinate his men and initiate their plan of attack. The sun was not yet overhead but the heat of the day was fast approaching.

"How much time do we have, Juan?" Stubblefield asked, pulling back the cuff of his shirt sleeve and revealing his digital Timex Ironman watch.

"Twenty-nine minutes."

Considering the vehicles and firepower available, as well as the time crunch, Stubblefield decided to split his men into two teams. Each agent carefully rummaged through the fifty pound duffle bag they had brought with them from El Paso. As they spread out on the tarmac, each man layered on his dark green BDU uniform, Nomex gloves and balaclava, and topped that with their Level IV body armor. Boots were laced tight one last time. Earpieces were in place and radios checked. Last but not least, fully stocked magazines were inserted into their M4 carbines with six spare magazines tucked in the pockets of their body armor for another layer of protection.

"I want two teams ready to go on the ground," Stubblefield said to the thirteen armed men standing in front of him. "And I want the hostage-rescue team in place first. You six will be "Alpha Team." This could just be a simple snatch and grab for us. I'm hoping there won't be a firefight, but let's not take anything for granted. Be on guard, act like we are going into hostile territory. I want snipers on the roof of the consulate. If you see anything suspicious – streets suddenly emptying of pedestrians or window curtains being shut – report in. The rest of us will be "Bravo Team" and we'll provide cover in case something goes wrong. The consulate will be our rendezvous point. Do we have a map of the area around the consulate?"

Guerrero pulled open his briefcase and fished out a map. He had one of every city along the U.S./Mexico border. He found the map for Nogales and spread it out on the hood of one of the vans waiting to carry the teams into Mexico.

"This is where your consulate is located," he said, pointing to the spot. "This is the street Calle San Jose that they mentioned. It runs on the east side.

The consulate also has streets running on its north and south sides."

"Do you have any idea on how this is going to go down?" Stubblefield asked.

Guerrero looked at the map with a blank stare. "I am not sure. Most of the cartel kidnappings don't end well."

Guerrero was well versed in the cartel's modus operandi. After the kidnapping of one of his sources, Guerrero received the man's pinkie finger in the mail along with a list of demands. The cartel once kidnapped a local mayor who had tried to crack down on the rampant drug trade infesting his city. When their demands were not met, the cartel sent the man's family a box containing his teeth – all of them. And they had most likely been pulled while the mayor was still alive.

"Most end in the discovery of a dead body. If a ransom is paid, the cartels will oftentimes dump the victim on the outskirts of town in the middle of the night. I hope and pray that this one will be different than the rest. But I don't think the cartel will decide to drop General Graham off at the front door of the consulate."

"So it could be any one of these streets?"

"Yes."

Stubblefield nodded and then looked at his men. "Okay. You snipers will have to be extra vigilant because we might not have an idea of which direction they're coming from. Keep an eye out for vans making sudden stops or a person walking the streets that looks like they might have been kidnapped and released – disorientation, wounds, bandages. Are they going to call again, Juan?"

"Yes."

"All right," Stubblefield said, whipping off his suit coat revealing a fully-loaded Glock .40-caliber in his shoulder holster. "Let's saddle up."

"Sir, what are our rules of engagement?"

After he pulled the bulletproof vest over his massive frame, Stubblefield gave his final pre-game speech. "Gentlemen, we want General Graham back in one piece. If something goes wrong, you are clear to engage any and all targets." He did not look at Guerrero or ask his permission on a possible response by the FBI on Mexican soil. He just gave the order. Guerrero, for his part, did not raise an objection on behalf of his country.

"Let's make sure we're all in radio contact. I want to know where each team is. We are in unchartered and unfamiliar territory. Keep your eyes open for anything suspicious. Expect something to go wrong and respond accordingly."

Director Stubblefield and Director Guerrero took the seats in the middle of the Econoline van that carried the driver, the front-seat passenger, and two other agents in the back row. The six agents of Alpha Team packed into the other van. The two snipers, both of whom were members of the FBI's elite Tactical Helicopter Unit, were in the dry Arizona air first with the intent that they would beat the two teams to the consulate and provide surveillance and cover for their arrival.

The streets of Nogales, the third largest city in the Mexican state of Sonora, showed a scattering of activity at that noon hour. Among the bevy of local merchants, there were bargains galore for tourists making the short trip south across the border and looking to spread around their American dinero. Mexican-made crafts, leather goods, and pottery were top sellers that would eventually find their way into the home decor of many Americans looking to highlight their southwestern themes. Sidewalk cafes also did a brisk business, and the near football-sized burritos at La Estacion de Sonora were highly recommended by the locals.

Five minutes after takeoff, the Sikorsky UH-60 Black Hawk crossed the Mexican border and made it to the consulate. As it thundered to a hover over the building with its two booming General Electric T700 turboshaft engines rattling the windows in the surrounding area, the two FBI snipers fast-roped to the roof and took their positions.

The lead sniper, D.A. "Duke" Schiffer, the FBI's most decorated marksmen, took his position on the corner of the consulate roof covering the south and east portion of the area. When the curious asked what the "D.A." stood for, the forty-year-old father of two would respond "Dead Aim," his eyes narrowing on the target with an intensity on par with Clint Eastwood. Those wanting to know didn't dare ask if he was joking.

A fifteen-year veteran of the Bureau, Schiffer crisscrossed the country whenever and wherever the best sharpshooter was needed to be the eye in the sky. Schiffer had attended the last ten Super Bowls but had never watched a snap. He usually found his way to the highest perch in the area with nothing more than a bottle of water and his Remington 700P .308 sniper rifle. From there, he could watch everything but the game to keep the spectators safe from any terrorists looking to blow himself up with a suicide vest or spray the crowd with a barrage of bullets. Along with the last three presidential inaugurations, he had also been to six World Series and five Rose Bowls. With his Remington at his side, nobody bothered to ask him if he had a ticket. He spent most of his down time training, sometimes firing two-hundred rounds a day. That would usually be followed by a ten-mile run, and he squeezed in at least two marathons every year just for the challenge. Lately, however, he had found himself on loan to the Secret Service, per Director Stubblefield's orders, to keep watch over President Schumacher's public events.

"Sierra One is in position," Schiffer said into his microphone. His companion sniper, "Sierra Two," was also in position on the northwest corner of the consulate. With its flat roof and four stories, the consulate provided an excellent view of the area. "FYI, Director," Schiffer said over the radio to Stubblefield. "You might want to tell those curious folks in the consulate to take cover and keep away from the windows."

Special Agent Andy Welch radioed in from the Director's van. "Will do, Sierra One. We are approximately five minutes out."

"Keep your eyes open fellas," Stubblefield said to those in the van.

From his prone position, Schiffer flipped open the cap on his rifle scope and scanned the streets below – the crosshairs moving from one pedestrian to another. The rifle had a five-round internal magazine, but Schiffer had his extended to hold seven. Each round could kill a man at eight-hundred yards and all the activity taking place on the streets and sidewalks beneath him was well within his range.

Juan Guerrero reached into his jacket and pulled out his phone. "I need to call them to see if they are still going to make the drop."

"I thought they were going to call you," Stubblefield said.

"No," Guerrero said as he pressed in the number. "I don't think they want you and your men around when they release General Graham. They don't want to be tailed once they dump him."

"So we let them go?" Stubblefield asked.

Guerrero didn't respond. He just looked out the side window and spoke into his phone. "We are getting close. Are you prepared to deliver General Graham?" Director Stubblefield looked at Guerrero and tried to judge the response his counterpart was receiving in his ear.

"And then you will let her go?"

Before another word could be said, the FBI radios crackled to life.

"Sierra One has a visual on a male three-hundred yards south of the consulate," Schiffer said. His attention had been grabbed by squealing tires followed by several screams down the street. Someone in a van had opened the rear doors and dumped a body out. The van took off down the street. Schiffer no longer had a visual on the vehicle, it being hidden by an endless row of buildings. His only visual now was of a naked man lying in the street.

"Is it General Graham!?" Stubblefield yelled into his radio.

"It is unclear," Schiffer responded. "It looks like a white male. The only thing he has on is a dark hood over his head. His hands are tied behind his back."

"Sierra One, is he walking?" Stubblefield worried the cartel simply dumped the General's dead body in the street. If so, the FBI might need to change its plans and go on the hunt to kick some ass.

"He is alive. He is getting to his knees and now he is up. We've got people converging on him. We need someone down there right now. He's on the street called San Jose that runs along the east side of the consulate!" Schiffer had the crosshairs moving between the heads of any one of the four people starting to surround the man. They appeared to be unarmed. One looked like a tourist – a plump gringo with a wide-brimmed hat and a camera dangling from his pale white neck. The other two, a man and a woman, were dressed like locals. One appeared to be a ten-year-old boy. All of them looked like they were trying to help the man.

"Ten-four, keep an eye on him," Stubblefield said. He didn't like that they had dropped off Graham before his teams were in position. "Alpha Team, go get him! Bravo Team will set up a perimeter when we get there."

The Director's van took a hard right. They had no siren or flashing lights to announce their presence so the agent driving the van pounded on the horn as he weaved in and out of the heavy Nogales traffic. The other agents all had one hand on their weapon and the other one gripping onto anything they could find to hold on.

In all the commotion, Stubblefield didn't even notice Director Guerrero yelling into his phone. "You let her go now!" he fumed. He banged his right fist against the inside of the van's door. "You promised to let her go, you bastard!"

"Alpha Team is on the scene!"

Six agents roared to a stop in the middle of the street and filed out of the van. Two agents covered the area to the south and another two covered the north. All four scanned the windows and the storefronts of the shops and restaurants surrounding the area. Those on the sidewalks were running for cover. Two of the good Samaritans froze in place in the middle of the street, not knowing what they had gotten themselves into. The gringo's hands shot straight up into the air. The boy ran off. The last agents hustled to the naked man with guns drawn and ripped off his hood.

"We got him!" one of the agents yelled into his radio as he steadied the disoriented General Graham. Although a bit wobbly, Graham managed a tired but thankful smile. "It's General Graham. He is alive. We got him!"

"Get him into the van! Get him into the van!"

Back in the other van, Stubblefield and his men were still four blocks away zigzagging their way through the traffic.

"Keep an eye on them, Sierra One! Get the General back to the consulate right now!" Stubblefield ordered.

"Let her go, you son of a bitch!" Guerrero kept yelling.

Stubblefield looked over at Guerrero and noticed he was not wearing an earpiece for an FBI radio. Maybe he didn't know what was going on. Maybe he was getting conflicting information. Or maybe his English wasn't that good. Stubblefield wondered why he kept saying "her," it was a "he" that the FBI was after. Guerrero knew that.

"Juan, it's okay," Stubblefield said, reaching over and grabbing Guerrero's wrist. "We got General Graham back."

Guerrero threw the phone into the back of the seat in front him. He unleashed a muffled string of profanities, his face in a contorted rage. He then looked over at Stubblefield. The tears were starting to well up in his eyes. "I'm sorry."

"No, it's okay. We got him back."

"I'm sorry, sir," Guerrero said, shaking his head. "They took my girl."

"What?"

"They took my girl." The tears were now rolling down his cheeks.

"Who? What girl?" Stubblefield didn't know what he was talking about. "What do you mean?"

"I'm sorry. They said they'd release her."

"Release who?"

"They took my daughter," Guerrero said, knowing he had been double-crossed. She was nine years old and had been snatched off the streets as she walked to school that morning. "They said they'd let her go if you came to get the General."

Three blocks from the consulate and before anyone realized they were falling into a trap, the driver of the Director's van suddenly slammed on the brakes.

"Hold on!" the driver yelled as the van crashed into a tractor-trailer truck that had stopped in the middle of the intersection. The occupants of the van lunged forward hitting with a violent bone-jarring thud whatever was in front of them – the dashboard or the seats the other occupants had just been in. The popping sound that soon followed told those inside that this was not a simple traffic accident.

"Bravo Team is taking fire!" Stubblefield managed to yell into his radio. He could feel glass from the van hitting him in the head. He thought he might have broken his left wrist bracing himself. He pressed in the button on his radio with his right hand. "Sierra One, we need cover!"

Hearing a muffled crash to his left, Schiffer had already taken his eyes off the van carrying General Graham to the consulate. To the east, the road was blocked by the tractor trailer. He repositioned himself and his sniper rifle, jammed down the bolt handle, and peered through its high-powered scope. The only part of the Director's van that he could see was the front grille that had wedged itself in between the truck's cab and trailer. He could make out a small fire beginning to take hold in what was left of the engine compartment. A black cloud of smoke could be seen coming up over the trailer. Schiffer then saw movement on both sides of the street.

"Sierra Two! Take the north side of the street!" Schiffer said into his voice-activated microphone. The second sniper had taken position on the northeast side of the consulate's roof and prepared his rifle.

Schiffer readied himself. The rate of his marathon runner's heart had spiked to ninety beats per minute. Someone without his level of training and competence would have their heart pounding at nearly twice that rate and possibly right out of their chest. He emptied his lungs with a giant exhale. His right eye closed, the left one intent on the crosshairs. His left index finger gripped the trigger. When the two men who jumped out of the trailer with AK-47s turned back to look at the Director's van, Schiffer pulled the trigger sending the speeding projectile into the back of the head of one of the men. By the time the second man looked down at the gaping hole in his fellow terrorist's skull and then up toward the west wondering what had just happened, Schiffer had cycled the bolt and squeezed off another round that whistled through the man's left eye. The man dropped to the pavement in a heap right next to his fallen compatriot.

With no other men jumping out the back of the trailer, Schiffer scanned the surrounding buildings with his scope and picked off two more men firing down from the upstairs window of a tailor's shop. Sierra Two had taken out two men on the opposite side of the street. One of the men who had leaned out of an upstairs window to take a better shot at the Director's van took a round in the chest and crashed through the awning of the store below him. The pungent smell of burnt powder hung in the air as the snipers looked for more targets.

Schiffer took charge of the situation. "Alpha Team, you gotta get the package into the consulate and then get east down the street! Now!" He then took out another armed man who had run down the roof of the buildings surrounding the Director's van.

The van carrying General Graham slid to a jarring stop at the rear entrance to the consulate and two agents hauled his ragged body into the safety and security of two armed MPs waiting inside.

From his perch, Schiffer scanned down the street toward the Director's vehicle. He wasn't seeing any movement.

"Director Stubblefield, do you copy?" he asked. After no response, he tried again. "Agent Welch, do you copy?"

Special Agent Welch was wedged in between the dashboard and the front passenger seat. The driver of the van was dead, not from the accident but from a bullet from one of the gunmen. One of the two agents who had been seated in the rear of the van had also been killed. The van was riddled with bullets, the windows gone and the glass strewn all over the inside of the van and on the street. The horrified pedestrians, tourists, and shopkeepers who had taken cover behind any pillar or solid wall they could find were now running away from the scene in a mass panic.

"Is everybody okay?" Welch asked to those in the van he could not see behind him. The firefight had left him short of breath.

Special Agent Jack Munson looked up from his position in front of the rear bench seat. He could feel blood running down the side of his face. His ears were ringing, and he had to reach his finger up to his ear to feel if his earpiece was still in. He had used his entire magazine after firing out the left side of the van. His seat mate had taken the right but caught a bullet in the shoot out. He was gone. Munson inserted a new magazine but didn't see any activity outside the van. He leaned over the seats in front of him and saw Director Guerrero's body in a lifeless heap. He could see two bullet holes in the man's chest. Without any body armor, he had no chance. Munson grabbed him by the neck with one hand and found Director Stubblefield lying underneath. Munson then sprang forward, and with both hands he threw Guerrero off of Stubblefield. He then reached for his radio microphone.

"The Director is down! The Director is down!"

CHAPTER 27

The White House – Washington, D.C.

President Schumacher had just finished an Oval Office meeting with the Israeli prime minister at ten minutes til two. The obligatory handshake photos were taken as they sat near the fireplace and chatted about Israeli security. The President gave his wholehearted support for Israel's efforts in protecting its homeland and vowed to supply Israel with the means to carry out those efforts.

Once the prime minister and the press had left, the President sat down at his desk and picked up the phone. He had left the matter involving General Graham to Director Stubblefield, figuring Ty would call if he needed anything. Plus, it didn't do any good for the President to pace the floor and wait for something to happen. The job of being President didn't stop when a national crisis hit. He wanted to look like the United States Government was open for business and functioning like normal. So he left the heroics to those on the ground. Of course, the Situation Room wasn't too far away if he was needed.

"Carla, can you get me Director Stubblefield on the phone?" he asked of his secretary. "I want to see how things are going down in Mexico."

No sooner had he finished the question than a red-faced Wiley burst into the Oval Office. He was out of breath and looked like he might pass out from overexertion. The President jumped out of his seat and ran around his desk. He worried his friend might be having a heart attack.

"Wiley, what in the hell is the matter!?"

Wiley tried to catch his breath by taking two deep gulps – both of which appeared to come up empty on any air. "Sir, it's Ty," he gasped. "There's been an attack on his vehicle in Mexico!"

With an outstretched arm, the President had to steady himself on one of the chairs, his mind trying to comprehend what his ears had just heard. The color went out of his face, now as white as Wiley's cheap dress shirt.

"The only intel we have is coming from the consulate in Nogales." Wiley was still out of breath. He had sprinted up the steps from the Situation Room and into the Oval Office after he took a call from the Deputy Director of the FBI. Now he was starting to feel a squeeze in his chest.

The President hurried to his desk and picked up the phone. "Carla, get the National Security Council in the Situation Room right now!" He then went to the door leading to his secretary's desk and found his military aide. He ordered him to make sure the Secretary of Defense and Joint Chiefs of Staff were brought directly to the White House.

And fast.

The President hurried back into the Oval Office and found Wiley with one hand clutching his chest and the other one steadying himself on the back of a chair. The President reached into his pocket and depressed the oversized Lincoln penny – his emergency button that would send Secret Service agents running in his direction in no time. He grabbed Wiley by the arm and moved him toward the door. He thought Wiley might collapse.

"I'm going to the Situation Room," he said. "And you're going to the medical office."

"No, I'm alright," Wiley protested, half bent over as they walked. The President could see the sweat rolling down Wiley's face, but that was not unusual.

"You might be having a heart attack. And I'm not going to lose two friends of mine in one day!"

Once out in the hall, he saw Agent Craig followed by two other agents who had their guns drawn. "I need some help here," the President said gesturing. "Wiley needs some help. He's out of breath and has some tightness in his chest."

Wiley stopped dead in his tracks. He couldn't go any farther. The President and Agent Craig lowered him into one of the chairs lining the hallway. Wiley was white as a ghost and dripping with sweat. He felt like he had a box of bowling balls on his chest. He grunted in pain. The President loosened what was left of Wiley's tie and unbuttoned the top two buttons of his shirt hoping to give him a bit of relief. Although his breathing was becoming labored, Wiley managed a faint whisper.

"Go," he told the President, his wide eyes motioning the way of the Situation Room. "Go."

"We've got him, Mr. President," Agent Craig said. Four more agents had arrived in the hall and cleared the way for Rear Admiral Curtis Shepard, MD, the director of the White House Medical Unit and the President's personal physician, along with two of the Admiral's medics. From the medical office on the ground floor, Admiral Shepard carried with him a bag full of supplies along with an automatic defibrillator just in case.

The President watched helplessly as they laid Wiley on the floor. But he had to go. One of his friends was getting the attention he needed. The President didn't know what was going on with the other. He finally relented and sprinted to the steps leading to the ground floor and the Situation Room, two Secret Service agents hustling along behind him. The wail of sirens could be heard piercing the capital afternoon as a bevy of vehicles brought the National

Security team to the White House along with a stretcher for Wiley.

The President entered the Situation Room and immediately felt uncomfortable. When something was going down, he had always asked Director Stubblefield what the problem was and how they could fix it. The terrorists had obviously become aware of how valuable Tyrone Stubblefield was, not only to the Federal Bureau of Investigation but also the President of the United States. And unless he wanted the terrorists to have succeeded in crippling the American President, he had better find the answers he needed from someone else.

National Security Adviser Carl Harnacke was standing at the table with a phone at each ear.

"What the hell is going on?" the President asked.

Harnacke hung up one phone and held the other away from his ear. "From what he can determine, Director Stubblefield split up his agents into two teams. The people holding General Graham dropped him off in the middle of the street and one team picked him up. While that was happening, the other team, which included Director Stubblefield, was ambushed as it was heading to the U.S. Consulate."

"How many FBI agents went down there with him?"

"Twelve agents, plus Director Stubblefield," Harnacke said as he looked down his list of notes. "The group also included Juan Guerrero, the head of Mexico's Federal Investigations Agency."

Now the President was getting pissed. The only way anyone would know Ty was coming to Mexico and where and when he was going to be at a particular place was if there was someone on the inside tipping off the cartels.

"I either want Deputy Director Patterson on line at FBI Headquarters or get him down here right now!"

"Yes, sir."

General Cummins barged into the Situation Room, made eye contact with the President, and fired off a snap salute. The President responded in kind. Both looked like they were ready to charge through the southern border and take on all-comers.

"General, where is your extraction team?"

Cummins had already made the call. "Mr. President, I have two Special Forces teams on their way from El Paso. Each Black Hawk helicopter will be flanked by an Apache attack chopper. I also have two F-16 Fighting Falcons and two Apaches from Luke Air Force Base just outside of Phoenix in the air and heading south."

The President nodded his head. He was having trouble concentrating. He kept wondering if Ty had told him that he was going to Nogales. Wasn't it Nogales, Arizona? Or did he say he was actually going into Mexico? Surely the President would have told him not to go into harms way. He was too valuable to the country to have him get into any trouble, and General Graham wasn't worth that level of a risk. He couldn't remember their last conversation.

"Sir?" General Cummins asked.

The President looked at him and snapped out of it. "That's good, General. As soon as we find out where he is, we'll be better able to give the go-ahead."

The Marine standing guard opened the door for the Secretaries of Defense and State.

Secretary of State Arnold hung up his cell phone, and wasting little time, he fired off what he knew. "Sir, I just talked with my counterpart in Mexico and they are advising that they have ordered the military to Nogales."

"Mike," the President snapped. "I don't know whether I can trust anything the Mexican Government tells me right now."

"They also wanted me to tell you that this is not a cartel hit."

"I don't care who did it," the President shot back. "I just want to find Director Stubblefield."

Harnacke put his caller on hold and pressed the remote control. "Sir, we are getting some video from the consulate."

The President and the others turned their focus to the flat-screen on the wall. The pictures showed a carpeted hallway in the interior of the consulate, the hurried camera operator obviously fumbling around with the camera as he walked. Once inside one of the rooms, the video showed General Graham sitting on a folding chair and drinking a bottle of water. His comb over was no longer over, just all over the place in a mess of hair. He had been given a pair of gray sweatpants and a blue T-shirt. After taking one last swipe of his face with a towel, he noticed the cameraman coming at him and managed to lift his tired old bones out of the chair. Everyone in the Situation Room had forgotten all about General Graham. They all leaned forward to take a good look.

"I am okay, Mr. President," Graham said weakly. His eyes were red and heavy, like they hadn't seen sleep for three whole days. He was able to show those watching his rows of teeth and give the camera a weak thumbs-up. "I'm okay."

An irate President Schumacher pounded his fist on the table. "I don't give a rat's ass about General Graham, damn it!" Several in the Situation Room were startled by the President's anger. He looked like he might reach through the TV and beat the crap out of the General. If it came down to it, and given that Graham was responsible for the mess they were now in, the President would have traded him for Ty right then and there. "I want to know what's going on in the damn street!"

The video was not a live shot, just one that those in the consulate cobbled together in haste to let those in Washington know that the package had been delivered safe and sound.

"Get me somebody on the phone who knows what the hell is going on!"

"Sir," Harnacke said. "I'm trying to get somebody who can give us some real-time intelligence."

Without thinking about it, the President picked up the phone and hit the speed dial for Ty's cell phone. He had called the number a hundred times before, and he didn't know why he hadn't thought about it sooner. But all he heard was a busy signal, the pulsing dull tone indicating something ominous had indeed occurred.

"Mr. President, I am receiving a report from one of the sharpshooters on the consulate roof that radio traffic from Director Stubblefield's van indicates he has been hit," Harnacke said, gulping hard. He said it again just in case it hadn't been heard. "He has been hit, and I'm afraid to say that there are fatalities."

The President paused to take a breath. His shoulders visibly slumped. Tyrone Stubblefield had been one of his best friends for over thirty years and saved his life on two occasions. Now the President felt powerless to return the favor. He had to keep it together. He closed his eyes to keep the tears from rolling down his cheeks in front of the others in the room. None of them said anything. Nothing needed to be said.

"They are attempting to reach the wreckage of Director Stubblefield's van."

The President nodded. He then picked up the phone.

"Would you get me the First Lady, please?" he asked quietly. He rubbed his forehead during the ten-second wait. "Elle," he said when his wife came on the other end of the line. "I'm going to need you to go be with Tina. There's been a problem down in Mexico. I'm not totally sure of what's going on but I think you should go be with her."

After a few seconds of silence, the President rescinded his order. "Elle, I've changed my mind." His mind was running at what seemed like a thousand miles per hour. "I'm going to have the FBI bring Tina to the White House. That way we can all be together once we find out what's going on."

The President gently returned the phone to its cradle. General Cummins had been whispering into the ear of the Secretary of Defense, filling him in on what he had missed prior to his arrival. The Secretary nodded and said something to the General under his breath. Both of them needed an answer from the President.

Cummins cleared his throat. "Mr. President, I have to ask. Our aircraft will soon be flying into Mexican airspace."

The minds of those in the room envisioned a royally pissed off Commander in Chief in charge of a heavily armed U.S. military force with orders to cross the Mexican border and carpet bomb the country with troops or missiles or everything else in the U.S. arsenal – maybe make the area between the Gulf and the Pacific a parking lot or a deserted wasteland. Given that the United States was not at war with Mexico, some were understandably skittish about sending an armed presence onto foreign soil.

"Sir, I need to know. How far can we go?" General Cummins asked.

After the subdued call to the First Lady, the blood in the President's veins was slowly starting to boil again. For a fleeting moment, he wondered what President Reagan would do. When the "Mad Dog of the Middle East" was barking up the wrong tree in the '80s, military leaders asked Reagan how far the U.S. could go if Quaddafi's jets attacked American aircraft over international waters. Reagan did not waver and simply said, "All the way into the hangar."

President Schumacher started punching his right fist into his left palm. The fury in his eyes indicated the President didn't want the military stopping to worry about diplomatic niceties or to ask permission to come aboard. He wanted them to go all out.

"All the way to Mexico City."

CHAPTER 28

Nogales, Mexico

The six agents making up Alpha Team were skidding to a stop near the wreckage of the Director's van. The acrid smell of a small engine fire hit their noses when their boots hit the pavement. The streets were eerily quiet, almost like an old Wild West ghost town. The locals had endured years of cartel violence and had learned early on it was best to ride out the storm of bullets by hiding inside the nearest building and away from windows. It wasn't that much different from Floridians taking cover from a hurricane. Except in this region of the world, the disaster blowing through town was always man-made.

Two agents took up a position on the east side of the tractor-trailer to keep an eye on anyone seeking to show up for a second assault. The other four headed to the Director's van. Once there, they found Agent Welch struggling to remove Guerrero's dead body so he could get Director Stubblefield out of the van.

"He took a round through the shoulder!" Welch said to the others. "He's got some blood on his thigh too."

The Director's body armor had stopped one round and Guerrero might have actually saved him from several other bullets hitting their mark. Through the shifting of bodies and protective apparel, one bullet had found its way into the Director's left shoulder. Another lodged in one of his muscular thighs. His large body had become so wedged in between the seats that Welch was having trouble getting him out.

"We're going to need a first-aid kit," Agent Welch announced.

"We've got one in the van," Agent Nick Boston said. "I'll go get it."

Welch climbed back into the van and ran his hands over the Director's outer clothing, looking for any other entry or exit wounds. "Director, are you sure you're not hit anywhere else?"

Slightly groggy and in pain, the fifty-five-year old Stubblefield responded he didn't think so. "I think it's the shoulder," he grunted. "My thigh feels like it's on fire, too."

"Director, we're going to have to get you out of the van and to a hospital," Welch said. He looked at the others. "Is there an ambulance coming?"

There were no sounds of sirens on the way, the streets were empty of not only the regular folk but also any first responders. But the agents didn't feel like they were alone. It was anybody's guess as to who was hiding inside the buildings. It made the agents want to get the hell out of there. Fast. And none of them wanted to barge into and secure a Mexican hospital anyway. They wanted to return to more friendly pastures north of the border.

"We need to get him back to the United States," Agent Boston said, returning with a case of medical supplies.

Agent Welch agreed. "We'll get him in the other van and have the Black Hawk pick us up." He grabbed his radio. "Sierra One, we need that Black Hawk and a safe landing zone to get the Director on board!"

"Roger that," Schiffer responded.

Agent Welch grabbed hold of Director Stubblefield's legs and two other agents tried to get their arms around his torso without moving his shoulder. He winced in pain and reached for his leg, which only caused the pain in his left shoulder to increase. After a bit of effort, the agents managed to get him outside of the van. They laid the Director on the sidewalk so they could remove his vest and attend to his wounds. His white dress shirt was soaked with blood in the shoulder and it wasn't stopping. Welch could feel some wetness on the back of the Director's slacks. Two packages of military-grade field dressing bandages were ripped open and applied to the Director's wounds. The necessary clotting would take place in a matter of minutes – if the bandages worked properly and there weren't any other more serious wounds.

"We're gonna have to get moving quick," Agent Welch said.

Director Stubblefield's mind was clear enough to issue one last order before they left. "Make sure you bring the rest of the team with us," he said, his eyes looking back at the van. "We don't leave without them."

Boston went back in to get the two downed agents. He pulled them out to the sidewalk. He left Guerrero's bullet-riddled body behind in the van.

After Schiffer called for the return of the Black Hawk, he reloaded his magazine. He then turned his attention to the area of the Director's van. From his perch, he saw a line of vehicles coming at him from the east, and the rooster tails of dust behind them indicated they were coming at a good clip.

Schiffer looked through his scope once again and made the call. "Alpha and Bravo Teams, be advised. You're about to have some company."

"Are they friendly?" Welch asked, looking east but unable to make out who they were.

"I can't tell who they are, but I do know that they are armed. Repeat, they are armed and coming fast."

Two black Dodge Ram trucks were speeding to the scene, and at least four men with large weapons were hanging on in the beds.

Sierra Two was looking through his scope. "It looks like it says 'policia' near the tops of the windshields."

"I'm not sure we can trust them," Schiffer responded. His right eye closed, and the middle of the crosshairs followed the lead truck as it sped to scene.

"Let's hurry up and get the hell out of here," Agent Welch said, grabbing hold of the Director's legs. "Sierra One and Two, we need you to hold 'em off for a couple more seconds!"

Both snipers zeroed in and fired off warning rounds into the grilles of the speeding Rams, blasting a hole in the radiators. That should have put any well-trained police force on notice that they might want to rethink about coming any more forward. Or at least consider slowing down to size up the situation. The trucks, however, continued on with full heads of steam. The drivers were intent on proceeding onward.

Sierra One then called for tire shots, and the rounds whistled through the Nogales sky, finding their way into the right front Firestones. With rubber shrapnel spitting into the air and the right-front quarter panels ripping apart, both trucks lurched right as the drivers tried to regain control before crashing to a stop in a drainage ditch. Two men were thrown from the back of the pickups. The remaining eight, none of them in any type of identifying uniform, decided to hoof it the rest of the way, taking their weapons with them.

"Let's go, guys!" Schiffer yelled over the radio. "Let's go!"

The relative silence on the roadway in and around the Director's van was broken by the skidding tires of a beat-up and rusty Chevy pickup that rear-ended Alpha Team's idling van on the west side of the tractor-trailer in a crash of metal and glass. The concussion rattled the members of both teams and stopped them in their tracks. The men jumping out with an array of weapons indicated they were not members of the Red Cross looking to render first aid.

"You've got four more coming from the west!" Schiffer warned.

Agent Welch dropped the Director's legs he was holding and hit one of the men in the chest with the Colt 1991 .45-caliber pistol that had been strapped to his thigh. Schiffer took out two himself and Sierra Two ended the attack with a shot to the head of the remaining gunman. But things were not getting any easier.

"Eight of them from the east!" Schiffer yelled. "Let's go, guys! Let's go!"

Agent Welch grabbed the Director's legs again as Boston grabbed hold under his right arm and back. Two other agents grabbed their fallen comrades. The rest started firing at the men running toward them. The agents hustled around the front of the tractor-trailer to find their van had been pushed into a light pole. With the attacker's crumpled Chevy stuck under the rear bumper, Alpha Team wasn't going anywhere in their van. Plan B would have been to load the Director into the back of the Chevy and haul ass to the safety of the consulate. But the Chevy would soon be fully engulfed in flames. The situation looked like their last resort would be a three-hundred yard sprint to the consulate.

"Sierra One!?" Welch yelled into his radio. He didn't ask a direct question, but the tone of his voice indicated he needed help finding a way out of the chaos.

Schiffer was surveying the scene and things were not looking good. The cartel and terrorist tag team had walled off a five-block area around the scene of the Director's van. Once it became known that the FBI agents were still alive and attempting to evacuate Director Stubblefield, the terrorists sent in the second and third wave to finish the attack. They knew they had to be quick because they couldn't control the situation for much longer. They had to take out Director Stubblefield right now.

Sierra One could see terrorist reinforcements racing up the streets to the north and south of the consulate and converging on both teams. The mound of spent and still smoldering cartridges were piled along the right side of his Remington like a bag's worth of discarded peanut shells. He loaded in another two rounds to top off. He wiped the sweat off his brow, the consulate's black tar roof making it close to a hundred and twenty degrees. He looked up and saw another truckload of terrorists heading from the east. With both Alpha and Bravo Teams about to become completely surrounded and without any vehicles available to aid their escape, Schiffer had to make the call.

"Alpha and Bravo Teams, you're going to have to seek cover! Seek cover!"

With desperation in his eyes, Agent Welch was looking directly west to the consulate when he got the word. He looked to his right and figured door number one would have to do. The restaurant looked abandoned – the windows dusty and the display menus faded from the time spent in the sun.

"Sierra One, we're heading to the restaurant on the corner! The restaurant on the corner!"

"Roger that!"

As they got closer to the door, they noticed the sign hanging in the window – "Closed for Business." Perfect, Agent Welch thought. There wouldn't be anyone inside. One agent blasted through the glass in the front door. Welch and Boston carried the Director inside, and the remaining agents, living and dead, followed right behind. The booths and tables were quickly overturned and thrown in front of the door.

"Sierra One, we're inside!"

"Roger that, I see your location. Sierra Two, get on the horn with the military and tell them we need air cover."

Ten seconds later, a cadre of terrorists skidded to a stop out front of the restaurant. Ten AK-47 wielding men took up positions on the east side of the tractor trailer and behind various vehicles preparing to unload on the windows and everything inside.

"Get to the rear of the building!" Schiffer yelled over the radio. "Get away from the windows!"

Spent shells from the AK-47s littered the roadway, and the sound of gunfire echoed off the buildings as the cartel opened up their own personal shooting gallery on the restaurant.

Schiffer and Sierra Two picked off two men who had made the mistake of sticking their heads out from behind the trailer and into their crosshairs. Schiffer took a chance and fired a single round into the bottom of the fuel tank of the tractor-trailer's cab. When the leaking diesel fuel hit the fire from the Chevy engine, the cab erupted into a ball of fire, the blast shattering the windows and killing the three terrorists who had staked out positions on the east side of the cab. One other had his shirt catch fire and he frantically waved his arms hoping the flames would subside before he burnt to death. The blast and ball of fire also scattered a handful of other gunmen, who were growing increasingly impatient with the lack of progress on the building.

"Get inside!" Raul Camacho yelled to his men. The leader of the Sons of the Devil himself was on the front lines to take out the Director of the FBI and rid him and his cartel of one of America's top law men. His right hand was pointing in the direction of the restaurant. "Get inside now and get him!"

Whenever one of his men made an attempt to enter, they were pushed back by the FBI agents inside firing over the counters and overturned tables. Welch and Boston could see some of the cartel members running for their trucks. They worried the trucks could be used to crash through the front window. If that happened, they were done. Welch and Boston knew they couldn't hold off the cartel much longer. They were running out of ammunition. And they were running out of places to hide.

"I'm going to see if there's a back door out of here!" Welch yelled to Agent Boston.

Crouched low and with his M4 raised, Welch kicked open the swinging door to the kitchen and a blood curdling scream echoed through his ears. The red dot from the weapon's laser sight landed in the middle of the forehead of a Mexican woman hiding behind a kitchen table. She had her arms wrapped around her six-year-old daughter. The little girl started crying at the sight of the man pointing a gun at her mother.

"Por favor!" the woman cried.

"How many others!?" Welch yelled back at her. He looked beyond her and around the refrigerators and shelves of canned goods. "How many others!?"

"No one," she said, shaking her head back and forth and covering her daughter's head. The two lived above the restaurant in a one-bedroom apartment. "It's just us."

Welch made a quick check of the rear of the kitchen and radioed Welch to get the teams inside. He realized he just picked up two more members of the teams. He told the woman and child to move to the corner and motioned for them to stay down.

"Sierra One, is there a way out the back!?"

Schiffer took his eyes off the front of the building long enough to see a truckload of cartel members readying to come in the rear of the building. They were all armed.

"Negative!" he responded. "Negative! You have two trucks and ten men coming from the north!"

Sierra Two activated his radio. "We've got two Apaches on the way for air support! Just hold on! Hold on!"

An exhausted Welch was able to drag Director Stubblefield into the kitchen. The men could taste the salt from the sweat pouring down their faces. The body armor and midday heat had left their BDUs drenched. It felt like they had been doing battle for a day and half. Those who weren't hunkering down to ward off an assault from the cartel were rummaging through the drawers and cabinets looking for knives, clubs, or anything else that could be used as a weapon if it came down to hand-to-hand combat. Agent Boston made one last attempt to find another way out of this mess.

"Director," Agent Welch said. "Air support is on the way. We just gotta hold 'em off a little while longer!"

Stubblefield nodded. The big man was growing weak. He winced in pain at least twice a minute. He reached his right hand into the shoulder holster still strapped to him. He undid the leather strap and handed over his Glock to Welch. There were seventeen rounds in the magazine. They didn't have much else left. He looked at the Mexican woman and the little girl crying in the corner. The girl was wearing a red dress and had a flower in her hair. Between sobs, she kept pointing to the opposite corner of the kitchen.

"La puerta," she whimpered. "La puerta."

Director Stubblefield took notice. "What's she saying?" he asked, his voice hoarse.

Boston had noticed too. "She keeps saying 'the door,' 'the door.'"

While Agent Welch crouched in the doorway with the Director's Glock, Boston went to check on the puerta. He thought it might lead to the street to the west of the restaurant and maybe they could make a run to safety.

"Get in there, damn it!" Camacho yelled. He couldn't take it anymore. It was time to finish off the Americans once and for all. "Get in there!"

He sprayed the front of the building with his own AK-47 in disgust. Unable to take any more of his men's failed attempts at entry, Camacho sprinted back to his truck. He reached inside and pulled out his gold-plated baby – a fully functional M16 with a M203 grenade launcher attached. Still in the shadow of the tractor trailer and out of the view of the snipers, he inserted the 40mm high-explosive round in the barrel.

"Get out of the way!" he yelled at his men.

With a pull of the trigger, the round lit up the barrel and snaked into the outer wall of the restaurant. The entire front of the building erupted in a billowing cloud of dust.

"Apaches are on their way!" Schiffer reported, seeing the helicopters a mile and a half from the scene. He could not will them to move any faster.

Camacho inserted another round and fired another shot into the opposite wall of the building. Schiffer could feel the tremor from the top of the consulate. The blast weakened the front facade and the bricks and mortar crashed to the ground in a thundering rumble. Without the support of the restaurant's wall, the wall of the basket shop next door could no longer hold its load and it collapsed in a heap on top of the rubble. Then the back of the restaurant caved in. The west wall crashed into the street.

Camacho had no more grenades. But he didn't need anymore. His mission was complete. He motioned for his men to move.

"Vamanos! Let's go! Let's go!"

CHAPTER 29

The White House – Washington, D.C.

"Mr. President," NSA Harnacke said. "We're getting live footage from Mexico's Telemundo network."

The flat screen on the wall of the Situation Room showed two Apaches hovering in a whirring rush a hundred yards east of the restaurant, one on the north side and the other on the south. Both looked like a pair of angry hornets poised to strike if necessary. Five minutes earlier, both had unleashed a hellish barrage from their M230 chain guns. At three-hundred rounds per minute, the Apaches sprayed the now outgunned cartel members with piping hot 30mm rounds. The helicopters took no return fire.

The bloody battle had finally come to an end.

Once it was clear that the shooting had stopped, the Telemundo cameraman cautiously made his way down the sidewalk, hugging the building just in case the Apaches had anything left in their weaponry for him. The street-level view showed the tractor-trailer fully engulfed in flames and thick black smoke billowing into the blue Mexican sky. There was no movement in the streets, just the remains of the carnage that had taken place within the last thirty minutes. Piles of dead bodies, some with little left of their skulls and one which was nothing but a charred skeleton. Spent shell casings littered the ground like rice after a wedding.

The Telemundo reporter yelled something at his cameraman and started pointing here and there in harried fashion. It was apparent the reporter had been running to the scene because he was out of breath, his dark hair out of place. He cautiously stepped in to the street and pointed a finger at the mound of rubble that used to be the restaurant.

"Oh man, General," the President said, taking a closer look at the pile of bricks and mortar. "Did we do that?"

General Cummins had a phone to his ear as he watched the footage. When he got the answer, he put his left hand over the receiver. "Sir, that's a negative," he said. "Both Apaches had sixteen Hellfire missiles and none were fired. The building apparently came down before they reached the scene."

"Mr. President," NSA Harnacke said, himself on the phone. "I have FBI sniper Schiffer on the phone. He was on the roof of the consulate when this all went down."

"Put him on speaker," the President said. "Agent Schiffer, this is Anthony Schumacher, can you hear me?"

"I can hear you, Mr. President." Schiffer said. Drenched in sweat, he was on his feet for the first time in what seemed like hours. He was looking east down the street and staring the Apache pilots in the face as they remained on guard.

"What can you tell us about Director Stubblefield and his teams?"

"The van carrying the Director and his team was attacked by gunmen while the other team picked up General Graham. After dropping the General at the consulate, Alpha Team went to provide cover for the Director and his team. Multiple waves of gunmen prevented any attempt of making it safely back to the consulate. They took cover in a restaurant, but the cartels or terrorists, whoever they were, fired multiple grenades into the building and the walls collapsed."

"Oh, man," the President sighed. "Agent Schiffer, we're getting some pictures on the ground of a mound of rubble north of a burning trailer. Is that the building the Director and his teams went into?"

"Yes, sir. I have not had any radio contact with the teams since the collapse."

"All right, thank you, Agent Schiffer," the President said grimly. "General, let's get search-and-rescue teams down there right now."

The President wanted everything the General had – dogs, heavy equipment, and sophisticated listening devices able to hear even the faintest of calls for help.

"Yes, sir." General Cummins picked up another phone and executed the order.

"And get General Graham back to the United States. We're going to have to debrief him and find out who the hell's ass we're going to kick."

"Sir," NSA Harnacke interrupted. "CNN just came on with a live report."

The anchor in the studio notified the world that breaking news was occurring in northern Mexico just south of the U.S. border. The flashing red banner underneath the map of Nogales included an icon showing an exploding cloud of something and a headline that blared "FBI Director Attacked."

"Let's go to Hernando Gomez who is live on the scene," the anchor said. "Hernando, what can you tell us?"

The President of the United States and his national security team sat staring at the TV screen, wondering what Gomez would indeed tell the world. NSA Harnacke reached for the remote and the green volume bars increased in number.

"William, I can tell you that it is a chaotic scene down here in Nogales." The scene behind him showed a convoy of Mexican police vehicles and a line of ambulances, the latter of which had finally made it to the scene once it was determined the bloodshed had ended and the medics wouldn't be in harm's way. Firefighters were opening up their hoses on the tractor-trailer's burning remains. "FBI Director Tyrone Stubblefield had traveled to Nogales with a dozen FBI agents to oversee the transfer of General T.D. Graham, the Democratic Party's candidate for Vice President, who had been kidnapped two days ago by Mexican drug cartels. The van carrying Director Stubblefield, as well as Juan Guerrero, the head of Mexico's Federal Investigations Agency, was ambushed and a bloody shootout ensued."

The cameraman focused the lens on the blood in the streets, and CNN split the screen with the live shot and a file photo of Director Stubblefield, clad in a dark suit and seated in front of an American flag.

"Director Stubblefield and a team of FBI agents were able to seek shelter in this abandoned restaurant," Gomez said, pointing over his shoulder. "But it collapsed as a result of the continued assault. William, I just talked with an anonymous Mexican official on the scene who told me Director Stubblefield was killed in the attack."

The President slumped into his high-backed leather chair. No one else in the room wanted to look him in the eye, some looked at the screen, others looked down at their shoes. Nothing was said. NSA Harnacke grabbed the remote again and turned down the volume of the TV, not wanting the President to have to hear the anchor repeat over and over again what he had already reported. It would just make him feel worse.

The President thought of Tina Stubblefield and wondered the emotions she must be going through right then. He wouldn't believe the news until he was absolutely sure, but he had to head to the White House Residence to at least tell Tina and the First Lady what he knew. He didn't want her to get any more of the details from CNN. It would be one of the longest walks of his life.

He pushed back his chair and cleared his throat. "General," he said softly. "Let me know when the search-and-rescue teams arrive on the scene."

"Yes, sir."

Texarkana, Arkansas

The smoke from the Dutch Masters grape cigarillo rolled out the passenger-side window of the white van and disappeared into the gray Arkansas sky. Mohammed Akbar sat at the end of a row of parked cars at the first rest area Arkansas had to welcome those traveling east on Interstate 30. He, along with the driver Moamar Abbed, had flown down to Nogales from Chicago last week and waited for the VX to come up from Mexico through the border tunnel. Now, they, along with Yousef Musharra and Habib Nasra, who were both hauling the VX, had finally made it out of Texas, a long and arduous journey through the Lone Star State that required them to dutifully obey all posted speed limits and the myriad of other vehicle laws that could slow them down or tip off law enforcement and derail their plans altogether. They stopped only for food, gas, and to empty their bladders. One would drive, while the other slept. Now they were two and half hours away from Little Rock, and with luck they could make it to West Memphis by nightfall.

"Can you believe it?" Abbed asked. He had asked the same question five times in the last ten minutes.

The AM radio had been on for the last two hours, and all that the talk heads were discussing was the attack on America's FBI Director. It was Akbar's time to nap, to rest up for his stint on the nighttime drive to Cairo in southern Illinois. But now was not the time to sleep. He thought he could make it all the way to Terre Haute without stopping. He was smoking the cigarillos to calm him down from the euphoria of the moment not from any bouts of anxiety that he was having.

"Brother Rumallah has come through just like he promised," he said.

"He has decapitated the FBI," Abbed said in a tone full of wonder. This was huge news, something that many terrorists had failed to do – take out those in the upper echelon of the United States Government. Muslim extremists would be dancing in the streets of Karachi, and Aden, and Beirut once the news reached their shores.

Brother Rumallah had the wherewithal to stay out of Camacho's war with the FBI. It was his plan to lure Director Stubblefield to General Graham's pickup spot. Rumallah convinced Camacho that it was his best opportunity to show his muscle and prove his worth in the criminal underworld, and Camacho could not resist the temptress of power. All Rumallah and his band of terrorists had to do was let Camacho do their work for them and watch the carnage unfold from a safe distance. Once the battle was over, Rumallah and his men slipped out of Nogales and headed to the United States through one of Camacho's drug tunnels. It had been a brilliantly executed plan on his part – the damage to the U.S. was done, and Rumallah hadn't even gotten his hands dirty.

Musharra and Nasra walked out of the rest area and stopped at Abbed's window. He told them what they had missed while inside, and they took great joy at the Americans' distress. Both of them gave praise to Allah.

"Camacho was killed?" Abbed asked, returning his focus to the radio and wondering if he heard the talk head correctly. He turned up the volume. "And thirty members of his cartel?"

Akbar couldn't care less about Camacho and his cartels or the loss of life. His focus was on those in power in Washington, D.C. He could just envision what was going on in the White House and in the Hoover FBI Building. "The Americans will be in total disarray. We have stabbed them in the eye with a dagger."

"But they will respond," Abbed said. "You know President Schumacher will respond with strikes in Afghanistan and Pakistan just like he did after the attack on the National Archives. Our brothers will be in the crosshairs once again."

"No, they won't," Akbar said. He flicked the cigarillo out the window, the butt end sparking in the plume of ash on the pavement. He shifted in his seat and looked at Abbed. "They will blame the cartels for the attack. They won't find any fingerprints of al-Qaeda. All of the Americans' energies will be focused on their 'war' with Mexico. They will build their walls and shut down their southern borders."

It was indeed a brilliant plan on Rumallah's part, the men thought to themselves.

"And we will strike the U.S. from within," Abbed said.

"Yes," Akbar said. He could imagine federal and state law-enforcement personnel looking at their televisions with shocked faces. They would assemble on the border looking to settle the score with the Mexicans and would be too distracted to discover what Akbar had planned for the President. His plan was coming together better than he could have imagined. He fished out another cigarillo from the pocket inside his jacket. "While they are amassing their personnel and weapons on the southern border, we will come up from behind them and slit their throats."

CHAPTER 30

Nogales, Mexico

Agent Welch crouched down on the last set of stairs and looked up. The air was heavy, and they were all out of breath. They had heard a thundering crash above them, which was followed shortly thereafter with a cloud of dust and pulverized plaster filtering between the door and the frame. The nine remaining agents, Director Stubblefield, and the woman and child had scurried through the door hidden behind the restaurant's once used but now empty shelves. Once inside the stairwell, one only needed to walk down two flights of stairs to find another door, which led to a long dark tunnel that had no end in sight.

The little girl had witnessed her two older brothers playing in the tunnel on multiple occasions and had watched men enter and exit for the past couple of years. But she was never allowed to go down to the subterranean depths. She didn't know where it went, but the activity that had gone there had sparked her curiosity for some time. Now, afraid of the armed men milling about, she simply cried in the arms of her mother.

Agent Welch had gone back up the stairs to determine the amount of damage that had been done and whether they should sit and wait for the rescuers or think of a different plan. The cartel had reinforced the entry with several layers of concrete blocks, but even looking through a sizeable crack on the side of the door and after a good hard push, Welch knew they weren't going to get out that way. At least not for a while.

And time was not on their side. Director Stubblefield had lost a good amount of blood, what with the constant jostling of his body from the street to the tunnel below. He needed to get to a hospital. The radios were useless so far underground, and everybody knew better than to try their cell phones.

Back to the bottom of the stairs, Agent Welch conferred with Boston and the others. "There's no way we're getting out up there. We probably have a ton of rubble in and around the entry."

Welch took one look at the Director and decided they were going to have to check out the tunnel. "Ask her where this tunnel goes," he said to Agent Boston.

The armed Boston approached the woman, who was seated on a wooden bench rocking the child back and forth, and asked her in broken Spanish where the tunnel led.

The woman started wailing in agony, her eyes filling with tears. She begged the men not to hurt her and her daughter. "Please don't kill my daughter!" she cried in Spanish.

Boston pleaded with her to calm down. For goodness sakes, if they wanted to kill her they would have done so by now. He held out both hands, palms down, and gestured to her to be calm. They needed to know where the tunnel went.

"Tunnel," he said, pointing into the dark abyss to his left. This caused her to wail even louder, like there was a giant monster at the end of the tunnel and forcing her and her daughter to march in that direction meant certain death. She thought they would shoot her and her daughter once they were far enough away and leave their bodies for the tunnel rats.

Boston tried again. He stroked the young girl's head like she was a scared cat, as if to say, look, I'm not going to hurt you. He then pointed to himself and back to the tunnel.

"Donde?" he asked. "Where?" He was hoping she would say just across the street or maybe next door.

The woman looked down the tunnel once more and then back at Agent Boston.

"Donde?" he asked again. "Where does the tunnel go to?"

The woman's eyes got bigger. Maybe the man wasn't going to shoot her in the back. Maybe he just wanted directions. "Los Estados Unidos," she said.

Boston looked down the darkened tunnel and wondered if he heard right. "The tunnel goes to the United States?"

The woman nodded twice. "Si."

"Hey, she says this tunnel goes to the United States," Boston said to the others.

With her fear slowly subsiding, the woman then pointed to the gray box on the wall. Boston went over, opened it, and found two red levers. Both were in the off position. He took the chance and pulled down the one with the lightbulb above it. With a snap of the lever, the fluorescent overhead lighting blinked on thirty yards down the tunnel and illuminated the whole place.

The FBI agents suddenly realized they had stumbled upon one of the drug cartel's underground highways. The four-foot-wide tunnel was held up by cinder blocks and twelve-inch thick wooden studs. The floors were lined with two rails capable of moving cargo at a quick pace. Agent Boston looked at the other lever, saw the fan symbol, and pulled it down. Though faint, the agents could hear the ventilation system kick in.

Agent Boston hurried down the tunnel, bending down all the way so as not to hit his head. He was five-eight but with the Kevlar helmet still on his head it made him an inch taller. Anyone over five feet tall had best duck or risk taking a pillar in the forehead. The tunnel seemed to go on forever. It had taken the Sons of the Devil cartel ten years to build, and the amount of man hours and materials that went into its construction put a multi-million-dollar price tag on it. But to the cartel, it was worth every penny as tens of thousands of pounds of contraband could make its way day and night into the United States virtually undetected.

After forty yards, Agent Boston came to a row of shelves high on the right. It was lined with bottles of water, just in case the drug smugglers got thirsty in the stifling heat, and two rolls of paper towels. After another ten yards, he found two five-foot-long flat carts leaning up against the wall. The bottom side of each had wheels that would run on the rails. Two steel poles could be inserted on both sides of the cart to give the pusher more leverage.

"Hey!" he yelled back down the tunnel. "I need a little help down here!"

Two agents bent down and hurried down the tunnel. Once they reached Agent Boston, they put the carts on the rails and headed back to the stairwell. Agent Welch met them halfway before running back.

"Director, we're gonna have to put you on a cart and hope to make it to the U.S. side," Welch said. "I think that's our best chance. I don't think we have time to wait around."

Director Stubblefield nodded. His mouth was too dry to speak, and he was growing increasingly weak. Agent Boston handed out his armful of bottled water to the others. He used one roll of towels as a headrest for the Director and the other he used to wrap around his leg wound. Boston then unscrewed the cap and held it to the Director's lips. He took in a couple of ounces and smiled, seemingly refreshed.

"Let's go," he whispered.

With the order given, Agent Welch took the lead down the tunnel. He had the Director's Glock pointed forward and ready just in case someone was waiting for them. He was followed by two agents, then the Director on the cart pushed by another two, the fallen members of the team were being wheeled down by two more. The last two, Agents Boston and Munson, kept watch on the rear of the group with the woman and her daughter right in front of them.

"Keep moving," Welch kept saying in the tight quarters. The lit tunnel appeared to go on forever. "We just have to keep moving."

The men on their feet were starting to feel the cramped nature of the tunnel in their own muscles and bones. Their backs were tightening from bending over and the slow, stunted walk was doing a number on their quads. The ventilation system was worthless, and the heat was suffocating. The little water the men had gulped down had gone out just as fast in the sweat rolling down their necks. The only thing that kept them from taking off their body armor to lighten the load was the unknown that lie ahead. After what seemed like a mile long march under the earth, Agent Welch slowed and held his left hand up.

"We've got another door coming up here," he said.

A noticeably ominous feeling came over him. If the door was locked, backtracking through the tunnel would only return them to where they started. And there wasn't any way out back in that direction. Agent Welch wasn't worried about a padlock or a couple of chains keeping out those heading to America. The FBI agents would find a way to break through. But he was worried that the U.S. Government had already found out about the tunnel and put an end to its existence by filling its side with a couple tons of cement.

"Take those two lights out," Welch whispered to the two agents behind him as he pointed to the ceiling. When he opened the door, he didn't want whoever might be on the other side to see his bright smiling face and the letters "FBI" in big yellow letters plastered across his chest. He didn't know the current location of his group or whether there would be a welcome home party waiting for them on the other side. A dark background behind him might give him enough time to scan the area and get off a few shots. The two agents, still bent over, reached up and took the fluorescent tubes out of their cover. They then gently laid them next to the tunnel wall.

"And push the Director back a little bit."

Once he saw the two agents return to their crouched and armed position behind him, Welch approached cautiously and put his ear to the door. He heard nothing – no voices, no radio. He reached for the knob with his left hand. His right hand was squeezing hard on the Glock. The knob turned with some effort, the rust indicating it had been there for awhile. Welch pulled the door back an inch and his eyes peered over his raised gun.

The eyes then looked up and widened with joy. Rays of sunshine could be seen filtering through the blinds of the windows above. He opened the door wider, the gun still held out in front of him.

"Stay here," he told the others.

Agent Welch moved cautiously forward up a ramp and stopped at the top behind a counter. He noticed through the blinds that cars were traveling in both directions on a road out front. And they were American cars. New model Chevys and Fords that looked like they had been washed and waxed and taken care of. The signs outside were in English, too. The one on the window read "Rosario's Floral Shop." If there were flowers being sold inside, it had been awhile. Welch sprinted back down the ramp and threw open the door.

"It's an old flower shop in the United States," he blurted out. "They've got a freakin' conveyor belt right up to the loading dock. Let's get the Director up here!"

Welch went running back up the ramp and unlocked the front door. In full HRT regalia and loaded weapon at his side, he bounded out onto the sidewalk and, as if a gift from above, he noticed an Arizona state trooper's patrol car heading in his direction. He whipped his badge out of his breast pocket and stepped right into the trooper's path. The car screeched to a halt in the middle of the roadway.

"Special Agent Welch, FBI! I need an ambulance at this address right now!"

The ambulance arrived within three minutes, along with twenty other law-enforcement vehicles from half as many agencies looking to offer whatever assistance they could. Welch and Boston, along with two paramedics, lifted Director Stubblefield's stretcher in the ambulance. Boston got in the front passenger seat. Welch hopped in the back. Before he closed the door, he told two of his FBI agents to get a ride with the troopers and meet them at the hospital. The others would stay at the flower shop for the time being to let those on the ground know what was going on.

"Let's move!"

The White House – Washington, D.C.

"Sir, it's somebody claiming to be a Special Agent Welch with the FBI." NSA Harnacke said with one hand over the phone receiver.

The President had returned to the Situation Room after breaking the news to the First Lady and Tina Stubblefield. All of them were crying before the President managed to get a single word out of his mouth. He consoled Tina as best he could and told her he'd have the FBI bring her children to Washington as soon as possible. He didn't know what else to say. He left with both women still crying. It undoubtedly had been the worst day of his life.

"Sir?"

The President didn't hear him the first time. He was so focused he couldn't take his eyes off the television – the screen showing rescue crews tossing cracked bricks and busted two-by-fours into a clearing on the street. He could see the search dogs poking their noses around the rubble, into and out of holes, smelling for any trace of human life. He was hoping and praying for an arm to poke out, maybe the dust covered head of his friend to emerge and give a smile to the cameras. Maybe he had taken cover under a table or a counter and it would just take some time to pull him out alive.

"I don't know him," President Schumacher said. His tone insinuated he didn't want to be bothered right now by someone he didn't know.

"Mr. President," Harnacke said. "The call came directly to the Situation Room."

The President took his eyes off the screen. "And?" What of it? That didn't mean he knew who Agent Welch was.

"Sir, he says he is with Director Stubblefield at a hospital in Nogales, Arizona."

"What is this some sort of prank?" the President asked. Whoever was on the other end had better hope not because, with his current foul mood, pissing off the President of the United States was just about to become a federal offense.

"Sir, the number is from Director Stubblefield's phone."

The President looked at Harnacke like he was having trouble comprehending everything that was being said.

Hospital. Arizona. Ty's phone.

The President reached over and pressed the button for the speakerphone.

"This is Anthony Schumacher. Who am I talking to?"

"Mr. President, this is Special Agent Welch with the FBI's hostage-rescue team. I accompanied Director Stubblefield to Nogales, Mexico, to pick up General Graham and we were ambushed near the U.S. Consulate."

"I was told you were going to Arizona," the President interrupted, still not believing.

"The kidnappers called and said the drop-off point was going to be in Nogales, Mexico south of the consulate. Once we were attacked, we had no escape so we took cover in an abandoned restaurant."

"That restaurant you apparently were in collapsed to the ground."

"Yes, I know, sir. I was there. We took cover in a stairwell that led to a tunnel. A tunnel used by drug cartels to smuggle drugs underneath the border. We came out in Nogales, Arizona, and Director Stubblefield has been rushed to the hospital. He was taken into surgery with gunshot wounds to his shoulder and his thigh. The doctors say he's going to make it."

President Schumacher wanted to cry. He wanted to believe the man was telling the truth – that his friend had survived and would recover. For a man who had every communication device at his disposal, he desperately wanted one inside that operating room.

"Mr. President, are you still there?"

"Yes," he responded softly. He dabbed at his runny nose with the back of his hand and cleared his throat. "I'm still here."

"Sir, Director Stubblefield told me to relay a message to you."

"Go ahead."

Welch looked down at the note he had scribbled down. "I'm supposed to tell you to call Tina and have her let David and Tisha know that the Director is okay. He is going to be okay."

The President collapsed into his chair and started crying. After a brief moment, he told Agent Welch he would let Tina Stubblefield know right now. She was still upstairs in the Residence with the First Lady. Jubilation erupted once Welch clicked off the phone. In the euphoria that followed in the Situation Room, with hugs and handshakes exchanged between Cabinet Secretaries and four-star generals all around, the President excused himself so he could tell Director Stubblefield's wife the good news. He was beginning to think it was all a dream. He walked out the door of the Situation Room where he was handed a note by the Marine standing guard. The note was from Admiral Shepard, the President's personal physician.

It read:

Mr. President,
Mr. Cogdon is resting comfortably at G.W. Medical Center. It was a mild heart attack, but he will be fine.
He's already itching to get back to work.

The President smiled and thrust his right fist into the air – a double dose of good news. The sprint upstairs would be made in record time.

CHAPTER 31

Benton, Illinois

"Son of a bitch!"

The Dutch Masters grape cigarillo was streaking to the ground like a missile. Mohammed Akbar had only lit it a minute and a half ago, but what he heard on the radio had caused him to fire the cigarillo to the pavement and unleash a string of profanities into the night sky. It was 8:30 p.m. on that Saturday evening, and Akbar and his crew had stopped at a rest area near Rend Lake, about half distance between Mt. Vernon and Marion on Interstate 57. The lot was empty save for three semis that were parked for the night. The men had reached Illinois with the wind of success at their backs and the hopes of jihad staring them in the face. It had been a glorious day with the demise of America's FBI.

At least until Akbar turned on the radio.

When the others came back out of the rest stop, they found their leader seething in a rage, pounding on the hood, and cursing like mad.

"Mohammed, what is wrong?" Abbed wondered as he hurried to the van.

"That son of a bitch is still alive!" Akbar yelled at him.

Abbed looked around at the semis and then shushed him. "Quiet down." Not only was he worried the truckers would hear Akbar, he was afraid the rest area's security cameras would pick up what was said. "Who is still alive?"

"The FBI Director," Akbar shot back with another fist banging the van's hood.

"They said he was dead." Abbed knew he had heard correctly earlier. It had not been a dream he kept telling himself over and over again on the trip north.

"Damn those Americans!" Akbar cursed.

While Akbar set to pacing back and forth on the sidewalk, Abbed, Musharra, and Nasra leaned into the van and listened to the radio. The announcer mentioned the attack, the collapsed building, and the tunnel from Mexico to the United States. It was almost too much for the men to comprehend. How could Director Stubblefield have survived? They heard the attack was very violent. But now they learn it was unsuccessful?

The radio broadcaster kept stalling for time, repeating much of what he had already said, and then he got word that the countdown clock was currently at ten seconds.

"Okay, ladies and gentlemen, the next voice you will hear is that of the President of the United States."

With several hurried waves of his left hand, Abbed motioned Akbar to come back to the van.

From behind his desk in the Oval Office and out to TV sets, computer screens, and radios around the world, President Schumacher gave his late-night address.

"Good evening. I come to you tonight to report on the events that have unfolded in the last forty-eight hours. Two days ago, Mexican drug cartels kidnapped General T.D. Graham, the Democratic candidate for Vice President of the United States, held him at gunpoint, and promised more bloodshed if the United States did not acquiesce to their demands. We declined.

"On my orders, I directed FBI Director Tyrone Stubblefield, Joint Chiefs Chairman Hugh Cummins, and Defense Secretary Russ Javits to coordinate a response that would free General Graham from his hostage takers and bring him back home. Director Stubblefield personally accompanied his dedicated team of agents to Nogales, Mexico, where they carried out their mission with great skill and precision. And I can proudly report to you tonight that General Graham is safely back on American soil.

"The rescue of General Graham was not without costs, however. America and the FBI have lost two of their most faithful servants – Special Agent Mason Hollister and Special Agent Ron Starnes. Both were ten-year veterans of the Federal Bureau of Investigation and members of its vaunted hostage-rescue team. Tonight, I ask that all Americans remember them in your prayers and keep their families in your hearts in this their time of need. We are thankful for the dedication Agents Hollister and Starnes have shown in their service to the United States.

"I also want to tell you Director Stubblefield himself was injured in the rescue attempt – taking a bullet in the shoulder and one in the thigh. He was rushed to a hospital in Nogales, Arizona. Thankfully, I can report to you tonight that Director Stubblefield has made it through surgery and is expected to fully recover from his wounds. As a dedicated leader of the FBI, Director Stubblefield has committed his life to preserving and protecting the Constitution of the United States and safeguarding the people of this great country. His service should make everyone proud to be an American. And I look forward to welcoming him back to Washington in the coming days.

"On one last note, our preliminary investigation leads us to believe the kidnapping of General Graham and the attack on Director Stubblefield were coordinated attempts by Mexican drug cartels and al-Qaeda terrorists intent on advancing their murderous agenda and bringing their drugs and jihad to the

United States. I can assure the American people that I will not rest until our borders are secure and our citizens are safe. To that end, I have authorized the United States military to take any and all action in defense of the southern and northern borders as well as the east and west coasts. Further, I have directed the Department of Homeland Security to increase its security presence at airports, train stations, and bus terminals across the country as we head into next week's election.

"My fellow Americans, we live in perilous times. The war against violent murderers and terrorist extremists will go on unabated. It must, lest our children and grandchildren be deprived of the freedoms we hold so dear in our hearts. And it will, as long as I am President. May God bless General Graham and the men who endangered their lives to bring him home. And may God continue to bless the United States of America. Thank you."

Abbed reached in and turned down the volume of the radio. The men nearly jumped out of their shoes when the semis' horns started blaring throughout the rest area and surrounding countryside – a good ol' fashioned redneck celebration of American victory. An incensed Akbar put a lit cigarillo to his mouth. His chest had been heaving up and down as the rage continued to boil inside of him. He looked over at the second truck. Its cargo containing some of the most lethal toxins known to man. And now it was all up to him.

"We must kill him," Akbar growled in the shadows of the rest area. He looked each man in the eye. "We *must* kill him. It is up to us. Our brothers and sisters are counting on us."

"We are ready," Abbed reported.

The cell phone on Akbar's hip angrily buzzed to life. He grabbed the phone with his left hand and his cigarillo with his right. "Brother Rumallah," he said. "Yes, we have heard the news. And we are not happy."

"We are on our way," Rumallah told him. Akbar could hear the man on the other end behind the wheel with an engine pushing the speed limit. Seated next to Rumallah was his brother, Ibrahim, and both were wide awake. Neither had slept much since they entered the United States, and the President's words lit the fire within them.

"When can you get to Indiana?"

"Indiana? Why do you want me there? I am going to Washington."

"No," Akbar huffed. "You must come to Indiana. That is where the President will be."

"The election is on Tuesday. He will be in Washington at the White House." Rumallah acted like he had the President's itinerary in the seat next to him.

"No, damn it!" Akbar said again. "Listen to me." He was growing irritated with Rumallah's intransigence. He was a terrorist from Yemen with no knowledge of the American political system. "The President will be in Indiana on Election Day. He has to vote and put on a show in front of the TV cameras."

Rumallah suddenly got the picture. He had been so focused on other matters that the little things escaped him. Akbar, however, had lived in the United States long enough to know how the scene would most likely unfold.

"We can be in Indiana by Monday morning," Rumallah said.

"Good," Akbar responded, glad that his terrorist cohort finally saw it his way. "We will have everything ready to go. Be safe, my friend."

The men with the VX were itching to get going. "What can we do between here and Silver Creek?"

"Did you rent that storage unit?" Akbar asked.

"Yes, two of them."

"Good, just get to the unit without detection. Unload the five-ten and make yourselves scarce so you don't draw any unwanted attention."

"We'll need two days' worth of provisions," Abbed added. "We will stock up before we meet up at the motel."

"That is where we will walk through the plan one more time." Akbar took one last drag and flicked the cigarillo to the grass. "Let's go. Judgment day is near."

CHAPTER 32

Bethesda Naval Hospital – Bethesda, Maryland

President Schumacher rode up the elevator with Wiley and a team of Secret Service agents. Wiley looked somewhat refreshed, like two days of bed rest was all he needed to recharge his batteries. He had complained long and hard enough that his doctors at G.W. Medical Center gave him his discharge instructions and pushed him out the door. His haggard look would no doubt return considering he wouldn't be sleeping a wink within the next forty-eight hours.

"So just a mild heart attack, huh?" the President asked Wiley as the elevator clicked off another floor.

Wiley had his eyes focused on his BlackBerry. The election was tomorrow, and he just knew that there was something he should be doing to get that one last vote out there somewhere? He had already directed several staffers and spokespersons to hit the airwaves and morning news shows. Twenty calls had been made to state Republican Party chairmen by the end of breakfast. The rest would wait until the sun peeked over the horizon in the states out west. But, as always, he worried there was something he was missing.

"What?"

"A mild heart attack," the President said again. He acted like the diagnosis should be a matter of grave concern to his friend.

"Yeah," Wiley said, uncaring and with his eyes back to his smartphone. "Three more and I'll catch Cheney."

"You have to start taking better care of yourself."

"I will, I will. As soon as the election is over."

The President gave him a look of disbelief. "You're going to start working out with me in the White House. Every day."

"Sure," Wiley said, his backup BlackBerry now on.

"We'll make sure we get out and walk a bit every day too."

"Sure."

"Maybe we'll run a marathon or compete in a triathlon."

"Sounds good."

The President looked over at Agent Craig who was smiling and shaking his head. It would be of little use for the President to continue on with Wiley now.

He had too many other things on his mind to start making resolutions.

When the elevator hit the twelfth floor, the agents fanned out and escorted the President to the end of the hall.

"I'll give you two a minute," Wiley said. He had to make a couple of calls anyway.

The President walked into the room and found Director Stubblefield propped up in bed looking like he was also eager to leave.

"Mr. President," the Director said, reaching out his hand, a wide smile forming across the face. "I was wondering what all those sirens were that I was hearing."

"My friend, good to see you."

The only picture released by the White House photographer of the meeting would show President Schumacher grinning from ear to ear at the sight of seeing his old friend Director Stubblefield, clad in a hospital-issued blue top, as they shook hands.

"Sir, I'd stand but . . .," he said, looking down at his leg under the cover. It was heavily bandaged, but the doctor said he'd be as good as new in no time.

"You had us worried about you for awhile there," the President said, pulling up a chair at the bedside.

"I was a little worried myself. It was a little too close for comfort."

"I was this close to storming the border with everything we had."

"I appreciate that."

"Well, don't do anything like that again because I cannot take looking into Tina's eyes and telling her any more bad news."

Director Stubblefield nodded his head. He knew little more needed to be said. He did thank the President for getting his wife to the White House to be with the First Lady. Both men had now been in situations where their wives thought they wouldn't be returning home. Just the thought was enough to make the President change the subject and lighten the mood.

"What's this I hear you smuggled two Mexicans across the border?"

The Director let out a laugh that could be heard out in the hall. He had forgotten about the Mexican mother and the little girl.

"That's not going to go over well with my GOP base."

The Director stopped laughing when he could feel the stitches in his shoulder starting to pop. "I thought they might be long lost relatives."

The President shook his head, figuring that wasn't much of an excuse. "Maybe I'll have to grant you a pardon."

Stubblefield thanked him but he was more interested in getting some inside news that he had missed since he was hospitalized. "How are things going out there?"

"I talked to Deputy Director Patterson, and he's got the FBI on high alert."

"I'm still worried about your safety, Mr. President," the Director said. He had a bad feeling about something. The terrorists were determined to make a big hit on the highest profile target there was.

The President didn't want him to worry. "The Secret Service will have the roads closed, the river blocked, and the airspace cleared all day tomorrow. I won't be out in public long enough for anything to happen." He then pointed at the Director's leg. "And how are you going to get to the polls with a bum leg? I was counting on your vote."

The Director smiled again. "I voted absentee last week."

The President didn't ask who he voted for. Didn't need to. He reached out and shook the Director's hand with both of his.

"We'll have you and Tina over to the White House once we get back to D.C." The President gave him one last wave before he reached the door.

Director Stubblefield waved goodbye and gave his friend one last warning. "Be careful tomorrow, Mr. President."

Covington, Indiana

Mohammed Akbar wiped the sweat pouring down his forehead. He had no time to light up a cigarillo. Plus, smoking would be impossible what with the respirator covering his face. The storage unit was the largest size available – a ten-by-fourteen on the end of a long row. It was a good spot – the security cameras were focused on the entrance, at least fifty yards away, and it was hidden from any passersby traveling down the main road. Only a stand of sycamore trees watched them as they worked in the near darkness. As long as none of the locals showed up in the dark of night with a load of junk to shove into their units, the men would have the place to themselves for the rest of the evening.

The ten drums of VX were lined up against the wall. They looked harmless. Nothing on the outside to indicate the contents could kill thousands of people. Akbar and his men had made it all the way to Covington, just a stone's throw from Silver Creek, without a second glance from the police. Communication by phone was kept short and encoded – the caller always making the connection from a pay phone, which was not always easy to find in those parts. They mentioned the five-ten and a "birthday party" they would attend the next day.

Akbar, Abbed, and the other two men all wore white protective coveralls and respirators given the hazardous contents of the drums. Abdi Rumallah, who hadn't slept in two days now, used only the respirator. He was too angry, too focused on killing the President to be concerned for his own safety.

After removing his suit, Abbed opened the garage door up three feet and crawled outside. He had driven the truck sprayer to the storage facility two hours earlier and parked it near the fence next to two large boats and a dune buggy that their Hoosier owners obviously had no room for in their yards.

Akbar had purchased the truck, two jet skis, and two other beat-up pickup trucks during the last month. When he made calls to his network of friends, the purchases were delivered to the rendezvous point. Rumallah's brother, Ibrahim, was making trips to the gas station to fill the trucks and jet skis with fuel.

Akbar motioned for Abbed to back the white 1989 GMC Mini Jimmy sprayer up to the unit door as close as he could. The truck was a used diesel with a tank that could hold 1,000 gallons. It was big enough to hold the VX in all ten drums, and Akbar wanted every last drop to be used. The spray mechanism could deliver the VX through the sixty-foot steel booms and thirty spray tubes, fifteen on each side of the tank. Akbar had purchased the truck off the Internet just two weeks ago, the online ad praising the truck's low miles, good condition, row-crop tires, and booms that were "like new." The seller promised the buyer would not be disappointed with the Mini Jimmy's performance. Not interested in dickering or even stating his best offer, Akbar agreed to pay the full $11,000 asking price.

The hose was hooked up to the sprayer's tank and to the first of the ten drums. No one was sure how this was going to go, but one of Akbar's engineering buddies said the siphon mechanism would move any liquid to where he wanted it to end up. The men went through the same process with each drum, careful not to spill any on them or anywhere else for that matter. Abbed, who was still out of his protective gear, stayed outside the unit and kept lookout.

Once every drum was emptied, Akbar and the rest of the men locked the unit's doors and pulled the truck over near the fence. They then traveled back to the motel near the interstate. They ate little and said even less. At 11 p.m., Akbar went through his final instructions.

"I want everyone up by four tomorrow morning," he said. "We must be ready to go at a moment's notice."

Laid out on the bed were pictures taken by al-Mutallab during his initial scouting trip to Silver Creek along with an aerial map of the surrounding area. Red dots indicated the places where the President was most likely to be on Election Day – his house, the polling place, the Donut Palace. Yellow highlighted lines delineated the possible motorcade routes. Blue lines with arrows marked the starting and ending points for the terrorist assault.

Akbar pointed his finger to the map. "As soon as Ibrahim sees the President leaving the polling place, he will alert the rest of us. Mumtaz and Habib on the jet skis will go first, then Moamar and Ibrahim will follow in the trucks for the second wave."

"Where will you be?" Abbed asked.

"Brother Rumallah and I will be in the truck sprayer," he said, pointing to a spot northeast of the President's property. "Once the Secret Service is distracted with the jet skis and the trucks, we will drive right into the heart of the President's property as soon as he drives up."

"But they will close the roads," Abbed said.

"Yes, but they will not close the farm fields to the east. Once they are distracted, we will have a straight shot." He traced the route with his index finger and stabbed the red dot denoting the President's house.

"Everyone will have an AK-47?"

"Yes," Akbar said. On the other bed, six AK-47s were lined in a row. Each was fully loaded and ready for jihad. "And they are to be used. If you are approached, you are to commence firing. This will cause further distraction and require the Secret Service to divert its resources so we can get to the house."

"What about the grenade?" All eyes in the room looked at the lone explosive sitting on top of a pillow. It had been smuggled into the country by Abdi Rumallah, who viewed it as an insurance policy in case things didn't go as planned. If the booms failed to operate properly, pulling the pin on the grenade would blow up the truck and spread the VX in a toxic plume. It would be the final dagger into the President's heart.

"It will be in the truck," Akbar said. "We will use it when we get to the house." He had no doubt they would make it to their intended target.

"What else do we need to do tonight?" Abbed asked.

"We are ready," Akbar said quietly. "Tonight, we pray. Tomorrow, the President dies."

CHAPTER 33

Silver Creek, Indiana

President Schumacher and the First Lady had been inside the polling place for twenty minutes. The gymnasium of the Abraham Lincoln Middle School contained a line of voting booths on the far wall and a full team of caffeinated poll workers ready to check the rolls and hand out the ballots. Once inside the gym, the photographers and cameramen took the obligatory shots of the President greeting the election judges, showing his photo identification, and then taking his ballot into the booth where he pulled closed the red-white-and-blue striped curtain. Once he was safely shielded from prying eyes, he filled in the oval next to his name with a ballpoint pen – the lever and the punch card having gone the way of the dodo bird. Once he was finished, he smiled for the cameras and inserted the ballot into the locked cabinet that would be opened later on that evening when the polls had closed.

Dressed in a pair of blue jeans and a long-sleeved red shirt with the wing and wheel logo of the Indianapolis Motor Speedway on the right pocket, the President placed the "I voted" sticker over the left pocket. Danielle did the same over her red turtleneck. There would be no blue shirts on that day. They smiled for the cameras and headed out.

Two ladies in a crowd of thirty outside the school took notice when a line of suits started filing out of the door. They had been waiting patiently for an hour just for this moment.

"Mr. President!" they both yelled when they saw the red shirts. "Mr. President! Over here!"

The President, surrounded by several layers of sixteen Secret Service agents, peered through the phalanx of suits and waved hello to those waiting patiently behind a row of bicycle racks.

"Please, Mr. President!" the women yelled, joined now by the rest of the group. The women frantically waved him over, one even folding her hands in prayer practically begging him to acknowledge their existence.

Not one to shy away from the locals, President Schumacher made eye contact with Agent Craig and told him that it would only take five minutes. Agent Craig gritted his teeth, nodded, and made the call.

"All units, Craig," he announced into his microphone. "Shadow is going to work the line."

When the President and the First Lady turned away from the limousine, the crowd erupted into cheers. The only ones who weren't overjoyed by the situation were the agents changing their perimeter positions. A swarm of armed men in nice suits changed directions and focused their attention on the people jumping up and down in great anticipation. The left lapels on each of the suits had a red pin with the Secret Service five-pointed star to thwart any would-be imposters from surreptitiously joining the protective detail. Yesterday, the pin had been green. Three agents had already checked purses and patted down a half dozen in the crowd. The two agents standing closest to the crowd repeated the orders they had already given in the event the President decided to come over and shake some hands.

"Would you keep your hands out of your pockets please. Keep them up so we can see them," the two men said, holding their palms above their waist. They were very polite. But the intense glare in their eyes and their thick necks were enough of a deterrent to make anyone think twice about disobeying them. "Hands out of your pockets, please. Thank you."

In the middle of the crowd, one man slowly took his hands out of his jacket. He then put them in the pockets of his jeans. He then took them out quickly. He wondered if the agents noticed. He could hear the shouts from the people around him and he saw the man walking in his direction. It was him – the President of the United States. Everything seemed to be going in slow motion, like he was having an out-of-body experience. He could feel the hair standing up on the back of his neck, the chills going up and down his spine.

The man's name was Ibrahim Rumallah. And the man he and his comrades were intent on killing that very day was only ten feet from him. Rumallah looked at the two people in front of him and down at the bike rack holding them and the rest of the crowd in place. The thought of leaping off the rack and lunging toward the President to snap his neck crossed his mind. He had not even dreamt of being this close to the target.

The President's limousine maneuvered within fifteen feet behind him and idled at the end of the bike racks closest to the school. The rear door was held open by an agent ready to slam it shut if the President was thrown inside.

"How's everybody doing today?" the President asked. The big smile was genuine, and he recognized a few faces in the crowd. Most were old-timers, up early hoping to see the President at his usual polling place. They were mostly white, and Rumallah's swarthy complexion had garnered a few looks. But the local residents figured he was with the big-city TV networks and didn't think twice about him.

The President started on the right side – first with the handshakes, using both his left and his right, and then out came his blue Sharpie for some autographs – a few pictures, a hat, a shirt, two newspapers, and five one-dollar bills. There were two agents on each side of him, looking intensely at the sea of hands for something out of place, something that didn't belong, a gun, a knife, a strange movement or quick thrust toward the President from out of nowhere. Agent Craig had his left hand in a death grip on the President's black leather belt, his right hand hovering close to the President's torso, just in case someone in the crowd tried to grab him.

"We love Danielle!" one excited woman yelled.

"So do I!" the President responded. He looked over at his Elle, who was working the line shaking hands as well. She blushed. The crowd got a good laugh out of it.

"Do you have your lucky GOP socks on today, Mr. President?" one woman asked. It was obvious she had known the President long enough to know he wore a pair of white socks with a red-white-and-blue elephant on them for good luck.

The President took a step back from the line and pulled up a pant leg on his jeans. Above his red Nikes were the socks that had been given to him by a neighbor prior to his first election to Congress. He only brought them out of his dresser on election days when his name was on the ballot.

"When are you going to go to the Donut Palace?" The trip was another Election Day tradition. These folks knew their favorite son well.

"We are going to head over there right now," the President said, returning to the sea of hands. The entourage had left early so the President could vote and then make a quick stop for breakfast before most of the locals even hit the snooze button. "My good friend Floyd Revson said he was going to make some victory iced cookies for us."

The President continued on down the line, and the limo inched forward with his every step to the left. A man wanted a picture of the President with his four-year-old daughter so the President picked up the smiling child and had her rest her feet on the bike rack. Picture taken, the President returned the girl and moved on down the line. With the President standing just three feet away, a sweating Rumallah blended in and held his outstretched hand over the shoulder of the two people in front of him. The President reached in and grasped his hand.

"Thank you," the President said to him before moving on to the next hand.

"How's ol' Wiley Cogdon doing?"

The President stopped and looked for the questioner in the crowd. It was a white male, standing right next to Rumallah. The man was a bit portly, maybe late fifties or early sixties. Perhaps he knew Wiley from his days frequenting the Silver Creek watering holes. The President was pleased somebody cared to ask. "He's doing great. He came back to Silver Creek with us, and I saw him walking around the house this morning."

"He wasn't exercising, was he?"

The President got a good laugh out of that one. "Goodness no. Unless walking around the yard in a shirt and tie and talking on his cell phone constitutes exercise. He's already counting the votes."

Rumallah took a step back and grabbed his iPhone. He had no weapons on him, the Secret Service had already checked. Although he was simply sent to keep an eye on the President and report on his whereabouts, he believed the chance encounter was a sign that the assassination would indeed take place that day. He quickly uploaded a picture of the President to Akbar.

"Where's the victory party?" another man asked.

The President smiled. He wasn't going to bite with the cameras rolling. The polls hadn't even opened in half the country. "We're going to stay in tonight," he said, pointing over to the First Lady. He did add, "We'll have a thank you party here in Silver Creek and in Indianapolis tomorrow, then it'll be back to Washington."

One of the Secret Service agents leaned into Agent Craig and whispered into his ear. He looked over the President's shoulder and noticed cars of all makes streaming into the parking lot. Word around town had spread quickly, and fifty people with just as many cell phones and dollar bills would soon be sprinting toward the bike racks looking to snap a photo or get a signature. Agent Craig gave a quick tug on the President's belt, not noticed by anyone else, and the President knew it was time to go.

"Did I get everyone?" he asked, backing away and looking over the crowd. Everyone seemed pleased. "Thank you all for coming out," he said with a wave.

"Thank you, Mr. President," the crowd said in appreciation. "Thank you."

The President and First Lady got in the rear of the limo on opposite sides. Once Agent Craig closed the President's door, he got into the front seat. He then waited for the rest of his men to get inside the line of armored vehicles.

"Shadow and Sunshine are moving out," he said. "All units proceed to the Palace."

During the four-mile drive, the President decided to make one quick phone call to Bethesda to see how Director Stubblefield was doing.

"Ty," he said. "How's it going?"

"I'm doing good, sir," Director Stubblefield said. He had been up for an hour, had a light breakfast, and was itching to leave and get back to work. The doctors, however, wanted to take things slowly and kept talking about lots of bed rest and little or no work. He was about to go crazy. He desperately wanted to get back to FBI Headquarters. For now, he had two assistants from the office who would keep him up to speed on what was going on.

"When are they going to let you go?"

"The doctor said it will most likely be this afternoon."

The President held his hand to the phone and told his wife the news.

"Well, I just wanted to check in. We'll be back tomorrow and maybe stop by the house to make sure Tina's waiting on you hand and foot." The President got a good slap across the arm from the First Lady.

"I might need a presidential directive for that to happen."

"Hey, one last thing before I let you go," the President said. "I read in the paper this morning that your brother retired yesterday."

"Yes, he did," the Director said. "I was just reading the story in the *USA Today* before you called."

"Was it a surprise?"

"He e-mailed me a couple of weeks ago and said he might be calling it a career pretty soon. His knees just couldn't take it anymore. I think he would have done it last week but for my little trip to Mexico."

Marcus Stubblefield had been an all-pro offensive lineman in the National Football League for the past fourteen years. The youngest of the Stubblefield brothers, Marcus spent most of his career on the gridiron with the St. Louis Rams. Although his older brother had grown up to receive the most notoriety in the family based on his groundbreaking rise to the top of the ladder at the FBI, Marcus did have something brother Ty could not lay claim to – a Super Bowl ring.

"Does he still like to tease you about his ring?"

"Every time I see him," the Director sighed. "He likes to pretend he's counting all 157 diamonds in the damn thing."

"What Super Bowl did he play in again? I can never remember."

"Super Bowl 34 with the Rams," the Director said before stopping in mid-thought. "I think that's XXXIV."

"Oh yes, I remember. It was against the Titans."

"That's right."

The presidential limousine was pulling to a stop in front of the Donut Palace so the President thought he'd better end the call. "We'll be back tomorrow. And if your brother is ever in town, tell him he's welcome to come over to the White House. I want to see that big ring again."

The Director shook his head. No one could ever talk about Marcus Stubblefield without referencing his Super Bowl ring. It was almost enough to make the Director want to suit up and give the NFL one last shot. "I'll let him know, Mr. President. I'll see you soon."

Covington, Indiana

The men were up at four, just like Akbar wanted. They said their prayers and washed thoroughly. At six, Akbar instructed Moamar and Ibrahim to take Musharra and Nasra and the jet skis down to the Wabash and get them in the water. The jet skis had been painted black, and the camouflage outfits of their operators would help them blend in to the fall surroundings while they waited for the command to attack. One would come from the north and the other from the south. And if the early morning fog blanketing the river valley held, they might make it all the way undetected.

Akbar and Abdi Rumallah were currently sitting at a rest area west of Covington and watching intently on Akbar's iPhone. From the website of the local CBS affiliate, they saw the President and the First Lady enter the middle school and then exit after voting. They watched as the President greeted the locals, and Rumallah argued strenuously that they should attack now while the President was out in the open.

"Brother Ibrahim is right there!" he said, pleading his case. "He can distract them at the school!"

Akbar rejected the idea, reminding him they were at least ten minutes away. Most likely, the President would be long gone by the time they got there, he told him. When Ibrahim called again to say the President's motorcade was not heading in the direction of the Schumacher residence, Akbar told him to not to worry. The TV cameras had picked up the President saying he was going for donuts – just as Akbar had expected.

"It will not be much longer," Akbar stated. "The Secret Service will not want the President to spend much time out in public. He will be in and out quickly."

"Why don't we hit him at the Donut Palace?" Rumallah snapped, his right fist smacking his left palm. He was desperate to kill, not wanting to wait any longer.

With the grenade sitting in a cup holder covered by a motel hand towel, Akbar lit a grape cigarillo and considered the pros and cons of the idea. There would be less security than what they would find surrounding the Schumacher property. But he realized a change of the attack plan would result in going forward without Musharra and Nasra on their jet skis.

"We need all the distractions we have planned for this to work," Akbar said after a good long puff. "If we were to go down Main Street with the sprayer, a light pole or traffic signal might snap off the sixty-foot booms. Then we'd be dead in the water."

"We could ram the limousine!" Rumallah argued.

"We wouldn't even be able to get close!" Akbar shot back. He pointed to his iPhone. "There is the motorcade," he said, looking at a local news broadcast of the convoy heading to the Donut Palace. "There are three limousines there. Which one has the President?" He then pointed to the other vehicles. "Four armored Suburbans flanking the limousines. We would most likely bounce off them and they would speed away. Then we would be dead!"

"We can do it!"

"No!" Akbar yelled. "We wait!"

CHAPTER 34

Bethesda Naval Hospital – Bethesda, Maryland

Director Stubblefield's doctor had been in to check on him, made some notes on the chart, and with some helpful hints, told the Director he could leave later on that afternoon. He would be required to undergo several weeks of outpatient physical therapy on his leg and his shoulder, but his prognosis for a full recovery was excellent. The doctor did, however, strongly advise him to get some rest and take it easy as he transitioned back to work full time.

"Rest," the Director repeated, just to let the doctor know he heard him. He promised to do so. Once the doctor left the room, Stubblefield figured the rest could wait and called in one of his assistants.

"What do I need to know?"

Special Agent Kent Ward carried an armful of briefing materials that other FBI agents had dropped off earlier for the Director's perusal and signature. He pulled up a chair and moved the tray table closer so he could set down the mound of paperwork.

"Here's the morning news from the CIA," Ward said, handing over the highly classified document that the President, the National Security Council, the CIA Director, Director Stubblefield, and their trusted staff would look over on a daily basis.

"NSA says signal traffic has dropped off dramatically from Mexico," Ward reported.

The Director nodded his head, thumbing through the pages. The intelligence drop off wasn't unexpected. Most of the cartels were in hiding, wondering when the U.S. was going to retaliate. Stubblefield stopped abruptly when he noticed the "five-ten" in connection with several phone calls that the NSA had been unable to trace. He hadn't thought about the five-ten in a week or so and, given the recent events, that it slipped his mind was not a surprise.

He mentioned the matter to Ward and looked up at the ceiling. The mystery still bugged him, like a crossword clue that he could not figure out. He ran the numbers in his head – forward, backward, different combinations – five-ten, ten-five, fifteen, one-zero-five, five hundred and ten. He remembered discussing the matter with the President, and then a fleeting thought about their earlier conversation regarding his brother's Super Bowl ring flashed through his mind. That sparkling diamond-encrusted monstrosity that Marcus had shoved in his brother's face a million times over the years. The bling would be forever etched in the Director's mind. On one side – the engraved name of Stubblefield, his brother's position, a Rams helmet, and the Gateway Arch; on the other side – the Lombardi trophy with XXXIV above it.

The shaking of the bed startled Agent Ward. It was like the Director had been struck by lightning, or at the very least hit by a violent spasm.

"Give me a pen," Stubblefield blurted out, reaching out his left hand and snapping his fingers.

Agent Ward thrust his hand into his jacket pocket and pulled one out. He handed it over. "Everything all right?"

Director Stubblefield took the pen and jotted the numbers 5 and 10 down on the top of the page. Beneath the five, he put a V. Beneath the ten, he put an X. He then put two and two together.

"VX," he said in disbelief. "Son of a . . ."

"What's wrong?"

"Give me your phone!" Stubblefield yelled out. "Watson! Watson! Get in here!"

Special Agent Mike Watson heard the yelling and almost reached for his service weapon. He opened the door and saw Director Stubblefield urging him inside.

"Get in here and give me your phone!" the Director yelled. He already had Agent Ward's phone to his ear. Hearing the commotion, nurses down at the end of the hall hurried to the room thinking something was wrong.

"Get me the Secretary of Defense," Stubblefield said, talking to his flummoxed secretary back at FBI Headquarters. She had not been expecting his call. "Hurry up!"

"What do you need?" Agent Watson asked. He had his phone ready.

"I want you to get Director Defoe on the line at the Secret Service. Tell him it's an emergency."

"This is Secretary Javits," the voice said from the phone.

"Russ, it's Ty Stubblefield. I think I know what that 'five-ten' might be."

"What?"

"VX."

"Oh, shit."

"You need to tell your men at the Pentagon to watch over the Newport Chemical Depot." Director Stubblefield was keenly aware of the proximity of the Depot to the President's hometown. He cursed himself for not thinking of it sooner.

The Secretary, however, had already done so. "Ty, I always put Newport on high alert when the President is in Silver Creek. We have fighter jets patrolling the sky. It's standard procedure." He didn't think there was much else they could do. "There's not enough VX remaining at Newport to do any damage anyway." "The intelligence says someone is still talking about the 'five-ten,'" Stubblefield said, not wanting to just let it go and hope for the best. "Something is going on."

"Director," Watson said, interrupting. "The Secret Service is still trying to contact Director Defoe."

Stubblefield figured Agent Craig wouldn't be taking any calls while he was busy with the protective detail. But the Director needed to get in contact with someone on the ground.

"Get me the number for Agent Schiffer," he said. "Now!"

Silver Creek, Indiana

The President of the United States had walked out of the Donut Palace carrying a box of two dozen sugar cookies with GOP elephants iced on top. They would be dessert later on that evening. He held up the box, smiled at the cameras, and entered the back seat of the limousine for the ride home.

Two minutes later, Ibrahim Rumallah watched as the motorcade hurried by him and a crowd of onlookers. He made the call.

"They are on their way home."

Akbar and Rumallah fired up the diesel and buckled up. They said nothing as they left the rest area at a good rate of speed. Once they crossed over the Wabash, Akbar pushed a button on his phone and gave the command.

"Yousef and Habib, go now."

Hiding in separate alcoves concealing their positions, both men throttled the jet skis, each with an AK-47 strapped to their back, and headed for the President's property.

"Moamar, get ready," Akbar said to Abbed who was sitting in his idling truck on the side of an old country road.

As they barreled down the interstate at eighty miles per hour, Rumallah pointed out the window as he looked to the south. Through his binoculars, he could see the helicopter roughly five miles away and heading west. He knew it was shadowing the President's motorcade.

"Let's go Yousef and Habib," Akbar said as he steered the truck onto the off ramp. "Let's go!"

Just off the interstate, Akbar exited the county road and hit the field just to the west of Maple Ridge Farms. Looking out the front window, the proprietor, Donna Sullivan, saw the sprayer making a mess of what remained of her soybean field across the road. And she was not happy.

"Doggone it," she said to no one in particular. She hadn't ordered any spraying to be done. For goodness sakes it was harvest time, and with beans at thirteen dollars a bushel, she wasn't going to let some idiot get away with a morning joyride. She grabbed the phone and called her neighbor, who had a nearly identical truck and sprayer in his farm implement arsenal. The neighbor also had a mischievous 16-year-old son with a brand new driver's license who had caused his own share of havoc over the years. When the boy's mother answered, Sullivan asked what in the world her son was thinking. The woman, slightly taken aback at the accusation, pointed out her son and her husband were sitting at the kitchen table eating breakfast. After a moment of silence and with the sprayer moving on to the field to the southwest at a high rate of speed, Sullivan knew something was wrong. She didn't even say goodbye before hanging up. She picked up the phone again and dialed the Secret Service command post.

Once Yousef Musharra passed under the interstate, the bells and whistles in the Secret Service command post started going off.

Agent Levrett walked up behind the agent manning the cameras. "What's up?" he asked, looking at the top row in the bank of monitors.

"Jet ski heading south on the river."

"Where?"

"Right there," the agent said, pointing at the black dot streaking down the river close to the bank.

Agent Levrett took a step closer to the monitor and peered at the screen. He didn't like the idea of a jet ski heading his way. The morning was too chilly for some recreational fun on the water. And he had never seen a black jet ski before. He activated his microphone. "Give me an Interceptor and a Prosecutor up north. One jet ski."

As soon as he gave the order, the buzzer sounded again. Another monitor showed the same black dot heading in the opposite direction. "Another one from the south!"

"Give me another Interceptor to the south. Another jet ski. All units – stop all river traffic!"

The county road leading to the President's house was blocked on the north end. With the motorcade about to turn north and make the two-mile trip to the Schumacher driveway, the Secret Service didn't want any unauthorized traffic.

"Ibrahim and Moamar!" Akbar yelled into his phone, bouncing over the ruts of a harvested corn field. "Go!"

A half mile away from his target, Moamar Abbed gunned his rusted pickup and headed straight for the road blocked with two police cars. The flashing lights on top of the cars should have warned anyone intent on approaching to slow down, but the revving engine indicated it was accelerating and not about to stop.

"Incoming vehicle!" one agent manning the road block yelled into his radio. He and three others then dove for cover. Just before the truck hit the two vehicles, Moamar ducked down behind the dash and braced for impact. The violent crash sent his truck and a vacant squad car off into the ditch. In the mess of crumpled steel that remained, he popped up with his AK-47.

"We're taking fire! We're taking fire!"

Two agents and two sheriff's deputies responded in kind.

Ibrahim had followed the motorcade as closely as possible without detection. Even though he was nowhere near the President's limousine, he was instructed to ram the last law-enforcement vehicle he could find. When he rear-ended a sheriff's deputy pulling up the rear, he opened up with his AK-47.

"I'm taking fire!"

Not long after that, the crew of the four Secret Service boats on the Wabash gave similar reports. "Shots fired! Shots fired!"

Agent Levrett gave the announcement. "All units we are under attack! We are under attack! Get Shadow back to the ranch! Get Shadow back to the ranch now!" He hit the emergency button for the Joint Operations Center in Washington, D.C., alerting all Secret Service details that an attack on the President was in progress. He then radioed the President's limousine to make sure the agents inside heard the transmission.

"Stagecoach, this is Levrett, do you copy?" He didn't have to wait long for a response.

"Levrett, Craig, roger that," Agent Craig said over the roaring engine. "Shadow is on the way."

On the roof of the President's house, Secret Service agents with high-powered binoculars scanned in every direction. Two snipers readied their rifles for the President's arrival. One other sniper felt a vibration on his right hip. He had two phones on him, but the one on the right would only be used in emergencies. He knew he had to take the call.

"Schiffer," he said abruptly. It was Director Stubblefield on the other end calling from Bethesda. "Sir, we've got problems," Schiffer said, the earpiece in his left ear telling him of the attack. The Director informed him of the possibility of VX. "Roger that."

The driver of the President's limousine was hauling ass with the two decoy limos and the four Suburbans right on his tail. The quiet bucolic surroundings of Silver Creek were now a cacophony of wailing sirens and speeding vehicles.

Given the wide open and flat terrain east of the river, Akbar and Rumallah could see the motorcade heading north as the sprayer charged through the Indiana dirt at a high rate of speed. Rumallah extended the booms and depressed the button for the VX. He looked in the passenger-side mirror and saw the drops of the misty spray coming out of the nozzles.

"It's working! It's working!" he yelled. "Go! Go! Go!"

"Allahu akbar!" Akbar shouted, fire in his eyes. "Allahu akbar!"

The Secret Service agent manning the phone at the guardhouse took the call from Donna Sullivan and relayed it to the others. "Watch the sprayer! Watch the sprayer!" he yelled, pointing to the east.

Flashing red lights on top of the telephone poles indicated something was indeed very wrong. To the east of the President's property, the farm field contained an array of biological sensors. And the flashing lights indicated they had picked up a problem. Akbar and Rumallah were two hundred yards from the road.

"Chemical attack!" Agent Levrett yelled into his microphone from the command center. "Chemical attack!"

At the entrance to the property, the driver of the President's limousine slammed on the brakes, and jerked the wheel left, the back end fishtailing before he regained control and gunned the accelerator. Agent Craig jumped over the front seat and lunged into the back.

"Mr. President, I'm going to need to put this on you," he said, reaching into a compartment of the rear door. He pulled out a chemical hood and placed it over the President's head. He did the same for the First Lady. Once he started the limo's stand-alone oxygen system, he yelled at the driver. "Get inside! Let's go! Let's go!"

Secret Service agents opened fire as Akbar and Rumallah crossed the road and headed for the driveway. Rumallah had one hand on the VX button and the other out the window as he fired his AK-47. He emptied his cartridge before taking a round in the head from an agent on the ground. Rumallah slumped over to the right, his left hand falling off the spray button. Now the only one remaining, Akbar leaned over behind the dashboard, his left hand on the steering wheel, his right hand squeezing the trigger for the VX, and his right foot holding the gas pedal to the floor.

Emerging from a stand of trees that circled the property, Wiley Cogdon had a phone to both ears. He was talking numbers with two Republican Party chairmen in New York. He had no clue what was going on around him. He never saw the truck coming at him or the man with the black gloves who grabbed him from behind.

"Oh!" Wiley let out. He was pulled backwards, the unidentified hand covering his nose and mouth and yanking him to the ground. He instantly thought he was being abducted, kidnapped just like General Graham. He just knew this was the end. If the man with the black gloves didn't kill him, his artery-clogged heart now pounding through his chest just might. He struggled with the man and tried yelling for help, screaming into the hand that was preventing him from even taking a breath. Nothing came out but a muffled shout.

For a split second, Akbar stuck his head up over the dash and gunned it for the small opening between the driveway and the trees. The counterassault team opened fire on the Mini Jimmy, the front windshield shattering into the cab. With his head now behind the dash being showered with glass, Akbar barreled through the front end of a Suburban trying to block his path and punched forward. The truck's left-side boom went scraping down the side of the Suburban, the right boom snapping off against a tree. Once he made it through, he finally saw what could not be seen from the main road. It was only seventy-five yards to the Indiana White House.

"Get inside the garage!" Agent Craig yelled to the driver.

The limousine left the asphalt and hit the concrete, still wet from an overnight shower. The driver slammed on the brakes, which sent the speeding eight-ton limo skidding into the back of the President's garage and slamming into the rear wall.

"Drop the door!" Agent Craig yelled. "Drop the door!" One agent inside the garage opened the rear door to the limousine. Stunned and his left knee aching from hitting the back of the front seat, the President limped out. With his chemical hood still on, he reached back for the First Lady's hand. But their hands never met. Agent Craig and another agent picked up the President and rushed him inside. One other agent grabbed the First Lady in his arms and did the same.

On the roof top, Agent Schiffer let out one final exhale. The bolt handle was down. His right eye went closed. He would only get one shot. The crosshairs settled on the area just above the steering wheel of the truck. All he could see was the driver's left hand gripping the wheel.

Knowing the end was near, Akbar grabbed the grenade in his right hand. When he raised his head to take one last look over the dash to check his direction and aim for the house, he brought the grenade to his mouth to remove the pin.

Before Akbar could clamp down on the pin with his teeth, Schiffer's left index finger squeezed the trigger of his Remington. The round whistled through the air and slammed into Akbar's skull. The violent whiplash caused Akbar's head to bounce off the headrest, his right hand dropping the grenade harmlessly to the floorboard and his left hand pulling down on the wheel as his body slumped forward. The truck veered toward the left of the house before it smashed into a tree. The agents on the ground didn't ask if the driver was hurt. They just unloaded on the cab with everything they had.

"Get 'em downstairs!" Agent Craig yelled. "Get 'em downstairs!"

Once in the basement bunker, Agent Craig took off the chemical hood and looked the President over.

"Are you all right, Mr. President?"

"I think so," the President said, grabbing his knee. "What's going on, Mike? I need to know what's going on out there."

Agent Craig spoke into his wrist microphone. "Levrett, this is Craig. I need a situation report."

The President looked over at his wife who was sitting on a couch. She was crying and shaking, the chemical mask now in her lap. The President hobbled over to her and put his arm around her. He then looked at Agent Craig. "Where's Wiley?"

Agent Craig put a finger to his earpiece but didn't look the President in the eye. The President's hearing was good enough to realize numerous agents were yelling into Craig's ear. Something was definitely wrong.

"Mike, what's going on?"

Out on the front lawn, a Secret Service agent was yelling for assistance. "I need an ambulance and a NAAK over here right now!" He was almost out of breath. He had dragged Wiley fifty yards in search of fresh air and a clear spot in the grass. He could feel a tightness in his chest so he corrected himself. "Two NAAKs and an ambulance."

The ambulance in the President's motorcade turned off the driveway and drove through the grass until it reached the two men.

Agent Clint Gilbert could see Wiley's muscles twitching. Then came the vomiting. His body was trying to fight off the toxin. Both had received a decent spray after the right boom broke off after hitting the tree. The medic inside the ambulance opened up the window and threw out the NAAKs – a nerve agent antidote kit. He then rolled up the window to prevent exposure. Agent Gilbert broke open one of the kits as fast as he could and removed the safety caps. He jammed the injector of atropine into Wiley's ample thigh and held it for ten seconds. He then did the same with the pralidoxime injector. Agent Gilbert yelled at the ambulance driver that he was going to need a haz mat team and a chem wash. He also told the medics to suit up. He then opened the second NAAK and jammed the spring-loaded needles into his own thigh. Wiley collapsed onto his back, his wide eyes looking at the blue Indiana sky. He never saw the four white suited men putting him on the stretcher and loading him into the ambulance.

It was all over.

EPILOGUE

Methodist Hospital – Indianapolis, Indiana

The President and the First Lady stepped off the elevator with his Secret Service detail and received a nice ovation from the assembled medical staff. The doctors and nurses had worked through the night keeping an eye on Agent Gilbert and Wiley to make sure their exposure to the VX didn't cause any long-lasting effects. The doctor told the President that the two men would make a full recovery. Although he did add that they were extremely lucky.

The FBI and Secret Service were putting the pieces of the puzzle together in the aftermath of the assassination attempt. Six terrorists were dead. The President's property was spared much damage because the wind had been blowing to the east at the time of the VX attack. Plus, the nozzles on the sprayer had clogged so much that little made it into the air. Haz mat crews had cordoned off a section of the farm field to the east that had received a small amount of VX.

The newspapers had giant headlines blaring on each page – terrorist attack, election results, and little else. The news anchors had been on the air for close to twenty-four hours with no shortage of stories to cover. The President had won the election by over seventeen million votes. It was a huge victory. Although it wasn't a surprise given that Sanchez essentially gave up campaigning after the General Graham fiasco.

Now it was time for the President to celebrate with the man who made it all happen. He entered the hospital room and saw a groggy Wiley looking up at him. It looked like he had been out of it for awhile. He was just starting to get his senses back. The TV, however, was off, and Wiley didn't have access to his BlackBerrys. They had to be discarded because of the contamination.

"Mr. President," he said, grabbing the President's right hand with both of his. "Did we win?" His voice was hoarse and dry. He needed water. But more important than water, he craved information.

The President squeezed Wiley's hand hard and smiled. "You did it, my man. All fifty states."

Wiley looked away. It wasn't long after that the tears started flowing down his cheeks. He had done it. A historic fifty-state landslide. All his hard work had paid off.

He turned his eyes back to his candidate. "It was a shutout?" It was Wiley's dream to lead the campaign to a 538 to zero electoral vote shutout, the first in American history.

The President took a seat. He knew it would hurt but he gave it to him straight. "I'm sorry, my friend, we lost D.C."

The District of Columbia has three electoral votes. The President won all fifty-states and the 535 electoral votes that went with them. It was ten more than Reagan won in 1984 after losing only D.C. and Mondale's home state of Minnesota.

Wiley looked genuinely pained, like his dream had been shattered.

"We won more than the Gipper in '84," the President said, trying to cheer him up.

Wiley nodded, relenting for the time being. He couldn't change things even if he wanted to. "Not bad," he said. "Not bad at all."

The President got up from his seat and patted Wiley on the shoulder. "And don't forget, my friend, the next election is only four years away."

THE END

Rob Shumaker is an attorney living in Illinois. *Chaos in the Capital* is his third novel. He is also the author of *Thunder in the Capital, Showdown in the Capital, D-Day in the Capital, Manhunt in the Capital, Fallout in the Capital, Phantom in the Capital, Blackout in the Capital,* and *The Way Out.*

To read more about the Capital Series novels, go to

www.USAnovels.com

··· ···· ··−